MW01615607

FLOWERS
OF
EVIL

HANI'S DAUGHTER MYSTERIES

N . L . H O L M E S

WayBack Press
P.O.Box 16066
Tampa, FL
⚱

Flowers of Evil
Copyright © 2023 by N. L. Holmes

The Lord Hani Mysteries™2020

All rights reserved.

Cover art and map© by Streetlight Graphics.
Author photo© by Kipp Baker.

No part of this book may be reproduced, scanned, or distributed in any printed or electronic form without permission. Please do not participate in or encourage piracy of copyrighted materials in violation of the author's rights. Thank you for respecting the hard work of this author.

This is a work of fiction. Names, characters, places, and incidents either are the product of the author's imagination or are used fictitiously, and any resemblance to locales, events, business establishments, or actual persons—living or dead—is entirely coincidental.

Dedicated to my husband, the "man of my heart."

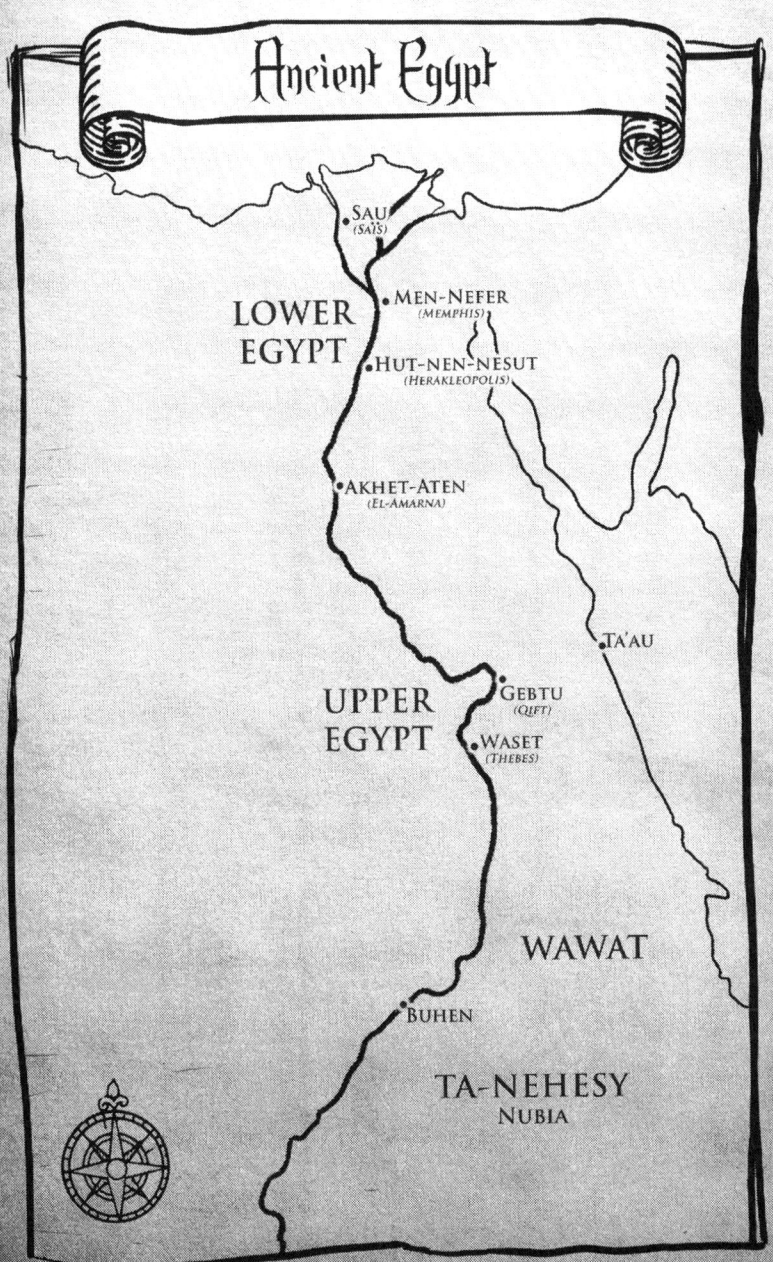

Ancient Egypt

SAU
(SAÏS)

LOWER
EGYPT

MEN-NEFER
(MEMPHIS)

HUT-NEN-NESUT
(HERAKLEOPOLIS)

AKHET-ATEN
(EL-AMARNA)

TA'AU

UPPER
EGYPT

GEBTU
(QIFT)

WASET
(THEBES)

WAWAT

BUHEN

TA-NEHESY
NUBIA

HISTORICAL NOTES

Our story takes place in Egypt in the first regnal year of the boy-king Tut-ankh-aten(amen), that is, around the year 1335 BCE. Readers of The Lord Hani Mysteries will recognize that it picks up shortly after *Pilot Who Knows the Waters* leaves off.

Egyptian medicine, primitive as it may seem today, was far and away the most advanced of its time. The *sunu* (m.) or *sunet* (f.) was a scientific practitioner, whose art was based on cause and effect empirically observed—and written down—over the millennia. Even without understanding principles such as germ theory, he or she had observed that certain treatments worked. In addition, there were magical healers, who dealt with disease as the presence of malevolent spirits, and closely related religious healers. Conceiving medicine as a holistic endeavor, the Egyptian physician treated mind, soul, and body to arrive at a cure. There were specialists of many kinds, as well as dentists.

In a traditional society like that of Egypt, each stage of life was clearly defined and marked outwardly. Children, who spent a lot of their time unashamedly naked, usually had their heads shaved, with only a braid hanging from one side. This "lock of Haru" configured them to the child god Horus and invoked upon them his protection. Boys were circumscribed at seventeen or so and were considered to pass into full manhood at that point, when they also cut off their childhood lock. Girls became women as soon as they were able to bear children, and their status as marriageable maidens was indicated by two clusters of tiny braids that seems to have varied a bit in design. Once they were married, they could wear any style of hair or wig, but especially the long, full style with sections that lay in front of each shoulder, which modern scholars call "tripartite."

Egyptians had no surnames, but they identified themselves as "Y son or daughter of X" (their father's name)—Hani son of Mery-ra. Sometimes, if their mother was from a more exalted family or simply to pay her homage, they might add her name as well—Neferet daughter of Hani and Nub-nefer.

A word about the vast priesthood of Amen-Ra at Waset. The entire hierarchy was headed by the First Prophet (high priest) and after him, the Second Prophet. These were both political appointments reserved to the highest aristocrats of the land and might be held simultaneously with a secular office such as vizier. There followed a Third and Fourth Prophet, both lifetime appointments that were hereditary and full time. Other priests fell into two ranks, the more prestigious *hem netjer* (man of god) and the *wab* (pure one), whose service was often physical. For example, *wabu* carried the god's barque in processions. Other priests were defined by specific duties, such as the lector priest, who read aloud the ceremonies as they were carried out, or the *sem*, who presided at funerals. Priests served for a quarter of the year at a time.

Originally, high-status women could occupy all of these positions as well, but by the New Kingdom, when our story takes place, their roles had been restricted to singers and musicians. Interestingly, the *weret khener*, or supervisor of all the musical personnel, was often a woman.

In addition to priestly offices, the temple had numerous lay administrators, who looked after various aspects of its enormous wealth.

The Egyptians saw the soul as having multiple parts. The *ka*, the vital essence of the person, could reside in his image after death, which occurred after the *ka* left the body. Every god and class of person had a special kind of *ka*, and that of the king was divine. The *ba* was the individual personality of the person. It was thought to fly out of the embalmed body at night in the form of a bird and if angered, could haunt the living. The *ib*, or heart was the seat of thought and emotion. It testified for or against the person at judgment when it was weighed against the feather of Ma'at. The *akh* might be called intellect or consciousness. In the blessed life after death, the *ba* and *ka* were reunited with the *akh* to form a perfect version of the deceased. The *shut*, or shadow, was thought to contain something of the person who cast it. The *sekhem*, or power, is a little-understood concept that seemed to reinvest the blessed *akh* with life. And finally, the *ren* or name by which a person was called actually formed a part of him, and his soul could be killed by erasing that name in its written form.

The Egyptian year was full of festivals, some of them

local and others national. I have conflated the ceremony of loosing paper boats, which was part of the Theban Wag Festival, held early in the year (late summer), into the Festival of the Beautiful Valley, which took part in late spring. Both holidays had a similar emphasis—the union of the living and the dead members of the family through visits to the west bank of the Nile, where family tombs were located.

And finally, a word about kings. Although we today call the pharaohs by their birth name (Amenhotep, Akhenaten), they would have been known in their own times by the unique throne name they adopted upon their coronation. Hence Amenhotep III would have been Neb-ma'at-ra; Akhenaten, Nefer-khepru-ra, etc. Altogether, they had five names used for formal occasions.

CHARACTERS

(* indicates a historical personage)

Aha: Neferet's eldest brother, lay administrator of the cattle of Amen-Ra.

Ah-mes: second wife of Sen-em-iah.

Ankhet-khepru-ra Nefer-nefru-aten*: the throne name of former Queen Nefert-iti.

Amen-em-hut*: Neferet's maternal uncle and Third Prophet of Amen-Ra.

Amen-mes: son of Djehuty-mes. Former star student of Hani.

Anuia*: wife of Amen-em-het.

Ay*: maternal grandfather of the king and vizier of the Lower Kingdom.

Baket-iset: Neferet's eldest sister, a quadriplegic.

Bener-ib, called **Ibet:** a *sunet* and the lady of Neferet's heart. Her name means "sweet heart."

Djed-har: neighborhood healer.

Djefat-nebty: Pentju's wife and herself a famous physician, she was the teacher of Neferet and Bener-ib.

Djehuty-mes: eldest son of Lord Ptah-mes, a *hem-netjer*.

Hani*: Neferet's father, the high commissioner of foreign affairs in the north.

Har-em-heb*: an infantry general and mentor of the young king.

Hu-may: twelve-year-old orphan boy adopted by Neferet and Bener-ib and apprenticed as a goldsmith.

Imi-seba: foreman of the flower-field workers of Amen-Ra.

In-hapy: royal goldsmith and mother of Maya. Hu-may and his late father were employed by her.

Iry*: "Shepherd of the Anus". A famous proctologist from earlier in the New Kingdom.

Khuit: old neighborhood healer with whom Neferet had first studied medicine.

Mahu*: former police chief of Akhet-aten, now in Waset.

Mai-her-pri: eight-year-old second son of Maya, Neferet's nephew. His name means "lion on the battlefield."

Maya: Hani's son-in-law and secretary.

Menna: infantry commander whose life Hani saved years ago.

Mery-ra*: Hani's father, a retired military scribe.

Meryet-amen: wealthy widow. The widowed Mery-ra's lady friend.

Mut-nodjmet: Pa-kiki's cousin and wife.

Mut-em-wia*: Ptah-mes's eldest daughter, a chantress of Amen-Ra.

Mut-tuy: thirteen-year-old orphan girl adopted by and apprenticed to Neferet and Bener-ib.

Neb-ma'at-ra Amen-hotep (III): a great king of the New Kingdom and paternal grandfather of Tut-ankh-aten.

Nefer-khepru-ra Wa-en-ra Akh-en-aten*: son of Neb-ma'at-ra and father of Tut-ankh-aten. Known as "the heretic" because of the disruptive religious and social changes he enforced.

Neferet: Hani and Nub-nefer's youngest daughter. A *sunet*. Her name means "beautiful."

Nub-nefer: Hani's wife, a chantress of Amen-Ra.

Pa-kiki: Hani's younger son, chief scribe at the military garrison of Waset.

Pa-ra-messu*: adjutant of General Har-em-heb.

Pen-amen*: Amen-em-hut's eldest son.

Pen-buy: son of Sen-em-iah and a florist for Amen-Ra.

Pentju*: vizier of the Upper Kingdom and a *sunu*.

Pipi: Hani's younger brother.

Ptah-mes*: Neferet's husband and the treasurer of the kingdom. A very wealthy high aristocrat, he formally goes by the nickname **Maya**.

Pu-im-ra: a *hem-netjer* in charge of cult objects for Amen-Ra.

Qen: six-year-old orphan adopted by Neferet and Bener-ib.

Sat-hut-haru, called **Sati:** Hani's second daughter; married to Maya.

Shu-roy: eight-year-old orphan adopted by Neferet and Bener-ib.

Shuttarna*: king of Naharin at the time it was partitioned.

Sit-amen: a dyer's wife, neighbor of Neferet and Bener-ib's dispensary. Her son is **Huy**.

Surer: a farmer whose land neighbors the flower fields of Amen-Ra.

Tetiky: lieutenant of Pu-im-ra in charge of gold vessels.

Tiry: three-year-old orphan girl adopted by Neferet and Bener-ib.

Tut-em-heb: bodyguard of Sen-em-iah.

Ullum-tishni: a Hurrian mercenary.

Wabet: maid of Sen-em-iah

GLOSSARY OF GODS AND TERMS

Akhet: the season of Harvest, the four months between the wheat harvest in spring and the Inundation of the Nile in late summer.

Akhet-aten: Horizon of the Aten, the city in Middle Egypt that briefly served as Akh-en-aten's capital.

Amen-Ra: In the New Kingdom, when a Theban Dynasty took the throne, the local creation god Amen, the Hidden One, was merged with the national sun-god Ra to become the major deity of the kingdom and king of the gods.

Ammit, the Devourer: a monster composed of crocodile, lion, and hippopotamus parts who consumed and annihilated any soul that failed the judgment in the afterworld.

ba: the part of the soul that contained the individual's distinctive identity. It flew forth from the tomb at night in the form of a bird and could haunt the living if not appeased.

Bak: a famous sculptor of the new realistic style promulgated under Akh-en-aten.

Bearer of Divine Offerings: the lay administrator responsible for floral offerings to Amen-Ra.

Bes: a lion-like dwarf god, protector of women and children.

***bulti*:** the tilapia fish.

chantress: a female singer in the service of a god. It was considered a kind of priesthood.

***deben*:** Egyptian commerce was based on barter, but values were reckoned in terms of *debens,* a given weight (usually 91g) of copper, silver, or gold in the form of big rings.

Djahy and Kharu: Palestine/Israel and Syria, respectively, regions which composed the northern vassals of the Egyptian empire.

Duat: the afterworld.

Gem-pa-aten: a temple built at Karnak (Thebes) by Akh-en-aten while he was still his father's coregent that prefigured the extreme artistic style of his reign.

the Great One: Ta-weret, one of the patron goddesses of women and children. She took the form of a pregnant hippopotamus with a crocodile tail and pendulous human breasts.

Hall of Royal Correspondence: the chancery or seat of government administration.

hem-netjer *(pl. hemu-netjer)*: man of god, a priest of the higher rank.

Hurrian: a person of Naharin (the Hurri) and their language.

Hut-haru's Lovelies: a bevy of beautiful divine girls who served as handmaids to the goddess of love and beauty (Hathor).

Im-hotep: an official of the Old Kingdom and designer of the Great Pyramid who became the patron god of physicians.

Inpu: Anubis, jackal-headed god of embalming. His workshop/temple was the **Per-inpu**.

Ipet-isut: the Greatest of Shrines, Amen-Ra's temple at Karnak. Often paired with the Southern Ipet at Luxor, it was the largest religious complex in history.

Isfet and the Apep Serpent: Chaos, representing everything in opposition to *ma'at*—falsehood, injustice, and disorder—and the serpent-demon Apophis who symbolized and caused such evil.

iteru: a unit of distance, approximately a mile.

ka: the life force of a person or god, hence an important part of their soul.

Kemet: "the Black Land", the Egyptians' name for their country because of the rich black Nile alluvium that distinguished it from the surrounding desert. It consisted historically of two kingdoms, the Upper (upstream, that is, southern) and Lower (downstream/northern), and so is sometimes referred to as **the Two Lands**.

Khonsu: Theban moon god, the son of Amen.

Lady of the West: Hut-haru, who, among her many other duties, welcomed the soul to the "West", the land of the dead.

ma'at: the concept of truth, justice, and cosmic balance. With a capital M, the goddess who personified these qualities.

Master of the Double House of Silver and Gold: treasurer of Upper and Lower Egypt, although much of the kingdom's wealth was held in commodities rather than precious metals.

medjay: originally Nubian tribesmen known for skill in archery, the term later came to designate the police, who were composed in large part of such archers.

Men-nefer: Memphis, the capital of Lower Egypt.

Montu: falcon-headed Theban god of war.

Mut: the consort of Amen-Ra. Her name meant "mother", and she was queen of the gods.

Naharin: a kingdom known elsewhere as Mitanni, which occupied what is now Kurdistan in inland Syria. The Hittites had just taken over half the country, and the other half was ruled by puppets of Assyria.

Osir: Osiris, the divine king of the underworld. The dead were thought to be conformed to him, so any dead person might be referred to as an Osir.

Peret: the four winter months between the autumn Inundation and the spring harvest.

persea: a large tree related to the avocado, whose fruit was eaten and used for oil.

the River: the Nile, which had no name nor was it personified by any god. Hapy was god of the yearly Inundation, which brought live-giving water and rich alluvial soil to the fields.

Royal Ornaments: the king's harem, consisting of hundreds of women.

Sau: Saïs, a city in the Delta of the Nile devoted to the goddess Sekhmet. Her temple was the site of a great medical school.

Sekhmet: the Powerful One, lion-headed goddess of disease and of healing.

sepen: juice of the opium poppy, employed as a painkiller in Egypt. There is some ambiguous evidence that it might also have been used recreationally in the New Kingdom.

speech of the gods: writing—in this story, specifically hieroglyphic writing as distinct from the cursive that Neferet had learned to read and write.

sunu (m.), ***sunet*** (f.): a physician of the more scientific sort.

sycomore fig: not to be confused with the sycamore (plane tree), this was a large relative of the fig that bore edible fruit.

Ta-nehesy: Nubia, modern Sudan, an area that had been conquered by Egypt and was ruled as a viceroyalty.

Third Prophet of Amen-Ra: a hereditary lifetime priesthood, this post came right after the High Priest and his second-in-command in importance.

User-het-amen: "Mighty of Prow is Amen", the golden processional barque of Amen-Ra.

wab (pl. *wabu*): "pure one", the lower rank of priests.

Waset: City of the Scepter (*was*), known to us as Thebes. This was the capital of Upper Egypt.

Wasshukanni: the original capital of Mitanni/Naharin, replaced after the partition of the country by the city of Taite.

weret khener: "great one (f.) of the musicians", the person in charge of the musical personnel of the temple.

weshket: a broad collar of beads or fresh flowers worn over the shoulders.

CHAPTER 1

After one last look up and down the street, Neferet finally pulled the gate shut and slid the heavy bolt. She heaved a dispirited sigh. The woman of her heart, her fellow *sunet*, Bener-ib, stood in the doorway of the little dispensary.

"Either this is the healthiest neighborhood in the Two Lands, or people just aren't coming to us when they need a doctor," Neferet said.

"Where are all the patients who used to go to that Khuit for healing? She was mostly just a witch, but look at all the people who turned to her for help," said Bener-ib disconsolately.

"It's because we're women." Neferet leaned against the gate.

"Khuit was a woman."

"It's because we're *young* women. Nobody can believe a couple of girls have any wisdom." Neferet clenched her teeth and thrust out her lip, an all-too-familiar anger rising in her. "People don't seem to care that we were the royal physicians for Akhet-khepru-ra. We're literate. We may be young, but we know all anybody has ever learned about medicine because we can read."

Bener-ib nodded. "Should we give up and go back to helping Lady Djefat-nebty?" she asked in a small voice.

Neferet wasn't so quick to accept defeat. "Never. We can make Lord Ptah-mes's servants come to us and Papa's too. And Uncle Pipi's and Aha's and Pa-kiki's and Sati and Maya's and—"

"They already do. They're just not sick very often." Bener-ib, a tiny, bird-boned person with a big head of slender braids, wilted with discouragement.

Here was their insurmountable problem. Two young women from good families who had studied medicine since their earliest adolescence under the greatest woman doctor alive—the physician of the Royal Ornaments—had given up a lucrative and prestigious post at the palace to serve the residents of this modest working-class neighborhood of Waset.But people were always asking why, as if they thought it betrayed some dishonesty on the part of the two well-meaning women. Neferet had always had the unconventional notion that even the poorest workmen should be well cared for, as her parents' own family servants were. It embarrassed her—pained her—to see ordinary people dragging through life with unset fractures and flyblown eyelids. Their lives were hard enough without all that. Besides, her honest, straightforward nature had been painfully constrained in the stifling atmosphere of court etiquette.

So here they finally were, full of idealism and the desire to do good. And nobody came to them. Not even the clients of the ancient healer who had inhabited their little dispensary before them. It made Neferet angry just to think of it.

She let out a breath through her nose like a blast of steam. "We're not babies. We're twenty-four years old. We've been studying for half our lives. There's no reason for this."

"It was nice of Lord Ptah-mes to make that tax collector of his come when he had a boil on his neck," said Bener-ib optimistically.

Ptah-mes was Neferet's husband—in name, at least. Despite the fact that she was younger than most of his children, the two had agreed to a union that served their mutual convenience. Ptah-mes, a friend of Neferet's father, was a grieving widower who wanted no more of women. The pro forma marriage kept away his avid suitors. And Neferet had just needed an appearance of respectable matronhood to cloak her relationship with Bener-ib. Lord Ptah-mes—who, since his first wife's death, had gone by his childhood nickname, Maya—was one of the richest and most blue-blooded personages in the City of the Scepter. He was also the Master of the Double House of Silver and Gold. He could certainly use his influence to steer patients to the two women, but those were people who could afford a good doctor anyway.

Neferet scrunched down her brow in an effort at hard thought. She looked around the courtyard of the little house, all neatly swept, with medicinal herbs planted in beds outlined by whitewashed rocks. Three dogs lay sprawled here and there in the shade of the wall, panting, following her with their eyes as if they would help if they could. A one-eyed cat angled his leg overhead and licked in improbable places.

"We'd better be going," said Bener-ib after a moment. "The children and their nursemaid will be home by now and wonder where we are."

"I guess you're right. It just makes me mad is all." Neferet checked the animals' water bowl and squatted to pet the largest dog, who grinned up at her. "You boys guard the house well. All right, Mangler? Cheetah, don't let any rats get our goose fat."

The shadows of a long summer evening stretched from house to house as they emerged into the street. Some of the neighbors were sitting on their doorsteps or leaning over the parapets of their roof terraces, enjoying a breath of cooler air while their children, liberated at last from a day of work, ran around and played. They nodded respectfully as the two young doctors passed.

"Evening, Hotep. Evening, Sit-amen," Neferet called cheerfully.

She knew them all and would have sworn they all liked her. Sit-amen, the dyer's wife, brought them fried bread treats in honey when she made them for her family. But nobody came for healing.

Neferet saw that one of the children had a stye on his eyelid. "You need to put something on that eye, little man. Tell your mama to bring you to our dispensary, and we'll get you all fixed up."

"Yes, Lady Neferet," said the mother from the doorway.

Neferet knew she wouldn't come.

The packed-earth streets of the southern capital, with its crowd of walled houses and yards, held in the early-

24

summer afternoon's heat and radiated it back like an oven at the end of the day. Neferet and Bener-ib were relieved to enter the lofty red-painted gate of Lord Ptah-mes's villa and find themselves in the cool and beauty of a garden full of color, fresh pools, and soul-tickling scents.

Neferet heard men's voices in the garden and cried in delight, "It's Papa!"

She grabbed Bener-ib's hand and drew the smaller woman after her at a run toward the pavilion sheltered by vines, where her husband received guests in the evening. Ducks scattered before them, squawking indignantly, as the two pelted up the gravel walk toward the stone building with its broad porch and delicate painted columns. Two men sat in comfortable low-backed chairs under its shelter, beer pots and straws before them on a pair of graceful stands. Everything in Ptah-mes's house was beautiful. At first, Neferet had felt awed by the perfection everywhere. But she wasn't the sort to stay intimidated long.

Lord Ptah-mes, as usual, was dressed to the same perfection, even in the relaxed privacy of his own home. In his late fifties, he was tall and slim and still strikingly handsome, with chiseled features and heavy-lidded black eyes. But more important, under his rather frosty exterior, he was a good man. He generously permitted Neferet to spend his gold however she liked and had welcomed the army of cast-off or disabled animals she'd collected. And he had opened his home to the six fatherless children she and Bener-ib had taken in after their mother abandoned them.

Not everybody would have done that, the young woman told herself gratefully. They were especially rowdy children.

Beside him sat Hani son of Mery-ra, Neferet's beloved

father. She observed with affection that he was the exact opposite of his friend in appearance—a broad, squat, heavyset man with a square jaw, laughter-crinkled little eyes, and a wide grin that bared the space between his front teeth. Everybody said she was a younger, female version of her papa, which suited her fine, even if—in spite of her name—she wasn't as beautiful as Mama and her sisters. She was smart like Papa, too, who could speak many languages and write them as well. He was high commissioner of foreign affairs in the north, right below the vizier of the Upper Kingdom, and she loved him more than anything except Bener-ib. But then, she had known Papa all her life—she was his little duckling.

The two men looked up as the women skidded to a halt in the gravel.

"Papa! You're here!"

"In the flesh and plenty of it, as Grandfather would say," Hani said with a laugh, extending his arms.

Neferet threw herself on him with such exuberance that a less solid man would have tottered. "Hello, Lord Ptah-mes. Are you eating here tonight, Papa?" She took her seat on her father's lap.

"No, my duckling. I just dropped in to ask your husband's opinion on something, and he was kind enough to offer me some of this delicious herbed beer."

Ptah-mes gave his cool, enigmatic smile.

"Ibet and I have been discussing how to get word of our practice out. Nobody's coming, and I just can't believe there aren't any accidents or diseases in that whole neighborhood."

"Surely your sister brings her children," Hani said.

Sat-hut-haru and her husband, Maya, lived in Maya's old family home, a former goldsmith's workshop just around the corner from the dispensary.

"Unfortunately they're healthy. I-I mean, fortunately." Bener-ib grew scarlet. She probably wouldn't say anything else for the rest of the evening, fearing she had disgraced herself.

"Our families and friends all together won't keep us very busy. It's just rotten, the way people won't give us a chance. They don't know what they're missing."

Papa gave her a squeeze. "Maybe it will just take time."

"Is there another practitioner in the area?" Lord Ptah-mes asked. "Someone who may be draining off your potential patients?"

"I don't know." Neferet shot Bener-ib a curious glance. "Have you heard anything, Ibet?"

The girl shook her head, but then her face lit up. "Oh! I think there is. I've heard mention of somebody called Djed-har. I don't think he's a real *sunu*, though."

"Well, there you go, my duckling. Either work out some division of labor with this Djed-har, as Khuit must have done, or see if you can't win some of his patients over. Maybe you take the women, and he takes the men."

At last, some progress. Neferet was ready to charge out and beard this fellow, but it was too late in the day. Perhaps they could negotiate some sort of partnership. The possibilities were a delightful challenge to her ingenuity.

The two young women bade Papa and Ptah-mes good evening and headed off to the nursery to have dinner with the children.

"Let's go see this Djed-har tomorrow," Neferet said as they walked. "Maybe he'll be reasonable."

Bener-ib looked dubious. "Men aren't always reasonable."

"If we can't charm him, we'll fight. We'll win—you'll see."

The children had been given permission to take over the rear area of Lord Ptah-mes's garden, behind the wall that separated the fancy part from the practical part. Under the shade of the huge sycamore figs planted by his ancestors, the younger ones were playing a noisy tug-of-war while the nursemaid looked on in boredom, fanning herself with a trimmed palm frond. Hu-may, the oldest boy, who was about twelve, and his thirteen-year-old sister, Mut-tuy, were hunched over a game of Hounds and Jackals. All at once, the girl gave a howl of frustration and surged to her feet, her face crimson and scowling. Hu-may shrank back and murmured something apologetic, but Mut-tuy stalked away. Then she glanced at the two young women and froze.

"Hello, Mut-tuy," said Neferet pleasantly. "Have you people eaten yet?"

The girl's scowl went blank with confusion. No doubt, she'd expected a reprimand. She was getting to be tall and gangling, like her mother, with a thin, pretty face usually disfigured by a glower.

"Uh, no," she said, almost civil despite herself.

Hu-may said meekly, "Nurse said we'd wait for you and Lady Bener-ib."

The nurse came hurrying up. "I hope that's all right, Lady Neferet. Qen and Shu-roy were fighting again on the way home. They ought to go without."

"Of course, we'll eat together—Qen and Shu-roy too. We're a family now."

Certainly, Neferet, for all her occasionally naughty childhood, had never been deprived of dinner. That kind of punishment seemed barbaric to her, given how convivial family dinners had always been at home. "You can tell cook we'll eat out here."

"We're not a family," growled Mut-tuy. "You're not our mother. Neither one of you."

Neferet and Bener-ib exchanged weary glances. Even after months of effort on their part, the girl wasn't ready to unbend. The other children had come around, to a large extent. Hu-may, like a little grown-up, was already apprenticed to Maya's mother as a goldsmith. Mut-tuy was hard as the kernel of a persea fruit, always bristling with resentment at the double tragedy that had struck her real family. Only a few months ago, her old grandfather, the last one left, had gone to join his ancestors. She had to feel thoroughly abandoned.

The servants emerged with tables and stools, and everybody took a seat, with much struggling over who got to sit where.

"Count off, now," Neferet said loudly. "We don't play favorites."

Still giggling, the children began to count off, but three-year-old Tiry only knew one number—*hamtau*, "three"—so another struggle erupted over who got to be third. The little girl found the chaos hilarious. At last, the children sat two by two at the small folding tables, and the ordeal of passing out food began. Neferet didn't know what the family had been given to eat, because they didn't seem to like anything that came their way except the roast duck stuffed with cracked wheat, which they gobbled down like starving animals. Only the baby—placidly seated in the nurse's lap, sucking his grubby thumb—had no comment.

By the time dinner was over and the youngsters had been marched off to bed, Neferet was exhausted. This happened every day. As soon as they were alone once more, she said to Bener-ib with a deflated sigh, "Do you suppose our mothers had it this hard?"

The girl shook her head. "I was the only child."

"I suspect Mama had her hands full with Pa-kiki and me. The others were older and pretty well-behaved anyway."

"We have to keep trying, though, Nef'et. Their father was brutally murdered." Bener-ib swallowed hard. Her own father had been murdered with equal brutality. "And they think their mother has died too." Her own mother was dead.

Neferet wrapped a compassionate arm around her friend. Nobody had a tenderer heart than Bener-ib. "Of course, we won't give up. We'll get through to Mut-tuy if it's the last thing we do, right? I swear to you on Mama's *ka*."

⁜

Early the next morning, the two young women set off through a city already warming fast, each leading a small child, the older youngsters trailing them like a line of unruly ducklings, with the nursemaid bringing up the rear, the naked baby in her arms. The inhabitants of the working-class neighborhood already knew them and could time their morning tasks by the noisy procession more regular than any water clock. Neferet tipped her head to the old grandfather who sat in the doorway across the lane from the dispensary and unbolted the gate. The three dogs greeted them with a joyous cacophony of barking.

"Somebody's ready for breakfast," she said, patting each furry head in turn. "Hu-may, do you want to see what the butcher has for them today before you head off to work?"

The boy obediently trotted off down the street, while the nurse organized the younger children for games and Mut-tuy slouched around, waiting until the house was opened. The *sunet*s were training her to become a healer—a painful task because she hated being told what to do. But the girl was smart. If she ever stopped resenting their kindness, she would make the young women an able assistant.

Cheetah burst through the cat hole, a mouse dangling from his jaws, as Neferet opened the door of the house.

"Somebody's doing his job, I see," she said in cheerful satisfaction.

She had just ushered Bener-ib and Mut-tuy through the opening and released the rolled-up fly mat when wild voices from the street caught her attention. An instant later, someone hammered urgently at the gate.

"*Iyah!* Open up, Doctor! We have a wounded man here."

Neferet flew back to the gate and threw it open.

A crowd of men, with a woman at the rear, stood before her. Two of them carried, slung between them, the bloody body of a well-dressed, expensively wigged man.

"Bring him in," Neferet said with professional calm.

There was a shocking amount of blood. Her heart

31

lurched into her throat. She didn't care much for his prognosis.

They all hustled across the narrow yard and through the doorway to the rustle of shuffling footsteps, leaving bloody splatters in the dirt. The woman, her hands to her mouth, trailed them uncertainly.

"Are you his wife?" Neferet asked quietly.

She nodded, her eyes full of fear. Kohl was running along her eyelids under the onslaught of tears.

"We'll do what we can."

Meanwhile, Bener-ib had cleared a place on the table, and the two servants lowered the victim gingerly. A groan escaped him.

At least he's still alive. "Mut-tuy, bring us hot water and cloths. We have to be able to see the wound." But the stench told Neferet that his intestines had been pierced. Somewhere not far away, the Lady of the West was waiting with outstretched arms to receive him.

Goggle-eyed at her first sight of a real patient, Mut-tuy handed Bener-ib the pot of water and cloths, and the *sunet* began to sop up the blood, which fountained endlessly from the man's middle.

He moaned restlessly but didn't appear to have the strength to stir.

"What happened?" Neferet asked, looking around at the crowd of servants and the victim's wife.

No one spoke. She turned back to the wounded man and wiped his brow with a towel moistened with cool water. Fever had already set in.

One of the men, a burly young fellow as bloody as a butcher, finally said in a trembling voice, "The master had just got out of his litter in front of his gate when a couple of fellows jumped out of the shadows and threw themselves on him. Us who was around, we grabbed the attackers, but they slashed their way free and disappeared. Hati-ah, here, got cut up too."

"It's nothing," Hati-ah insisted. His forearm was covered in blood, apparently his own as well as his master's.

"Can you do anything?" the woman cried tremulously, clutching at Neferet's arm.

But Neferet could think of nothing encouraging to say. Her insides had that hollow, leaden feeling that meant the worst was about to happen.

"There's no point in stitching up the outside," she said gently. "He's lost a lot of blood, and they've chopped him up pretty seriously inside. As the medical books say, 'This is not a case I will treat.'"

The woman understood and began to whimper. She reached out a hand to touch her husband's shoulder but then drew back as if she'd just discovered it was someone else. A gloomy silence fell over the group, broken only by the increasingly weak huff of the patient's breath. His lips moved feebly, and Bener-ib leaned over his face.

"I think you'd better stand with him, mistress," Neferet said. "His soul is ready to fly. He might have something to say to you."

The woman drew closer fearfully. "Sen-em-iah, my brother, I'm here."

At first, Neferet wondered if she'd misunderstood and the woman was really his sister—although from her age she might have been his daughter—but *brother* and *sister* were terms of endearment often used by married people.

Everyone stood, hushed, waiting for a final word from the threshold of the other world. Sen-em-iah said nothing. His head lolled finally, and a tiny sibilance of breath escaped him.

They all stared at him expectantly until Neferet said in a quiet tone, "I think he's passed to the West, mistress."

She took the patient's hand and pressed her fingers against the inside of the wrist. No pulse.

The woman stared at Neferet as if she couldn't believe her. She made no move to wail or tear her hair.

"Who is he? Why might someone have done this?"

Since the wife was frozen, one of the servants answered. "Sen-em-iah son of Nakht is—was—Bearer of Divine Offerings of Amen, mistress. Chief florist of the Hidden One's temple, like his father before him."

Yahyah. That explains why he was just coming home at this hour of the morning. Florists work all night, while it's cooler.

"Who would want to kill a florist?" she asked. "They don't hurt anybody."

"Maybe it was just a random attack," suggested another of the servants. "Maybe they were going to rob the master."

"Were you all with him when he was attacked?"

"Not me," said an older man. "I'm the steward. I came out with the mistress of the house when the others yelled. These young fellows are the litter bearers and bodyguards. Yes, they were with him."

No casual robber would have attacked anybody protected by eight stalwart young men. And Neferet knew what the servants didn't—the attacker had not just stabbed Sen-em-iah but had ripped viciously. He had aimed to kill.

The steward said, "We brought him all the way here because we didn't know where else a *sunu* could be found at this hour of the morning. One of these fellows lives in this neighborhood."

Bener-ib, who had been listening intently, leaned over Sen-em-iah and drew down his eyelids.

That gesture brought his wife out of her shock, and she began to cry, quietly at first, but soon she was howling, keening, raking at her face with her nails.

"Perhaps mistress would like to go home, notify the children?" suggested the steward, taking her by the elbow. "If we could leave the master here briefly until we can call the servants of Inpu...?" He raised inquiring eyes to the two *sunet*s, one after the other. Already, he was edging the distraught widow toward the door. The block of servants crowded after them.

"Of course," said Neferet. "Is it all right if we come by later to ask a few questions? We'll have to report this murder, now that we're involved, and we'll need to explain what we see's been done to the body."

The steward nodded distractedly over his shoulder, and the entire crowd disappeared through the door. The woman's wails trailed off as they exited the gate, and soon Neferet, Bener-ib, and Mut-tuy were left staring at one another in silence. The young girl's eyes were round as plates and scalpel sharp.

Mangler had entered and was lapping blood from the smooth plaster floor, his tail wagging in pleasure at the windfall.

Neferet gave her partner a long significant stare. "Do you realize what this is? Our first murder case."

"Our first? Will there be more?" Bener-ib said faintly.

"Look at that wound. Somebody wanted to be sure this florist died. Somebody who knew what they were doing. A soldier, maybe. A professional assassin." Neferet turned to the body of Sen-em-iah, whose eyes had popped open a slit. He seemed to be watching them. "If only he could tell us who did this. I feel sure he knew. But he didn't have any final words."

"Oh yes, he did," said Bener-ib, brightening. "I distinctly heard him say something just before you called his wife over."

Neferet's heart stepped up its pace. She seized Bener-ib's hand. "He did? Quick, Ibet! What did he say? This could be the clue to his murder!"

Bener-ib looked around as if searching for witnesses to support her, then she pronounced firmly in her girlish voice, "He said... he said, '*Sekhat.* Rabbit.'"

CHAPTER 2

"RABBIT?" Neferet repeated, disappointed. "You're sure? That doesn't make any sense."

Bener-ib's eyebrows crumpled in apology. "I'm not sure, no. But that's what it sounded like."

To Neferet's surprise, Mut-tuy said, "It was 'rabbit.' I heard him too." The girl's eyes sparkled with sudden interest. Her mouth was still stubborn, but there was nothing resentful about it.

"Wasn't there anything else?" Neferet asked.

Bener-ib and Mut-tuy shook their heads in unison.

Neferet stuck her lip out in thought. "I wonder if that was a pet name for his wife."

"There was something odd about her," said Mut-tuy eagerly. "She behaved very strangely toward her husband. Did you notice?"

Yahyah, this has really woken our girl up, thought Neferet, amused.

The three of them looked down at Sen-em-iah, still prone on the table among them.

He knew something. Come on, my boy. Tell us your secrets. "Let's clean him up a bit before the servants of Inpu come. It looks like a slaughterhouse in here."

She and Bener-ib set to work, and Mut-tuy went off to boil more hot water. At that moment, Hu-may pushed through the fly mat, a basket full of freshly butchered bones in his arms.

"He had a lot, mistress. He said—" The boy broke off in shock at the sight of the blood-drenched dead man on the table. "Bes protect us…"

"Divide them among the three dogs, Hu-may. There's a helpful fellow. Don't let Faithful take Hedgehog's. Then you can go on to work," Neferet said hastily to the young goldsmith. She could explain to him later what had happened.

She turned back to the corpse lying before her. Sen-em-iah was middle-aged, a little paunchy but not enough to distract a knife looking for his vital organs. He was coarse featured but well cared for, with clean, manicured nails and a neatly shaved scalp. A prosperous man, as his expensive clothes and wig confirmed, with a beautiful collar of colored faience beads around his neck.

"If he was in charge of all the floral offerings at the whole Ipet-isut, he must have been an important person," said Bener-ib as if she had read Neferet's thoughts.

"But I guess he was out of work for the period when the temple was shut down. How long was that? Twelve or thirteen years?" Neferet grinned at their young assistant, who had reappeared at her side. "As long as Mut-tuy is old."

"I'm thirteen, not twelve." said the girl, automatically contrary. But her attention was glued to the body of Sen-em-iah. An awkward silence fell over the three until Mut-tuy added, "My father was stabbed to death too."

And Bener-ib said in a small voice, "Mine too."

Oh, no—all this blood. It's probably awakening their worst nightmares. "But they were clean strikes, both of them. Just a nice, instantaneous blow to the heart. Neither one of them looked like this. They wouldn't have lingered and suffered." In fact, Neferet had no idea of the conditions of their deaths. Papa hadn't shared such details with his family when he had investigated.

Bener-ib drew in a big sniff. "Do we really have to report murders that come to us?"

"No, but I think we should find out who did it, don't you? To appease the Osiris Sen-em-iah's *ba*. And the killer is still wandering around. He could hurt somebody else."

"We should," Mut-tuy said fiercely. Her skinny frame quivered like a cat anticipating its pounce.

Maybe she ought to be a medjay—*a policeman—instead of a healer*, Neferet thought, both amused and surprised. She was tempted to say, "Not you—you're too young." But she remembered how offended she would have been by such a judgment when she was thirteen. That was the age she'd begun her apprenticeship to Khuit, right in this house. Old Khuit, too, had met a violent end.

Instead, Neferet said, "Let's talk to Papa this evening. He can tell us how to get started."

They had barely finished tidying up when two shaven-headed priests of Inpu arrived with a pair of sturdy servants. They went through all their prayers and wafted their incense around and dribbled their consecrated oils on Sen-em-iah's forehead. Then the servants loaded the deceased on a stretcher, draped him with a red linen sheet, and set off for the Per-Inpu, where the long embalming process would begin.

Bener-ib mopped up the floor and scrubbed until the stains on the tabletop had faded, then Neferet heaved the basin of bloody water out into the court for the dogs to enjoy. The air seemed suddenly fresher.

"What did you say that other healer's name was, Ibet— the one who works around here? We need to pay him a visit. See if we can't divide the practice somehow."

"Djed-har. Why don't you go, Nef'et? Somebody needs to be here in case we get another patient," Bener-ib said.

Neferet sighed. "What an optimist. All right. Mut-tuy, stay with Ibet and—"

"No," the girl said flatly. "I want to go see this Djed-har."

I've never met a more headstrong creature in my life. But Neferet knew she had much the same reputation. She could remember a few times in her childhood when her papa had had to lock her in the house to keep her from following him.

She shrugged. "If Bener-ib's in agreement."

"I don't really expect anybody, unfortunately."

Neferet led the way to the gate, unsure exactly of what she was doing but no less determined for all that. "Mut-tuy and I will be back before lunch," she called to the nursemaid.

The woman had Tiry and the baby each on a knee, nursing, while the others played, screeching, in the shade.

Neferet saw from the corner of her eye that the flourishing bed of calendulas had been trampled and the flowers scattered. She sighed.

They were out in the street when it struck her that she had no idea of where this Djed-har might live. *One of the neighbors will know. In fact, they probably all do, I'm afraid.* She made *hoo-hoo* noises at the door of the dyer across from their house. As usual, a sour, penetrating odor drifted out from the workshop out back, where they kept the urine they collected as a mordant for fabric to be dyed.

Sit-amen, the mistress of the house, appeared under the mat hanging in the doorway, her usual pleasant smile on her face. "Ah, Lady Neferet. I was just going to come over. I made sesame sweets this morning and thought the children might like some."

"That's *so* nice of you, mistress. I'm sure they would," Neferet said enthusiastically, the water rising to her mouth in expectation. "You're always so generous with us. I wish we could do something in return—I'd treat your children for free. How's that stye on the little one's eyelid?"

Sit-amen looked evasive as she folded a cloth around a basket full of sweets, still warm and radiating toasty sesame smells. Her capable brown hands deftly tucked the corners under, the creases of her knuckles and quicks stained bright red.

I guess we're doing a red batch today, Neferet thought.

"Oh, his eyelid is better. We put some salve on it."

"Did Djed-har give it to you?"

Sit-amen glanced up and away. "I think so."

"Could you tell me where he lives?" Neferet said. "Ever since we moved in, we've wanted to pay him a visit—colleagues to colleague, you know."

The woman looked flustered, but then she shrugged. "Why not? Turn left at the next corner, then go all the way

41

to the River. It's a fancy house opposite the royal magazines. There's a palm tree that bends out over the road." She held out the basket, her smile returning. "My children always love these, but I don't make them too often. With the festivals coming up, I thought it was time."

"May the Hidden One bless you! We'll return the basket."

The basket on her arm, Neferet backed out the doorway, waving goodbye, and Mut-tuy slouched after her. "It's my medical opinion that we should fuel our journey with a few of these before we set out for Djed-har's," the *sunet* said as soon as they were out in the baking sun of the street. She peeled back the towel and offered the basket to Mut-tuy, who took a treat, an expression of scornful disengagement on her face. But she went back for another even before Neferet had finished one succulent cake soaked in honey. "Mmm! She could be a professional baker."

"Not if everybody knew she had her hands in pee all day long," Mut-tuy said.

"She doesn't have her hands in pee. They trample the cloth with their feet. So you don't want her to kick you in the mouth."

Mut-tuy gave a snort of laughter despite herself, spraying sesame crumbs up the front of her sheath.

Suppressing a grin, Neferet eyed her appraisingly. "We need to let your hair grow. It won't be long till it's time to cut off this Haru-lock and replace it with braids."

"Mother already let me wear a dress for more than a year now."

Neferet knew better than to tangle with the sainted memory of the girl's mother, who had, in fact, been a slatternly, irresponsible, and wildly temperamental woman who beat her children. She just said, "There, you see?"

After a space of silence punctuated only by the twittering of birds and distant calls of workmen, Mut-tuy said, "Why do you and your family call your husband Lord Ptah-mes and everybody else says Lord Maya?"

"He went by Ptah-mes until a few years ago, when he was sent up to Azzati. Then he started calling himself by his childhood name. A lot of people whose names end in *mes* do it, like Maya, my brother-in-law. He's really Amen-mes."

Mut-tuy twisted her mouth skeptically. And indeed, it had been more complicated than that. Papa had hinted that Lord Ptah-mes's life had been unhappy at that point—he had been, in effect, exiled—and that he'd perhaps wanted to be someone else, if only the fortunate boy he had once been.

They wheeled left at the corner, as instructed, and set off in the direction of the River. Their bare feet padded in unison down the packed-earth street, which was almost empty of passersby at this hour. But the crowd began to grow as they neared the royal magazines—mostly porters and men driving donkeys and ox carts loaded with supplies for the storehouses. They saw the magazines to their right, one after another—long, low mudbrick buildings with vaulted roofs—and a steady stream of porters entering, sacks and jars on their shoulders. Shading her eyes, Neferet looked up and down the blank-faced row of small houses on her left. Most of these people probably had jobs at the palace. But it wasn't a pleasant block to live on, with the perpetual noise of trundling carts and the dust of endless feet. Up close, she saw that a good many of the houses looked uninhabited.

Only one stood out. It was considerably newer and larger than the others and had a fresh coat of whitewash. A tall, skinny palm tree stretched diagonally across the wall, leaving a little puddle of shade in the middle of the road.

"I guess this is our Djed-har's," she said, examining the high wall and gaudily painted gate. *Can a gate look unfriendly?* This one did.

After passing the basket of sweets to Mut-tuy, Neferet banged on the door with her fist. The two of them waited for a long time. Then she knocked again.

From within came the pad of bare footsteps and a deep, grumbling male voice. "All right, all right. I'm coming."

The gate swung back with a creak, revealing a stooped, skinny old man with very few teeth, whose appearance certainly didn't match his voice. His expression was chilly. "If you've come for the doctor, he's seeing a patient. Very important. Come back later."

He tried to pull the gate shut, but Neferet had already inserted herself in the opening. "We'll wait in the yard," she said with a good cheer that would have struck those who knew her as a little dangerous. One didn't say no to Neferet.

Mut-tuy, who enjoyed nothing so much as defying people, squeezed through as well. The two of them stood planted there, backs to the gate, and looked around.

The narrow court was bare, garnished only by a few reluctant sprigs of grass. The soil was trampled hard, and the only shade that relieved it was that cast by the wall, the one tree having abandoned its allegiance. It hardly looked as if anyone lived there. The house, on the other hand, was new and garish and too big for the lot. An eye-burning stench of ammonia filled the air.

They must pee on the walls, Neferet told herself in disgust, trying not to screw up her nose.

The old man turned back to the door of the residence with a sniff.

Neferet said casually, "You might tell Djed-har that the wife of Lord Maya, Master of the Double House, is waiting for him."

The man's eyes widened, and he hustled inside. A noticeably short time later, a small, dry, hollow-chested personage of about Papa's age burst across the sill, cleaning his teeth with his tongue in a way that suggested he had sprung up from his breakfast table. He bobbed up and down in an exaggerated gesture of respect. "My lady! What an honor! I apologize for making you wait. I had a patient. Please, come in, you and your daughter."

"I'm not her daughter," said Mut-tuy.

And he probably thinks I'm not Lord Maya's wife, thought Neferet with a silent chuckle. In terms of age, she could almost have been Ptah-mes's grandchild, and with her shaved head, bare feet, and unadorned working-class shift, she hardly fit the image of a great lady.

"This is my assistant. My partner and I are your new colleagues around the block. We just wanted to drop in and say hello."

Djed-har frosted over. He drew himself up and crossed his arms. His dark-ringed eyes flickered over her with the rock-hard hostility of jasper. "Permit me to say with all paternal goodwill, my little lady, that the practice of medicine, which is an honorable and learned science, seems like an unsuitable hobby for a girl of good birth. And it could be dangerous for the innocent people who commit themselves to your care."

Neferet felt the slow burn of anger rising up her cheeks, building steam in her nose. *So that's the way it is, eh?* She forced herself to maintain a civil expression, but her smile rattled a little at the edges as if it were coming undone. "Actually," she said too brightly, "we studied in the household of Lord Pentju, the vizier and former royal physician. We were the royal *sunet*s ourselves under Ankhet-khepru-ra. If you don't believe me, ask our Sun God."

Instead of looking impressed, Djed-har burst out laughing—a metallic, contemptuous whinny. "I'm sure you were. Just be aware that people's lives are at stake in your little fantasy, my dear."

She gritted her molars. "What are your qualifications, if I may ask? Because if you're a specialist, we may want to refer our patients to you." *Over my dead body.*

"I studied at the greatest medical school in the world at Sau," he said, lifting his chin. "My teacher was the inimitable Lord Iry, who proudly bore the title Shepherd of the Anus."

"So you specialize in shit. Good to know." Neferet bared her teeth in an icy smile. *There's no point talking about any division of labor with this dung heap. He doesn't think we're even real* sunet*s.* Then an idea wiggled its naughty way into her thoughts. She asked innocently, "Would you mind writing down a good poultice to cool the anus? We've got lots of patients who are... overheated."

Djed-har's eyes shifted back and forth in a flash of fear, then he tossed his head and said in a belittling tone, "Real professionals don't give away their cures so lightly, little lady."

"Little lady." That does it, thought Neferet, her simmer becoming a furious boil. But she realized she had learned something. *This man doesn't know how to write. I'll bet he's never been near Sau.*

She held onto her temper just long enough to say a semi-civil goodbye and get back out into the street. The gate slammed behind them. "What an utter and abominable fraud!"

"Isn't Lady Bener-ib from Sau? She'll know whether he studied there."

"She certainly will. Her father taught there at the House of Life." Neferet stumped away, heading inland at a fierce pace, propelled by her outrage. She thrust out a hand to Mut-tuy at her side. "Give me one of those sesame treats, please, my girl. I was going to let Djed-har have some, but he started lying the minute he showed up. He wasn't seeing a patient—he was eating."

"Grown-ups are disgusting," said Mut-tuy, and there was real disenchantment in her voice. She'd seen a lot of evidence in her thirteen years. The two of them ate as they walked, chewing with as much gusto as if it were Djed-har between their teeth.

"I'll bet anything he's warned everybody away from our practice. I really, really want to see him exposed for the fraud he is," Neferet growled.

"What if Lady Bener-ib doesn't remember whether he was at Sau or not?"

Neferet gave a carnivorous smile. "Oh, she'll remember. Ibet has the most formidable memory in the Two Lands. She could repeat to you word for word what her first nursemaid told her at the age of three."

They walked on in silence, jaws working. Only five sesame treats were left by the time they entered the brightly painted gate of the infirmary.

Bener-ib greeted them hopefully at the door of the dispensary. "Did you have any luck, Nef'et?"

Neferet was ready to vent. "He's the biggest dog turd under the sun. He said he trained at Sau, but he doesn't even know how to read, I'd bet anything. I think every word that comes out of his mouth is a lie. And then he gave me the 'little lady' and 'my dear' routine. Aagh!" She stamped her foot. "When I think that our neighbors are in his clutches, and here we are, well trained and ready to serve, and everybody is afraid to come because he tells them we're just rich little dilettantes, I want to *scream*."

"How awful." Bener-ib's very hair seemed to droop—she was so crestfallen. "I don't remember anybody at Sau named Djed-har, but maybe he's older."

"Our parents' age, I'd guess, although there was a dried-out look about him. He said he studied under somebody called Iry."

"The Shepherd of the Anus? But he lived more than a hundred years ago. My father mentioned him as if he were a god from ancient times."

Neferet and Mut-tuy exchanged looks of disgust.

"If Djed-har's been around for a hundred years, that explains why he looks dried out," said the girl with a sneer.

Neferet pounded one fist into the other palm. "We're going to win over that liar's patients if it takes the rest of my life, I swear. May Sekhmet make my hair grow in green if we don't. May I sprout a tail, and may worms come out my nose—"

"Oh, don't say that! What if it really happened?" Bener-ib cried in horror. She made a frantic little gesture to ward off bad luck.

But Mut-tuy laughed savagely. "I want to see it."

All at once, Neferet remembered that Bener-ib hadn't had any of the sesame cakes yet. She held out the basket. "These are for you, Ibet. Eat them now, and we'll take the basket back to Sit-amen. I'd like to hear what Djed-har has told everybody."

Her hand hovering over the basket, the young woman asked with her usual self-effacement, "Have the children had all they wanted?"

Neferet slapped herself on the forehead. "Oh no! Sit-amen gave them to us for the little ones, and we ate them all!"

Mut-tuy suppressed a snort of laughter—in her household, it had been every child for himself—and Neferet said matter-of-factly, "Well, we'll eat lunch at our house, and Mama will have her cook make some more. They're just as good—believe me. Go ahead and take those."

The two doctors lingered a while longer on the off chance that some patient might happen in. Then, having discovered that the nursemaid had already marched the younger children home for lunch and a nap, the three of them took off for Mama and Papa's house. It was closer than Lord Ptah-mes's and a lot more comfortable. Besides, she hadn't had a chance to talk to Papa about the dead man and how to pursue his murderer.

As they drew near to the southern suburbs, with its old

family villas, Neferet noticed for the first time that the large houses were surrounded by clusters of poorer ones—no doubt residences of the servants of the rich and the artisans who catered to them. She tried to remember if such blocks huddled around the magnificent estate of Lord Ptah-mes. In any case, the idea of a working-class neighborhood was nebulous, she saw. *I wonder who the neighborhood healer down here is.* Her own family had always consulted a real *sunu* when one of the children's escapades had ended in a broken arm or a split lip. And then, of course, there was Baket-iset's accident.

They drew near to the familiar red gate, and Neferet was flooded with the warmth of all her happy childhood memories. She had never known any other home until the day she married. Well, she and Ibet had lived at the palace on and off, but this had always been home. Like the farm, it had belonged to Grandfather and probably his father before him. A haven of love, the modest villa was always open to guests and relations. The married children and their families were still frequently to be found here, as if strong cords bound them to the big, friendly house and its peaceful gardens, drawing them back and back if they wandered overly far. Her parents were never too busy to welcome visitors.

Neferet knocked eagerly, and the gate was opened not by old A'a, the perennial doorkeeper, but by Iuty, the younger gardener.

"Mistress Neferet! Mistress Bener-ib! The master and mistress will be happy to see you. Your sister is here too." He stepped back and let the three young women pass.

"But where is A'a?"

"Here, mistress," said the old man from a stool in the shade of the garden shrine. He grinned and waved a bony hand.

"He's supervising now," Iuty said with a wink. "Training me for the job."

"We'll have to call you Great One of the Gatekeepers," Neferet said. The old man was as much a fixture of her childhood as the house.

The three young women passed up the white-graveled walk toward the dwelling, which was set well back in the vegetation, at its lushest in the late-summer-harvest season. Among the bushes, the cicadas blared, and the familiar scent of thyme and sage simmered under the filtered shade of date palms, jujube, and acacia trees. Papa's pet heron stalked elegantly down the path as if coming to greet them.

"Too bad we ate all the sweets," murmured Mut-tuy.

Bener-ib looked stricken. "Oh, I should have left some."

"She'd rather have a juicy frog," said Papa from behind the pomegranate bushes. He stepped out in front of them, arms wide, and Neferet hurled herself into them.

"What are you lurking around outside for, Papa Duck?" She laughed.

"Observing my fellow ducks." He gestured vaguely back toward the long rectangular pool, where the family raised carp and *bulti*. As usual, a flotilla of aquatic fowl paddled about among the waterlilies. "Are you girls going to join us for lunch? Where are the children?"

"They went home with the nurse before we decided to come here. Do you think the cook can make sesame treats before we leave?"

Hani threw up his hands in defense. "You're asking the

wrong person, my duckling. The kitchen is your mother's domain."

And when Neferet looked up, there stood her mother in the doorway, tiny and beautiful and as perfectly groomed as if she were singing for the Hidden One. "I thought I heard your voice, my love! Come on in, girls, and join us. Lunch is on the table. And Sati and Maya are here."

Neferet and Bener-ib hugged her—Bener-ib was marvelously fond of Lady Nub-nefer, who took the place of the mother she had lost too soon. Mut-tuy nodded a self-conscious adolescent acknowledgement, and the five of them trooped into the house.

Even from the vestibule, they could hear the laughter in the salon—Neferet's two sisters and Maya, her brother-in-law and Papa's secretary. Then Grandfather said something, and everybody laughed again.

Yahyah! They're all here! Neferet thought in delight. But then she realized that would make it harder to get into the second reason for their visit. *How will I talk about our murder case in front of the family?* They would warn her away from it, every one of them.

At her side, her mother said to her father, "You know, my love, a terrible thing happened on the temple grounds last night." Mama was a chantress of Amen-Ra, and her brother was Third Prophet. Thus, the family knew everything that happened within the sacred walls of the Greatest of Shrines. "The man in charge of floral offerings was stabbed. Who would want to murder a florist?"

CHAPTER 3

"THAT WAS *OUR* NEWS," NEFERET cried in disappointment.

Any further discussion was cut short by the clamor of welcome as they entered the salon. The doors to the garden were wide open to lure in even a warm midday breeze, and a fluttering greenish light, rich with all the herbal scents of the out-of-doors, washed the normally shadowy room. The family members were seated two by two at the folding tables Neferet had eaten from since she was old enough to sit up—Sati and Maya, Mama and Papa, and Grandfather by himself but leaning over Hani's just-served plate, probing, no doubt, for pickled turnips. Baket-iset, paralyzed since she fell from a boat half a lifetime ago, smiled happily up from the couch where she lay. Mama went off to tell the servants to set three more places and bring more stools.

"*Iyah!* Here are our medical girls," Grandfather said with a big grin that everyone said was identical to Neferet's and was certainly just like his son's. "Feel free to eat cabbage, my friends, and let indigestion do its worst."

"We don't have cabbage, Grandfather," said Baket-iset with a laugh. She turned to the newcomers. "Neferet! Bener-ib! And Mut-tuy! How nice you could join us."

"We came partly to ask a favor of Mama's cook."

"Surely Lord Ptah-mes has a cook. Even we have a cook," Maya said dryly. He was touchy about social status, having been born the son of a goldsmith. Mut-tuy's late father had been an artisan in her workshop.

"Yes, but nobody makes sesame treats the way Mama's cook does."

"It's our family recipe," said Mama as she entered at the head of two servants bearing stools and tables. As soon as the latter were unfolded, she set three plates upon them, seating Neferet and Bener-ib together as she would any couple, with Mut-tuy joining Grandfather.

"That florist who was stabbed died in our infirmary." Neferet washed her fingers in the little dish of perfumed water, enjoying the looks of surprise on the faces of those around her.

His bushy eyebrows rising, Papa said, "He was stabbed on the temple grounds, and they brought him all the way up to you ladies?"

"I think he was actually attacked at his gate as he came home this morning. And one of his litter bearers lives in our neighborhood, so I guess that was the only place they knew about."

"If they know about it, why don't they come to us for care?" muttered Mut-tuy.

"It sounds like they did, my girl," said Maya a little sharply. Neferet knew he didn't like children to be so forward—except for his own, who regularly monopolized the attention of all the grown-ups.

"Is he the one you said did such beautiful work, Mama?" asked Sati.

"Oh yes. His bouquets are magnificent. I'd love to see the fields where they grow all those gorgeous flowers. And thousands of them—you can imagine how many bouquets the Hidden One enjoys every single day."

Mama lifted a quail to her mouth with dainty fingers, and Neferet attacked her own with less daintiness, swabbing it in the sorrel sauce. It was definitely an excellent idea to have come here for lunch.

"It seems barbaric to kill a person who makes such beautiful things," Baket-iset said.

Neferet saw from the corner of her eye that Mut-tuy had stiffened—her father had made beautiful jewels for the king. "And they really cut him up inside. Whoever got him wanted to be sure he was dead. And they knew how to do it. They didn't just stab—they ripped. All his entrails—"

"Do we have to talk about this at the table, Neferet?" Sati looked a bit green.

"I suppose he had a family," mused Mama. "Perhaps we should pay our respects. I'm embarrassed to say I'm not sure I even know his name."

Bener-ib said, "Sen-em-iah son of Nakht."

"Well, well," Grandfather said with a belly-shaking chuckle. "I used to do business with old Nakht before he limited his clientele to the king of the gods. I couldn't compete, I'm afraid."

"What were you doing with a florist, Father?" asked Papa.

"Why, buying flowers—what did you think? We used to have parties rather frequently in our youth. You were sent up to the nursery, I'm afraid. I remember once Pipi fell down the stairs, where he had crept to spy on the grown-ups. We heard it, of course, and we all came running. There is no perfect crime."

Papa let out a guffaw. "I remember that too. I was with him, but when he fell, I hotfooted it back up to the nursery. *My* crime was perfect!"

"But now it's come to light." Mama laughed and wagged a warning finger. "Ma'at will make her exaction of you now."

"My punishment seems to be that we're out of quail." Papa eyed the empty serving platter mournfully. He dipped a finger in the congealing sauce and licked it.

Bener-ib pushed her plate toward him. "I haven't touched this yet, Lord Hani. Please take it. We came unannounced."

"No, no, my girl. I thank you for your generosity, but this is Ma'at's way of telling me I don't need another one."

At that moment, the serving girl emerged from the kitchen, bearing a second platter piled high with the small golden carcasses in a lake of tart green sauce, trailed by a plume of steam and fragrance.

"Your sacrifice is in vain, my love," said Mama with a smile. "I told cook to make more when the girls arrived." She turned a tender gaze on Neferet. "And she's making sesame treats."

Papa, with a guilty grin, speared himself a second quail. "Don't tell the live birds how much I love them cooked."

When they'd all finished and Grandfather and her

sisters had dispersed to their siesta, Neferet hissed, "Papa, I need to talk to you about something. That florist…"

"Should I wait for you outside, Lord Hani?" asked Maya, sliding from his stool. "We were going to do some work, remember?"

"No, my boy. Stay. You can hear whatever Neferet wants to tell me—can't he, my duckling?"

She made a disappointed moue. "I suppose."

Maya had aided her father in his investigations over the years. As a dwarf, he could go places the bigger people couldn't. The one she really would have liked to send off to nap time was Mut-tuy, but the girl refused to catch Neferet's eye and sat as immovable as a skinny rock next to Bener-ib. They had all drawn the stools into a circle so they could speak quietly.

"Papa, the only thing we know is what Sen-em-iah's litter bearers and bodyguards told us—he had just arrived at his own gate this morning when a couple of men attacked. The servants succeeded in fighting them off but not before they'd inflicted a fatal and *very* messy evisceration wound. He was barely alive by the time they got to the dispensary, and he died almost immediately."

"Well, then," said Papa, "no culpability on your part. You couldn't have done anything to save him."

"Oh, I know. But we need to find out who killed him, don't we?"

"I don't know. *Do* you?" asked Maya in a tone that implied they did not.

"We're supposed to report murders," said Mut-tuy defiantly as Neferet gestured for her to shut up.

"At least, it would be nice to appease his *ba*, don't you

think? We don't want him haunting people. And there was a lot of odd business around this man, Papa. I think he knew his murderer."

Papa looked thoughtful. "What makes you say that?"

"I don't know. I just have a feeling, like Grandfather says, *in here.*" She slapped herself on the belly. "Besides, his dying words were mysterious."

"And what were they, little duck?"

She turned proudly to Bener-ib, who said in a sepulchral tone, as if revealing a cosmic secret, "Rabbit."

There was a long silence while the others digested this enigma. Finally, trying hard to suppress a snort of laughter, Maya said, "And you think he was telling you that a rabbit murdered him? I know they can kick hard, but to eviscerate a man…"

"It would have to have been standing on a table," Papa agreed with a suspicious twitch at the corners of his mouth.

They aren't taking this seriously, Ammit take it. Neferet's face flamed like coals. "I didn't say that was the murderer's name, people. But you have to agree it's mysterious. Why would that be Sen-em-iah's last word, poised at the edge of the Duat? It must be important."

Papa, clearly still fighting down the urge to laugh, nodded. "And how do you plan to find the killer?"

"We need to talk to the bearers and guards again. See what they remember." Neferet held up a hand and began folding down one finger at a time. "We need to talk to his widow and any grown children. See if he had any enemies. I'd like to visit his workshop and flower farms to find out if anyone knows anything there. I want—"

"See here, Neferet," said Maya, serious now. "Do you

think this is appropriate? You two are physicians, not investigators. People have no obligation to talk to you. And worse still, you may happen on the murderer without knowing it. He may decide to rough you up or worse."

Papa gave her a tender smile. "We know you're brave, my duckling, but he's right. This could be really dangerous—two young women falling afoul of a criminal."

"Three young women," Mut-tuy corrected with a scowl.

Neferet made a huge effort not to yell. "It's all right for two men to investigate without a mandate but not for two—three—women? I should have known." She crossed her arms as if to keep from throwing something. "I thought you would help us, Papa, but no. Nothing but discouraging words. It's the same story as always. Men can do it, but women can't. If I had a copper *deben* for every time someone said that to me about practicing medicine, I'd be rich."

"You *are* rich," Bener-ib murmured as Neferet stared at her in disbelief. "It will be dangerous, Nef'et. They're right about that."

"What if I told you two we were required by law to report the circumstances of a murder whose victim we treated?" Neferet asked.

"I wouldn't believe you," said Maya.

"How are you going to have time to do this, anyway?" Papa asked. "You're busy taking care of your patients."

Raising her hands to the heavens, Neferet exploded. "What patients? They're all going to a male witch doctor who lies about his credentials."

Maya cast a glance at Lord Hani and lifted his eyebrows.

"We haven't told you about that yet, have we? That's why I'm so mad." With plenty of descriptive gestures and changes of voice, she outlined their frustrating visit to Djed-har. "Here he is, accusing us of being rich little frauds when he's the biggest liar on the bosom of Geb. He claimed to be a student of Iry when Iry's been dead for thousands of years."

"Well, a hundred," Bener-ib corrected timidly.

"Might as well be a thousand. He thought we wouldn't know. If he was just an honest witch doctor, fine. But I'm sure he's telling everybody he's a trained *sunu* and that we're ignoramuses. You should see that fancy new house of his. Don't tell me a neighborhood healer can afford such a place."

Papa shook his head sadly. "I'm sorry to say there are a lot of people like that, my duckling—people who have no respect for Ma'at and her truth. He's doing real harm by keeping people away from your care."

"We bring the children to you," said Maya defensively. "And we tell our friends to do the same."

Neferet doubted that many of Maya's friends lived in the same modest neighborhood where he had grown up, but he meant well. "Thanks," she said, deflated after her angry recital. "We'll just have to change everybody's mind."

"Maybe we should be getting back," murmured Bener-ib.

Neferet snorted bitterly. "In case someone else has brought a dying man to our door."

The young women rose to depart, and Papa and Maya pushed back the stools and prepared to spread out their work for the afternoon.

From the kitchen, Mama appeared with a towel-covered basket. "Now, don't eat these again before the children get any," she cautioned with a knowing smile. "Bener-ib, dear, see to it she stays out of them."

Neferet thanked her mother with enthusiasm, voluptuously sniffing the warm toasty scent of sesame. "Maybe we should hand out free treats to anybody who comes to the dispensary."

To her surprise, Maya said, "Not a bad idea, at least until people get into the habit."

However, the real jolt came from Mama. "You'll never believe this, but Cook says her sister works for this Sen-em-iah. She was shocked when I told her what had happened. I asked her where he lived. I think I'll pay the family a visit of condolence tomorrow if you want to come. I'm off duty until the afternoon."

Neferet's eyes popped with excitement, and she exchanged eager looks with Bener-ib. "Oh yes! I think that's the least we can do, don't you? Since we couldn't save the poor man."

"But don't harass them with questions, my girl," Papa cautioned. "You don't need to get involved in the murder. Just pay your respects."

"Of course, Papa." Neferet gave a mischievous snicker. "We'll bring them flowers."

"I hope she doesn't think you were encouraging her to investigate," Hani said next morning as he and Nub-nefer dressed. "You know Neferet. She'll be saying, 'Mama told me to.'"

He knotted his kilt and laid upon his shoulders a

sober dark-blue beaded collar that seemed appropriately mournful.

Nub-nefer reached up to tie it behind his neck. "I didn't encourage her, Hani, my love. I just think it's appropriate for her to express her condolences since they treated the poor man. Don't you?"

Hani made a noncommittal noise.

His wife said a little tartly, "Give her credit for some sense. She's grown up a lot. I think Bener-ib is a good influence."

"I agree. Neferet is a sensible girl under it all. But this determination of hers to find the man's murderer has me concerned." Hani knew that itch to see *ma'at* restored to the world. And he also knew from painful experience what dangers it could drag down on a person's head.

Nub-nefer stood back to give Hani a final look, and he was able to take her in as well. Perfectly beautiful, for all her fifty-three years—trim and golden and as smooth skinned as the day he married her, or almost.

"You're superb, my dove," he said, beaming with pride. He caressed her cheek with a hand. "I bless the inexplicable day you accepted my suit!"

"I told the gods I wanted the kindest, most loving man on earth, and they heard my prayer," she said tenderly.

"And the handsomest," he added with a grin. "After your own brother, of course."

She laughed and stretched up to kiss Hani's cheek. "Amen-em-hut is coming to the house of the Osir, too, or so he said."

"The Third Prophet of Amen is paying his respects?

This florist seems to be quite the important fellow for a working-class sort."

"Oh, he was supervisor to hundreds of people—he no longer did the work himself. And they did a magnificent job."

Hani held open the bedroom door for his wife, who preceded him to the stairs. "Who will take over his establishment? I guess his children will continue to run it?"

"I suppose we'll find out," she said over her shoulder.

They clattered down the staircase and entered the salon, where they found Neferet, Bener-ib, and Mut-tuy standing. The young girl—tall, flat-chested, and angular—wore the usual expression of suspicion and disgust. He wondered if Neferet hadn't met her match in the orphan.

"Good morning, ladies. Who's minding the dispensary in your absence?"

"Mangler. He's promised to lick the wounds of anyone who shows up," said Neferet cheerfully. She kissed her parents. "You know where we're going, I guess?"

"Mama does," Hani said. "Lead on, my dove."

In a block, they followed Nub-nefer to the door and crossed the garden, chattering and laughing. They encountered Mery-ra on the path, a bunch of cornflowers and a kitchen knife in his hand. He looked up in surprise.

"Revered father! You're up early. Have you decided to replace our late florist?" Hani slapped his father on the back, grinning with affectionate mischief.

Mery-ra's cheeks flushed. "Morning, son. Morning, ladies. No, no. I, uh, felt I needed a little peace offering to take to Meryet-amen. Blue's her favorite color." He looked at the flowers in his fist with embarrassment and stuck them behind his broad back.

"*Yahyah!*" Nub-nefer smiled. "Don't tell us all is not well between you." Meryet-amen, a wealthy widow, was the old man's lady friend. "What will Hani do for court gossip if she and her nephew are no longer part of our circle?"

"Nothing serious, I hope. I just need to pour a little honey on the wound, as our girls would say." Mery-ra's gaze swept over the familial crowd headed to the gate. "Where are you all going at this hour?"

Neferet said eagerly, "We're going to pay our respects to the man who died in our dispensary yesterday. We thought we might learn something that would help us track down his murderer."

Hani shot an I-told-you-so look at his wife, whose serenely amused expression never altered. Then he caught his father's glance.

Mery-ra's little brown eyes were alight. "So, you're on the case, eh?"

"No, Father. It's a job for the *medjay*." Hani sent a sideways glance at his daughter, who seemed not to have heard.

Bener-ib, at her side, looked anxiously at her.

They left the old man to his picking, Neferet calling over her shoulder with a naughty grin, "Include some mandrakes. They make love bloom!"

The morning crowds had filled the streets with noise and turbulence by the time they located the late florist's house. It was quite a splendid place, not far from the Ipet-Isut itself, thus in the same neighborhood as Lord Ptahmes's ancestral villa. But whereas the grandee's property exuded the perfume of old wealth and understated taste with nothing to prove, Sen-em-iah's mansion couldn't have been more than a generation old. It dominated its neighbors with its high walls and impressive gateway, painted with the owner's name and "Bearer of the Divine Offerings of Amen." Young trees rustled above the whitewashed expanse of wall. The gate panels stood open, and a pair of doormen welcomed the guests who came and went, most of them in white mourning scarves.

"Oh dear," said Hani. "Will we look disrespectful with our bare heads? Maybe we should throw a little dirt on our faces."

"No, no, my love," Nub-nefer reassured him. "We aren't family or close friends."

They passed through the gate, and no one asked them to identify themselves. Hani's eyes grew wide in admiration at the modest-sized garden. Whatever it lacked in mature shade trees, the area more than made up for in floral splendor. Among their irrigation runnels, the beds were densely planted in blocks of color—white chamomile and gold calendulas, blue cornflowers, and even the butterfly-delicate wings of scarlet poppies. He had never witnessed such profusion. He couldn't even see the ground between the plants. *It's clear a florist lived here.*

Beneath the young sun of an early-summer morning, the blooms shook their perfumed locks, and delicious scents rose like incense. The languid strum of cicadas was as amorous as the sistra of Hut-haru's own Lovelies. *This is one of the most beautiful places I've ever seen*, Hani thought, impressed. He had accompanied Nub-nefer out of a sense of duty, but all at once, he was glad he'd come.

Around the family garden shrine, lightly shaded by a pair of tamarisks in plumy pink flower, well-dressed visitors had gathered, chatting. Bouquets lay, overflowing, at the feet of the household gods and ancestors. Other people mingled on the porch and drifted in and out of the tall doors of the house.

"I'm impressed, my dove," he murmured to his wife. "The Osir seems to have had a lot of friends."

"A good many of them are temple personnel. I recognize a number of the priests and chantresses," Nub-nefer said. "Yes, it is impressive. Surprising, really."

They milled around and eventually drifted into the salon, where the family sat on colorful mats on the floor, receiving the condolences of their friends. The widow was a dull-eyed woman without makeup, who stared in a strangely expressionless way around her. Her short, natural hair was disheveled and drab with sand, which certainly didn't improve her appearance. At her side, a plump, glum-looking young man of about thirty kept watch over her. Hani assumed this to be Sen-em-iah's son. Several younger children clustered about them, wiping their eyes and every so often puckering up for a wail.

The poor family. One moment, they're happy and safe. The next, their father has been taken from them. It made Hani conscious of the fragility of life. Too often, he'd exposed himself to danger without much thought for what would befall his loved ones if the worst happened to him. He trailed Nub-nefer to the foot of the dais where the grieving survivors sat.

She introduced herself and spoke admiringly of the artistry of the deceased. The widow smiled listlessly and thanked her for her wishes. Hani remembered that Mut-tuy had described the woman's behavior as odd in her husband's last moments. He had to agree, although he couldn't put his finger on what was missing. People often responded to death with numbness.

Hani and his wife moved on, pushed gently by the line of those behind them. Then, from the rear, he heard Neferet's loud voice saying emphatically, "I don't know if you recognize us, mistress, but we're the doctors you brought your husband to yesterday. I'm sorry we couldn't do anything for him."

"I understand," the widow said faintly. "It was nice of you to come."

"Is there any time we could talk to you or the servants who might know anything about your husband's business? We need to get a sense of why someone might have done this to him and who it might be—you know, for our report."

Hani rolled his eyes. He might have known his youngest daughter wouldn't have forgotten her self-appointed mission so quickly.

A masculine voice said, "I'll talk to her, Mother. We want to be sure everything is done properly."

"But, Pen-buy, we've never had to do anything like this before..."

"And we've never had a murder in the family before." The man's voice had turned into a grunt, as if he were getting to his feet as he spoke.

By this time, Hani was too far away to hear any more, but he turned surreptitiously and saw the son of the family leading Neferet by the elbow toward the door into the interior of the house, Bener-ib and Mut-tuy in their wake. *I hope this isn't a bad idea. I may need to rein her in.*

67

CHAPTER 4

NEFERET FOLLOWED THE MAN DOWN the corridor and into the little courtyard, half-covered by a reed mat, that served as the family's kitchen. Several servants, in the midst of preparing refreshments, looked up at their master's approach.

"Go away for a minute," he said loudly. "Take those things into the salon if they're ready. I need to talk to this woman."

He then turned his attention to the three young women. He wasn't good-looking—*sloppy* was the word that came to Neferet's mind, despite his neat, expensive clothes. Soft flesh spilled over everywhere, and his face seemed to be composed of a beard-shadowed landscape of vague lumps rather than distinct features. But he appeared to be taking the women seriously.

"My name is Pen-buy son of Sen-em-iah. How can I help you, mistress?"

"Did your father have any enemies, Pen-buy? Business

rivals? Anybody who might have profited from his death?" Hands on hips, Neferet faced him with her most serious air.

Bener-ib pulled out a potsherd and a stick of charcoal and began to take notes, and Pen-buy's eyes flickered toward her and widened. *You didn't expect to find a literate woman, did you, my boy?*

"She can write?" the man asked.

"We both can. She studied at Sau. We're literate and highly trained *sunet*s who have served the palace under Lord Pentju, who's now the vizier." Neferet couldn't disguise her satisfaction as she watched his rising eyebrows. "If we couldn't save your father, it's because nobody could have. Someone intended him to die and took no chances."

Pen-buy swallowed hard. Then he said pensively, "I can't think of anyone who would want Father dead. He was well thought of by his colleagues and employees."

"He hadn't seemed preoccupied or anxious lately?"

"No. Well, maybe, but…" Pen-buy seemed to be weighing his duty to be frank.

"Anything you recall might be helpful to the *medjay*."

"Maybe I should just talk to them directly. They may make me say everything over again anyway." He looked around him restlessly, and Neferet realized they might be losing him.

"That's up to you," she said with an air of indifference. "By the time they come to you for information, more time will have passed, and more clues will be cold."

"We just need to make our report," Bener-ib said.

Mut-tuy's eyes flickered from one face to another. Her lips were pressed tightly together, and she looked like she wanted to say something.

Neferet said hastily, "Does the word *rabbit* have any significance for you?"

Pen-buy looked confused, almost offended, as if he thought she was teasing him. "No. We don't raise rabbits. We don't even like them—they eat flowers."

"It was your father's last word—I thought you'd want to know."

The man frowned. "It doesn't mean anything to me, but I'll tell my stepmother. She may recognize some significance in it. Thank you for making us aware."

He doesn't know a cross-eyed thing, Neferet decided, disappointed. "We'll let you get back to your guests, Pen-buy. Would you object if we came to the workshop and asked some of the workmen a few—"

"You're *in* the workshop. We work out of the buildings in back of the house. At night, of course, so the flowers will be fresh in the morning." He opened the door behind him and ushered the three back into the corridor. "You're free to, but I don't think you're going to learn anything. Everybody loved Father. He took good care of his people. He was... He was a good man in every way."

When the four of them trooped back into the salon and Pen-buy had disappeared into the crowd, Neferet sighed. "That was a waste of time. But at least he didn't call me 'little lady.'"

"We know now where the workshop is." Bener-ib was the perpetual optimist.

Although, Neferet thought, *she's probably* trying *to be an optimist since she really expects the worst.*

After partaking of the extravagant food offered by the bereaved family, Neferet's group took their leave. Once they stood together in the street once more, Papa put a hand on Neferet's shoulder and steered her a little apart.

"You mustn't harass these people, my duckling. They've just suffered a terrible loss," he said quietly enough that the others couldn't hear. "Just make your report and forget about it. The *medjay* are probably already working on finding the killer."

She could feel the sticky wave of stubbornness creeping over her like rabbit-skin glue, starting to harden into something unmovable. "You know the police, Papa. They don't really care about the people who die. They're just doing a job."

"Now, that's unfair. I'm sure there are many compassionate *medjay* who really want to help restore *ma'at*." He gave a bitter little chuckle. "Not everybody is like Mahu." Papa and Mahu, the former chief of police in the Horizon of the Aten, had been sworn enemies. Neferet, too, had fallen afoul of his antipathy toward the family. "No, no, my girl. You three need to leave this case alone. Concentrate on winning over patients. You have so much to offer."

He patted her fondly on the shoulder and drew her back to the group. Everybody was watching them, perhaps guessing what they had said. Mut-tuy's skeptical eyes zigzagged back and forth between Neferet and Papa as if to demand a report.

Neferet's jaw grew tight. His words had been a gently phrased paternal command. She didn't want to make too glaring a display of her rebellion because Mut-tuy was already only too inclined to resist everything her elders told her.

But as they parted from her parents, Neferet couldn't help saying, "Well, we're off to our grown-up occupation, people. Where we'll use our judgment in matters that affect people's lives. They trust us to do the right thing."

"Of course, my dearest," Mama said, waving. "I hope you get some patients."

After a moment of confusion, Papa just threw back his head and laughed heartily. He gave Neferet a wink, and her parents set off—Mama in the direction of home and Papa, still shaking his head, toward the Hall of Royal Correspondence. The three young women headed north toward the more modest neighborhood where their dispensary stood. Neferet was steaming, her steps heavy and violent.

Bener-ib, who observed her for a while in anxious silence, finally said quietly, "What's wrong, Nef'et? What did Lord Hani tell you?"

"To stay out of it, of course. To let the *medjay* take care of it." Neferet stopped walking and stamped her foot. "I'm *so* disappointed in him. I thought Papa would understand why we needed to investigate this case. After all the times we've helped him in *his* investigations."

"But why *do* we need to investigate? It has nothing to do with us. It could be dangerous. Somebody out there is willing to kill."

"Ibet, my girl, we're physicians," Neferet said with deep earnestness. "Everything we do is to help the living—to heal them, if possible, or at least to comfort them in dying. And once they're dead, do we just dump their souls like a load of bandages too dirty to bother washing? No. We couldn't save this Sen-em-iah, but we can at least be sure his *ka* can rest at peace without his poor abandoned *ba* flying around every night, looking for justice, for the rest of eternity. Even at the risk of our lives!"

Mut-tuy clapped heartily, her expression fierce and exalted. Neferet would have liked to tell her, "Not you, you're too young," but it would have seemed ungrateful to squelch an ally.

Bener-ib looked back and forth between them uneasily, her sharp features drooping in defeat. "If you say so…"

Neferet felt a sharp stab of guilt. *Do I want to do this more than I want Ibet to be happy?* Finally, she said, "All right. We'll go notify the *medjay*."

"What about his poor abandoned *ba*?" Mut-tuy squawked.

Neferet quelled her with an imperious hand and said piously, "We can't harm the living to help the dead."

They set off once more, Mut-tuy looking thunderous. But Bener-ib touched Neferet's arm with timid gratitude. Before they had gone too far, Neferet realized that, while she'd once been incarcerated in the police garrison at Akhet-aten, she had no idea where the comparable building was in Waset.

She stopped once more. "Let's drop by Papa's office, if he's gotten there yet, and ask him where the *medjay* are. He'll probably know."

The idea of him gloating over her capitulation sent a curl of smoke fuming up in her heart. Still, she was committed to doing this deed. Let the gods send her the least sign, and she might change her mind, but for the moment, that mind was made up, and she was as implacable in pursuit of the new course of action as she had been against it. Besides, Papa wasn't a gloater.

The crowd of pedestrians was growing denser as the morning wore on and as they approached the heart of the city. There was a strong reek of dung in the air and the bitter smell of heated metal. A fishmonger cried loudly the virtues of his catch, and a body of laundrymen, headed for the River with their baskets on their heads, pushed past, all but naked and already sweating under the powerful early-summer sun.

The House of Rejoicing, the late King Neb-ma'at-ra's jubilee palace, was on the west bank, but the warren of low whitewashed buildings that housed the House of Royal Correspondence lay on the city side of the River, where the older residences of Theban kings had stood for generations. The young women trudged up the ceremonial way that linked the mighty Ipet-isut to the Southern Ipet. The road was broad, sun-drenched, lined with ram-headed lions. On festival days, the *wab* priests carried the Hidden One's golden land barque in a glittering procession from one temple to another, but now an everyday crowd pushed and jostled the three. An occasional high-level bureaucrat in a splendid chariot galloped past, whipping on his sweaty horses despite the crowds. For all Neferet knew, one of them might have been her husband, who had a fine team.

Across from the temple of Mut and Khonsu, the young women turned left toward the River into the warren of low buildings that marked the scattered seat of the chancery. Papa's office was at the northern edge. The edifices were nondescript cubes of unwhitewashed mudbrick with bleak sunbaked little courts between, where busy scribes passed this way and that, heads swiveling at the unexpected sight of three females walking with brisk purpose toward the foreign office.

They entered the vestibule, a lofty-ceilinged space dimly lit by high windows. On the floor, a variety of petitioners sat cross-legged, patiently awaiting their turn. A few were dressed in the colorful garments of Djahy or Amurru, which Neferet recognized because of the many foreign visitors Papa had hosted during her childhood.

A prune-faced scribe sat at the front of the room, acting as receptionist. He looked up at them with eyebrows lifted in skeptical inquiry. "How may I help you, mistress?" he asked Neferet coolly.

"I want to speak to Lord Hani if he's here yet. Please tell him that the wife of Lord Ptah—I mean, Maya—wants a word with him."

The man scrambled hastily to his feet. "Of course, my lady. Please be so good as to have a seat. Er, er, I'll find you a stool."

"Not necessary," Neferet assured him cheerily. "You won't be long." She dropped to the floor and folded her legs, despite the constraint of her shift, and her two companions followed suit. Neferet could feel the curious eyes of the other petitioners on her back.

A brief interval passed, then Papa's office door opened, and the receptionist burst forth. He approached the young women with a bow. "My lady, the high commissioner will receive you."

"Of course he will." Neferet led the way into Papa's private audience hall.

He stood in front of his official chair. His scepter of

office lay in the seat. Papa was chewing something but swallowed hastily and greeted his visitors with a big smile and open arms. There were sesame seeds in the corners of his mouth.

"My duckling! Girls! Had I known you were coming this way, I would have waited for you. To what do I owe this invasion of feminine beauty?"

"Papa, can you tell us where the police garrison is in Waset?"

He looked at her, head cocked, a question in his eye.

Neferet hastened to say, "We want to report the murder of Sen-em-iah."

Papa nodded. "Excellent decision. It's not far—just south of here, almost at the edge of the administrative district. A tower similar to the one in Akhet-aten. If you get anywhere near it, you'll see it."

"Thanks." She turned to go then faced her father once more. "What are you eating, Papa?"

He laughed guiltily, his cheeks flushing, like a little boy caught in the act. "Sesame treats. The ones cook made for you yesterday were so delicious that we had her make more. I'd offer you ladies some, but I just scoffed down the last of them."

Neferet crowed with laughter. "So that's why you made us wait. Well, we're off. Give Mama and Grandfather and Baket-iset our love."

The three of them trooped out one after the other, past the curious stares of the petitioners and past the gawping scribes who haunted the courtyard. Once they had made their way to the street that outlined the southern border of the bureaucratic district, they stopped.

Neferet shaded her eyes with her hand. "Does anyone see a tower?"

The other two lifted similar hands, and they all stood back-to-back in matching positions, staring out over the sun-glaring lane in every direction.

"What's that thing that's taller than the other buildings?" asked Mut-tuy, who was herself taller than the others.

"That must be it." Neferet started to walk again but then stopped suddenly. "Oh."

Bener-ib bumped into her back. "What is it, Nef'et?"

"I've just had a wonderful idea. What if we offer to treat the *medjay* for free? They must get injured a lot. We wouldn't make anything on them, but they would tell their families. Imagine how many policemen there must be in a city this size!"

Bener-ib's eyes grew wide in admiration. "That *is* a wonderful idea. You're so clever!"

With a brisker step, the trio set off once more, keeping in sight the crenelated rooftop that loomed over the low houses around it. As they drew closer, they could see that it was indeed a tower of three stories with a modest walled court beside it. The stout gate was open, and a policeman with a spear and a cowhide shield stood guard. It looked intimidating—the sort of place one might enter and never emerge from.

Neferet's steps slowed as they drew up to the gate. The *medjay* said nothing, although his eyes flickered toward the three as they passed inside the court. Unlike the garrison in the City of the Horizon, there was an air of age about the building—the brick was softened and the wood scoured by generations of sand and wind. Things were a little untidy.

Neferet fully expected to hear the caterwauls of tortured prisoners, but the only sound was that of a cicada in the yard.

She turned to the others. "Let me do the talking. When we come to the part about Sen-em-iah's last words, I'll turn it over to you, Ibet."

The door was open for the breeze, the fly mat mostly rolled up but hanging at an angle. The three young women marched up to the entrance in a resolute line. Inside, several men stood conversing, among them a barrel-shaped, middle-aged specimen in civilian dress, who looked up as Neferet crossed the threshold.

A sudden lightning bolt of mutual shock and disbelief widened the eyes of both. Then Neferet spun on her heel and marched back out, the others trailing in confusion. Her heart pounding, she kept walking hurriedly to the end of the block and only slowed down when they had turned the corner.

"What is it, Nef'et?" cried Bener-ib, gaping at her. "You look pale."

"Mahu is in there!"

"Who's Mahu?" asked Mut-tuy, staring at both women in turn.

"He's a mean, corrupt police chief who used to be in Akhet-aten. He hates our family. He put Ibet and me in jail once." Neferet felt a clammy sweat on her forehead. She wasn't afraid of much, but she had no desire to confront Mahu's brutality again. "There's no possibility we're going to report this murder to Mahu. If there was ever anybody who hadn't the least teeny-tiny concern for *ma'at*, it's him."

"I thought he'd been put out to pasture," said Bener-ib in a worried voice.

"Well, it looks like he's back. And in Waset."

A chilled silence descended upon the three.

At last, Mut-tuy said, "I guess we're not going to offer to treat the *medjay* for free either."

"So right, my girl. If Mahu ever came in, I'd be too tempted to poison him."

CHAPTER 5

"So, we're going to investigate this murder ourselves after all?" Mut-tuy looked as eager as her affectation of boredom permitted.

"Yes, and we'll start by going to Sen-em-iah's workshop to talk to the florists. Somebody may know of a workman with a grudge or something." Neferet dusted her hands ostentatiously as if to shake off every grain of the *medjay*.

"But we can't leave the dispensary unmanned all morning. What if somebody comes?" Bener-ib said, looking dismayed.

"We can leave Mut-tuy."

"But she can't do anything for them. I should stay."

"I can bandage," the girl protested, but then she seemed to realize she was arguing against herself. "Only, I want to come with you to the florists'."

Eyes rolling to the heavens, Neferet heaved a sigh. "Look here, Mut-tuy. You're supposed to be apprenticed to become a healer. If you're never in the dispensary, what are you going to learn?"

"Who said I wanted to be a healer?"

"You didn't want to be a goldsmith like the rest of your family," Bener-ib reminded her.

"There are more than two professions." The girl gave a sniff of disdain as if the fact were self-evident.

That does it, Neferet thought in irritation. *She's still stuffed full of unreasonable expectations. As an orphan, she's lucky to have any opportunities at all.* "If your parents were still alive, you'd be a goldsmith, like it or not, my girl. People don't usually have a choice—they just do what their family does."

"Neither of you did."

Neferet wanted to snap, "We're aristocrats," but it wouldn't have been kind to rub Mut-tuy's nose in the rather large difference in social class between them. Besides, the loving tolerance of her parents, more than anything else, had enabled her to study medicine. Not to mention learning to read and write. Literate women were rare. Men scribes just didn't want to give them a chance. Both she and Bener-ib had been fortunate enough to have scribes in the family who had been willing to teach them.

"*I* did. My family are all doctors," Bener-ib said.

Apparently realizing she'd cornered herself, Mut-tuy gave an elaborate shrug. "I suppose you just followed along because you were supposed to."

Neferet pounced on her, wagging a finger under her nose. "Easy there, Mut-tuy. You aren't showing much respect for your elders."

But Bener-ib, uncowed, said firmly, "I became a doctor because I wanted to help people."

With a bad grace, Mut-tuy fell silent.

Neferet's heart swelled with pride and tenderness for her friend's noble soul. To the thirteen-year-old, she said, "Come on, then. We'll go to the florist, and Ibet will watch the dispensary."

Bener-ib shot Neferet a shy smile of gratitude, and Neferet squeezed her hand reassuringly. Mut-tuy might hold the little *sunet* in contempt for her timidity, but Neferet appreciated her friend's moral courage.

They parted company, Bener-ib heading back up to the neighborhood of the dispensary, and Neferet and Mut-tuy peeling off south toward the suburbs that lapped about the southern Ipet. The day was already on its way to becoming a sun-scorched furnace. Crowds thinned out as they left the center of the city, and soon, only the padding of their own bare feet in the packed-earth street broke the silence, except for the distant bray of a donkey.

Neferet tried to organize her thoughts. "After this, we probably ought to visit his flower farms. And some of the priests he worked with at the temple of the Hidden One."

"What sort of thing are we looking for?" Mut-tuy asked.

"Anything that might give us a clue as to who would have wished him harm. Did anybody have a grievance, for example? Was there a rivalry?"

The girl nodded thoughtfully. "Maybe we should talk to other florist workshops. They'd be the rivals."

"Right." *She's sharp. That's a good idea,* Neferet thought. But she could see the horizons of their investigation spreading like a water stain up the hem of a garment. *Where does this stop? Do we have to interview everybody he did business with?* For the first time, a sense of discouragement poked its gloomy nose in her stomach.

At last, Sen-em-iah's elegant little villa stood before them, its gate closed and silent this time. Within, no doubt, the sad family tried to go about its duties.

"Let's look for a service entrance down this street." Neferet set off around the corner, with the others following.

An open door soon greeted their eyes, where a group of sun-blackened men clad only in breechclouts loitered about. Pen-buy supervised as each was loaded with a bundle of long pole bouquets and set off at a brisk stagger under the rustling weight. A faint fresh perfume lingered around the space.

Of course, thought Neferet in disappointment. *They're finished with the night's work and are taking it all to the temple. I'll bet nobody's left inside.* "The lord of the horizon greet you, Pen-buy."

The florist looked up, an indecipherable expression on his nondescript face. He might have been annoyed, or he might simply have been tired and harassed. A mourning scarf drooped across his forehead. "You're too late if you wanted to talk to the workers. There's nobody here anymore but the girls cleaning up. You'll have to come back at nightfall."

Neferet changed tack glibly. "We just wanted to ask you where your flower farms are. We thought it might be a good idea to ask around there first. Before the weather gets any hotter."

Pen-buy pursed his lips and nodded slowly. "It's hard to describe to you just where they are. Perhaps I should take you." He dried his hands on his kilt and yelled over his shoulder, "Finish up for me, Roy. I'm going to the farms."

Pen-buy pulled off his wig and wiped his short-cropped hair with an arm, then he led the way toward the River.

Neferet disliked being part of a parade of ducklings in Pen-buy's wake, so she drew up level with him. His steps were weary, so it wasn't hard to stay abreast. "How is your mother doing?" she asked.

He lifted his eyebrows. "My stepmother, you mean? I can't tell. She seems to be alternately stunned and terrified. I'd almost say she acts like she's afraid she's next." His eyes shifted to hers. "If there's anything that can be done for her—medically, that is—maybe you should drop in on her. But don't tell her I said so. She'd think I was trying to kill her."

"Really?" Neferet said. "Are things that tense between you?"

"Not normally. But as I say, she's been acting very strange. I'm not even welcome in my own father's house anymore." After a moment's silence, he sighed. "I don't know why I'm telling you this. I've already told the police. I guess I wasn't happy with the way they treated us all."

Neferet, picturing Mahu questioning a grief-stricken family, could well imagine why. She stopped walking and turned to the man, staring him in the eye. "Pen-buy," she said earnestly, "*ma'at* must be done here. Somebody murdered your father, and his family doesn't know why. No wonder the widow is uneasy. That murderer is still out there, and your father's *ba* is crying for justice. My partner and I are *sunets*, not investigators, it's true, but we're trained to look for causes and effects. What are symptoms but just clues to a mystery? We feel a responsibility for Sen-em-iah since we couldn't save him. Let us do some asking around, see if we can't find out who has ruined your family's life."

He stared at her seriously, and she could almost see the thoughts whirring behind his mild brown eyes. "You seem awfully young," he said but not dismissively.

"We were the royal physicians of Ankhet-khepru-ra Nefer-nefru-aten. If the late king trusted us with her life, why shouldn't you?"

"I'm not sure I'm willing to pay you, though. The police are working on the case, after all. If you want to do it out of the goodness of your hearts, that's your business."

"You don't have to pay us. I'm the wife of Lord Maya, the treasurer." She relished the look of surprise that lit his plump face.

"Well…"

"All we ask of you is cooperation. We'll do all the work. And seeing *ma'at* restored will be reward enough." She faced him eagerly, like a hunting dog begging to be let off leash to run for the scent.

After a moment of reflection, he nodded. "All right. What harm can it do? Just try not to upset my stepmother." A fleeting smile twitched at his mouth. "But you're a physician—you know that."

The florist kept a small fleet of rowboats to ferry his flowers from the farm to the workshop. They hailed one at the water's edge, where the oarsmen stretched out lazily under the shadow of the hull. The men sprang to their feet at the approach of their master and eased the boat into the water.

There was barely room for Pen-buy, the two women, and the pair of rowers, but the River wasn't high, and they swung out into the current. Neferet watched the city receding in their wake, its ochre-and-white buildings, graceful palms, and lush garden trees shimmering, doubled, in the water. The biggest city in the world, Papa said. The great temples of Amen-Ra and his family dominated everything, of course, their high, undulating walls towering over the residences of men. In the distance, the pale-reddish mountains seethed in the summer air against a sky the color of beaten electrum. This was the horizon that had shaped her childhood. How good it was to be back in the City of the Scepter after those strange years in Akhet-aten.

Mut-tuy was looking in the other direction, toward the west bank, the land of the dead, where her father's home of eternity stood, thanks to the generosity of his employer, the goldsmith In-hapy—the gods only knew where her mother was. But in fact, they weren't headed to the other side of the stream, only sliding an *iteru* or two downriver to where the city gave way to the green of planted fields and the rich brown of fallow ones. Pen-buy's flower farm wasn't hard to spot when they approached it—suddenly, behind a screen of date palms, shades of green erupted into brilliant carpets of gold and red and white and blue. It was an extraordinary sight.

"My father would love to see this," Neferet said, ebullient. "He loves gardens."

"So do I," said Pen-buy, gazing raptly at the flower fields. "So do I."

Neferet eyed him surreptitiously. Despite a rather unattractive exterior, he seemed to have a soul. A lot of people might become florists because it was lucrative—and his expensive clothes proclaimed that fact—or because that was what their family had always done. But here was one who worked with flowers because he loved them.

They glided toward the land and maneuvered into the end of a narrow channel, where the two boatmen secured their little vessel and helped the three passengers up the steep bank with the aid of stone steps. Reeds grew thick in the channel mouth, arching in a feathery canopy over their heads until the travelers emerged. Once they were on ground level, the sun struck them once more with unseasonable ferocity. They started off up a well-worn trail inland, following the irrigation channel. Here and there, wooden sluice gates stood open. Neferet could smell the stagnant water, which straggled into an increasingly complex web of runnels. And all about her stretched the glorious fields of color.

"*Iyah*," whispered Mut-tuy as if she had just noticed.

"When you buy a bouquet, you don't think of where the flowers come from, do you?" said Pen-buy. For all that he had probably been awake the entire night, his weariness seemed to have fallen away, and he led the two briskly up the path toward a small, whitewashed building. Dark-green tufts of mandrake made a line around its foundations, already bearing the pale-green fruit that would turn golden then orange as the summer wore on. "I'll introduce you to the foreman. Probably most of the pickers are sleeping. A lot of them stay here during the work week."

He pushed under the fly mat into a long dark hall, its ceiling supported by a row of brick columns up the center. Narrow clerestories let in a modicum of light and air heavy with dust motes. A pair of swallows flew in and stitched a flittering path to the other end, where they disappeared into the shadows that shrouded the ceiling. On the floor, some thirty or forty men and boys were stretched out on reed mats, asleep—to the ragged sounds of snoring—or shaving or sitting quietly. The stench of sweat was overpowering. Pen-buy leaned over a dark-skinned older man who hunkered watchfully on his heels. He whispered something and drew the man toward the visitors.

"Imi-seba, here, is the foreman. He's more likely than anyone else to know what conflicts my father might have had. He's worked for the family since he was a child." Pen-buy clapped the man on the shoulder and gave him a pointed look then turned to Neferet. "If you'll excuse me, I need to get back to the city. When you're ready to leave, Imi-seba will find you one of the boats."

"Thank you, Pen-buy. You've been very helpful. May the lord of the horizon bless you," said Neferet. *Thank you for taking us seriously.*

Imi-seba followed his master to the exterior of the building, where a reed awning provided a strip of flickering shade. While Pen-buy set off toward the irrigation ditch, the foreman confronted the young women, with a frosty expression on his thin face. He was dressed in a long kilt but no shirt and, like his master, had a white mourning scarf tied around his gray-stubbled head. A little square tuft of graying beard decorated his chin. Neferet thought he was probably high up in the hierarchy of florists and maybe even literate, based on the disdainful lift of the nose he turned on them.

"How may I help you, my lady?"

"I don't know if Pen-buy told you who we are, but I'm Neferet daughter of Hani and Nub-nefer, one of the royal physicians. This is my assistant. Your master was brought to us, dying, and though we weren't able to save him, we swore to find his killer. If you know of any enemies Sen-em-iah might have had—any disgruntled workmen, any rivals—it might give us a place to start looking."

One thing was clear—Imi-seba did not think well of women asking him questions. He eyed Neferet up and down in a way that was just short of rude, his lips pressed together in disapproval. At last, he said brusquely, "Certainly no disgruntled employees. The master treated everyone with great generosity."

"What about other florists? Were people jealous because of his trade with the Ipet-isut?"

"The master wasn't simply a tradesman who did business with the temples, my lady. He was a lay official of the god's household." He folded his hands before him smugly as if this were the final word.

"Ah, like my brother, who's chief overseer of the cattle of the Hidden One," Neferet said. She couldn't resist. She suspected that such things would impress this man. "My uncle is Third Prophet, you know."

Imi-seba's eyes widened momentarily, and he straightened a bit. "Like that, yes, my lady."

"Anything else? Trouble with suppliers? Disagreements over land?"

"The land belongs to the king of the gods."

Neferet wanted to yell, "Well, what, then? Somebody hated him enough to disembowel the man!" Instead, she just stared at him, interrogatory eyebrows raised.

He pursed his lips thoughtfully. "There have been some

89

run-ins with the neighboring farmer but surely nothing serious."

"Ah, now we're getting somewhere. What sort of run-ins?"

"His animals have gotten into the flower fields a time or two. Eventually, the master had to go speak to him. They must have reached an understanding because it hasn't been repeated."

Neferet waited for more details, but nothing seemed forthcoming. "What direction is his property, if I should want to talk to him?"

Imi-seba pointed downstream. "It's a choice piece of agricultural land, which is wasted on husbandry."

Hmm, thought Neferet. *I detect a little bitterness there. I'll bet they had a land dispute, all right.* "Do you think any of the workmen might have something to add? Might they have witnessed a confrontation?"

"The men need to sleep, my lady. They'll be back in the fields by twilight," the foreman said sniffily.

Which doesn't exactly answer my question. The man is either being evasive, or he just doesn't want to talk to me. She was starting to find his whole manner annoying.

On his route home that evening, after his son-in-law Maya had split off to go his own way, Hani decided to drop in on the girls to see how their visit to the police had gone. He hoped they hadn't already left the dispensary. To his relief, he could hear the shouts and laughter of the children at their games even before he knocked on the gate. Bener-ib drew back the panel, and immediately, a ball rolled out, followed by a giggling posse of small people and large excitedly barking dogs.

Hani threaded his way in through the scrum, chuckling. "Bener-ib, my dear. Is Neferet around? I just wanted to see how your trip to the police station went."

"She's not, Lord Hani," Bener-ib said. He followed her narrow back with its mop of braids as she led him into the dispensary. The room was as clean and empty as ever. Bener-ib gestured him to a stool and sank, cross-legged, to the ground. "Our visit didn't go well."

Hani observed that the girl's face was pallid and her somewhat close-set eyes wide and uneasy. She looked almost frightened. "What's the matter? What happened?" he asked in a lower tone.

Her high-pitched voice trembled as she said, "That Mahu is here in Waset."

Hani was as taken aback as if she had reached out and smacked him. He stared at her, his mouth hanging open. "You're sure? It must be nearly two years now since he was forcibly retired."

"Nef'et saw him, my lord. And so did we all a little."

"Is he in charge of the *medjay* here?"

"We don't know, but he was in the station, talking to a couple of policemen. We saw him and turned right around and left."

A wave of dull anger rolled up Hani's cheeks. Mahu, the son of a jackal, had roughed up Hani, brutalized his daughter, and deliberately wrecked the property of his friend Ptah-mes. Eventually, the chief of *medjay* in the capital, suspected of corruption, had been packed off to his country properties, and Hani had thought that the Two

91

Lands were rid of him. *Can he really be back? Does Lord Ay, the regent, have more dirty work for the wretch to perform?*

"So you didn't make your report after all?"

"No, but the family must have, mustn't they? Nef'et and Mut-tuy went off to talk to Sen-em-iah's workers." Bener-ib twisted her fingers together in her lap. "I don't know why they haven't come back yet."

She fears the worst, Hani thought in compassion. Mahu had once accused Bener-ib of killing her father, and the two young women had spent a terrifying night locked up in the police garrison of the City of the Horizon. The memory—and Bener-ib had a good one—had clearly left a scar. He was just opening his mouth to say something reassuring when loud voices at the gate told him that Neferet had returned.

She burst into the room on the usual tidal wave of energy, talking away. Then she saw her father and threw herself on him exuberantly. "Papa! What a surprise! Did Ibet tell you about Mahu?"

"She did, my duckling. Do you know what that's all about?"

"No, but if he's got even the teeniest bit to do with the police here, I'm not getting near them. He could rot the best pile of fruit." She plopped to the floor, her square face fiercely determined. Her nose and cheeks were glowing with sunburn. "So we're going to investigate this ourselves after all. And"—she grinned at Bener-ib—"Pen-buy has given us his blessing."

Hani cocked a dubious eyebrow. Still, he knew better than to object.

"He may not look like much, but he's a decent fellow.

Never once did he say anything like 'Women doing something that requires thinking? *Iyah!* No, I rather like him. He took us to the flower farms, and we talked to his foreman. Listen to this!" She wiggled her way closer. "There's a farmer next door whose cattle have been getting into the flower fields. Sen-em-iah apparently had to have words with him."

"Just be careful, ladies. If passions are running that high, you don't want to get between the antagonists." He could only hope that Bener-ib's prudence would rein in his daughter's often unthinking boldness.

Neferet said, "After dinner, I want to drop in at the workshop again. The workers will be there at sundown when the fresh flowers arrive."

"Where is Mut-tuy?" Bener-ib asked.

"Outside with her brothers and sister. They're all waiting for Hu-may, and then the nurse will take them home. I didn't mention going to the workshop because she'd want to go." Neferet rolled her eyes. "That's the most headstrong girl under the light of Ra."

Hani suppressed a grin and made a point of avoiding his daughter's gaze. He and Nub-nefer had said the same thing a million times in the course of their youngest's childhood. Apparently, she had met her match.

"Well, I'm off to the house. May the lord of the horizon give you ladies a good evening. Convey my greetings to Ptah-mes."

CHAPTER 6

THE FLY MAT TREMBLED, AND a big tomcat with one eye pushed his way through, a bird dangling from his jaws. *Little murderer.*

In the cat's wake, however, a strapping young man shouldered through the front door, a child in his arms, her face tearful, red, and screwed up in misery. "Forgive me, doctors, but I opened the gate. My little girl has broken her arm, I think."

He addressed himself to Neferet and Bener-ib, Hani noted with surprise. The fellow must have known them. Otherwise, he would have assumed that the *sunu* was Hani, the only male present.

"Bring her over here on this bed," Neferet directed, while Bener-ib hustled into the back room to round up supplies. Neferet bent over the little one with a kindly smile. "Now, my girl, which arm have you hurt?"

"Dis one," said the child in a trembling voice, pointing at her left arm, which she cradled across her body.

"She fell off a wall," the father said. "She followed

her older brothers up there, although she knows she isn't supposed to. They were after the beehives."

"Don't tell your papa, but I like a girl who isn't scared to go where the boys go." Neferet gave a complicit grin as she felt the arm, and a feeble smile lit the child's face despite her pain. "However, now we have to deal with this bone. It hasn't broken the skin, and that's good. We're going to tie it onto a board so it heals straight, and we'll put it in a sling for a while. All the other children will want one too. Look! Even Cheetah, here, wants one."

Sure enough, the cat had jumped up onto the bed and was watching everything with interest through his single eye.

Bener-ib entered, with her arms full of bandages and a few slim strips of wood covered in linen for splints. Hani watched in fascination as the two young physicians drew out the little arm, surrounded it with pieces of wood, and tied it into an expert package, slipping an amulet or two among the bandages. His heart warmed with admiration for the pair, so competent and levelheaded.

"You can give her some of this water lily," Bener-ib said, offering the man a little pot with a wooden cork. "Three times a day if needed. It's very mild, but it will take the edge off her pain."

"How can I thank you?" The father hefted the child into his arms.

Her eyes were sparkling with tears, but she smiled bravely and wiggled her fingers at Cheetah.

"Can I bring you a goose?" the father asked. "Would you prefer grain?"

"Oh, something smaller. It was only a crack, no broken

skin." Neferet eyed the man. "Do you live around here? You look familiar."

He grinned. "I do. I'm one of the Osiris Sen-em-iah's bodyguards. That's why we brought him to you."

"Ah! I remember you now. Tell me—what's your name?—how's the family doing?"

"I'm Tut-em-heb. I guess they're all right. The mistress of the house is very fearful. We accompany her everywhere. I think—" He turned apologetically to Hani. "Excuse me, my lord. We probably cut in front of you. I don't want to tie up the doctors if you're waiting to be treated. I did have a little something to tell them, though. If they're really interested in investigating my master's killer, that is."

"No, no," Hani assured him. "I'm Lady Neferet's father. It's probably I who should be going."

"Stay, Papa. If Tut-em-heb has something to say to us, you may be interested too." Neferet turned to the bodyguard. "He's going to help us in this investigation. He's tracked down killers for the king—life, prosperity, and health to him."

Hani started to protest, but he picked up on his daughter's maneuver. Now, instead of showing defiance, she seemed willing to draw him into her escapade. She must have something specific to do that required a masculine presence.

"I wanted to tell you that my master had been uneasy for a while before he died. That's why he always took guards with him when he went out, even to and from work. He was nervous and—well, sharp. Usually he was kindness itself, but lately, he was likely to bite off your head for nothing. The young master was worried about him, I think."

Neferet made a pondering hum, her straight dark eyebrows drawn down in reflection. "Do you have any idea why? His foreman told us there was some trouble with a neighboring farmer over animals getting into the flower fields. Might he have threatened Sen-em-iah?"

"It's possible. I really don't have any idea of what the problem was. But the mistress seemed aware of it. She was frightened too. And still is—more than ever. I think she's even afraid of the young master."

The little girl in the man's arms stirred fretfully and whined, "Papaaa..."

"I should go," he said. "If I think of anything else that might help you, I'll let you know. And I'll give you a duck—how's that?"

Neferet gave him a dazzling gap-toothed grin. "Perfect. Tell your friends to bring their sick to us. We're far better trained than that Djed-har."

The man took his grateful leave, his daughter waving over his shoulder. Through the door, Neferet saw Mut-tuy accompany them to the gate. Neferet and Bener-ib exchanged congratulatory looks.

Then Neferet turned to her father. "Maybe our luck is changing, eh, Papa?"

"If you mean your medical practice, clearly," he said with a crooked smile. "And Sekhmet be praised. If you mean your investigation, well..."

"He had a good piece of information, I'd say. Something had the florist scared. He *did* know who killed him."

"Ah yes, the rampaging rabbit."

Neferet rolled her eyes in an expression of filial disgust

Hani had seen a lot of over the years. "Oh, Papa, can't you take this seriously? I'm counting on you to give us a hand."

"My duckling, I have nothing to do with such matters—less in my present position than ever, unless your perpetrator is a foreigner. I have no jurisdiction at all over domestic crimes." Hani spread his hands in a gesture of helplessness.

"Even if the king commands you to help?"

He stared at Neferet. "What does the king have to do with it? Now, now, my girl. Don't be bothering our Sun God about this. He has more important things to deal with."

"He likes me, you know. We used to take care of him when he was the crown prince."

"Neferet!" Hani felt trapped. His daughter was perfectly likely to beard the young king, who would, in fact, be only too happy to grant her request, no matter how extravagant—he was a lad who wanted to be liked. "You can't do that!"

Hani realized immediately that he had made a strategic mistake. He should have known better than to tell Neferet, "You can't." She would set out straightaway to prove that she could.

"We'll see," she said, glaring from under her lowered eyebrows. "Pen-buy is depending on us to find his father's killer, and a girl has to take whatever steps she needs to."

⁂

That evening at dinner, Neferet said to Bener-ib—quietly so that Mut-tuy couldn't hear her—"We'll go back to the florist's workshop after we've eaten. As I suspected, the workers probably will know more about what's going on than the family—or be more willing to talk. Nobody else had told us about Sen-em-iah acting strange."

"Pen-buy hinted," Bener-ib said, ever literal-minded. She finished off a cube of beef. "Do you really intend to get the king to make your father help us, Nef'et?"

"If he won't do it voluntarily. You'd think after all the times we've helped him, he'd feel obligated without being forced."

"What if somebody who doesn't want to talk to us reports us to the police? We could get in trouble."

Neferet lifted her hands in exasperation. "For what? Is it illegal to talk to people? We only want to do right by Sen-em-iah's soul. His own son wishes us success."

Bener-ib hung her head. "I just don't want to tangle with that awful Mahu again."

Neferet's frustration melted into pity. She could only imagine what it must have been like to be arrested for murder and to have to face a capital sentence. She herself had fought tooth and nail to save Ibet from capture and had been struck and thrown around painfully by the police, but her real danger had only been minimal.

Her eyes growing misty, she squeezed Bener-ib around the shoulders. "I won't let anything happen to you, my Sweet Heart." That was what "Bener-ib" meant, and to Neferet, it was the most beautiful name in the world.

From the next table, Mut-tuy stared at the two young women with her piercing glare of sullen humor.

"Mut-tuy, do you know how to play Hot-Hand-Cold-Hand?" Neferet said loudly.

"Of course," the girl said with bad grace. "I'm not that stupid."

Neferet ignored her sassiness and said cheerfully, "No, you're not stupid at all. So I'd like you to teach it to the others. You and Hu-may can show them how."

The adolescent shrugged, but her glance was suspicious.

She knows I'm trying to keep her occupied for a reason. Too bad. I don't have to tell her everything.

As soon as the meal was concluded, Neferet told the nursemaid, "Let them play in the garden until sundown. We're leaving for a bit. Mut-tuy is in charge of the games." She knew the girl was listening.

The two *sunet*s took their leave. As they passed through the forepart of the garden, they saw Lord Ptah-mes sitting alone in his pavilion. He had a tall cup of wine in his hand but wasn't drinking it. Instead, from his beautifully carved chair, he gazed out over the shady garden in meditative silence.

"Lord Ptah-mes," Neferet called. "Have you eaten yet?"

He looked up, and his somber expression brightened. "No, my dear, I haven't. Will you ladies join me, or are you going out?" With his usual impeccable courtesy, he rose as they approached.

Neferet felt a little guilty. She and Bener-ib had completely abandoned her husband's company since the children had arrived. He was of a solitary nature and probably didn't mind—especially after a day of being besieged by petitioners—but nobody liked to be alone all the time. She resolved to dine with him once a week.

From behind the dividing wall, a burst of raucous high-pitched laughter and taunts and Mut-tuy's voice, raised imperiously, suggested that the youngsters had begun their game.

"We're going to that dead florist's house to interview some of the workmen. They work at night, you know."

"Perhaps you should take the litters. It may be dark by the time you get back."

"Oh, that's all right," said Neferet breezily. "It's not far."

"Then may I suggest you let one of the servants accompany you? There's a surprising amount of crime on the streets at night. The police don't seem to be doing their jobs very well."

"I think that's a good idea, Nef'et," Bener-ib said nervously.

Neferet shrugged to be sure everyone understood she was indifferent to her own safety. "If you want to, Ibet, I have no objection."

Lord Ptah-mes clapped for his steward, who appeared as if by magic upon the steps of the salon. "Get one of the stauncher young servants to accompany these women. Be sure he has a stave."

"Yes, my lord."

In a heartbeat, the steward returned with a sturdy, fuzzy-haired young fellow who belonged to the garden staff. He had a businesslike cudgel in his fist.

"Accompany these ladies and keep them safe." Ptah-mes reseated himself.

Neferet bade him good evening, and the four set off toward the gate. She wondered if her father had been talking to Ptah-mes. It was still far from sundown on a summer evening, but the shadows were already long from the direction of the River. They headed inland through tightly settled neighborhoods and groves, the servant trudging stoically behind his mistresses. At the gate of Sen-em-iah's estate, they turned up the side street and followed his garden wall to the broad door that marked the workshop.

Inside, everything was an anthill of activity. Men ran to and fro, stacking bouquets of different sizes, as an old fellow with a branch of myrtle and a bucket of water sprinkled each layer to keep them cool and moist. Farther into the semidarkness of the building, another crew unloaded fresh flowers, branches of green leaves, stacks of reeds, and jars of cut water lilies. The perfume was intoxicating.

Pen-buy stood, hands on hips, supervising the porters. "You there, careful!" he cried. "We don't want to bruise them. They have to last all day." When the women approached—their guard remaining at the door—he greeted them distractedly. "Good evening, my ladies. You can talk to anyone, but don't keep them long. We have to finish before daybreak."

That wasn't as long a time at this season, Neferet realized, as it might have been in the winter months of Peret. The florist's face was glossy with sweat, although the shadowy hall was almost cool. His small eyes flittered restlessly around at his workers.

"Where are they actually making the bouquets?" she said loudly over the noise.

He pointed through an interior door that apparently opened into a large court. The two *sunet*s threaded through the porters and growing stacks of vegetation and emerged into a throng of women, children, and a few men seated cross-legged and as close together as possible in the vast enclosure, with only narrow aisles so they could be reprovisioned as needed. Each had beside her a pile of flowers and greenery and the basic structures of pole bouquets, the reeds tightly bound into staffs as long as a man was tall. Overhead, rickety shelters of reed protected the workers and their flowers from the last full blast of the sun. Burnt-out torches still hung here and there, whose flames, no doubt, prolonged the light throughout the nighttime hours. The employees busily threaded large needles with strips of plant fiber or folded persea leaves or expertly bound water lilies to the tops of their poles. Neferet stared around in fascination.

From a few cubits away, a big-bosomed middle-aged woman was waving at them. Neferet led the way to her side. She looked up at them, bright-eyed, but her fingers never stopped their work.

"You must be Lady Neferet," she said.

Neferet nodded. "Your master gave me permission to ask if anyone might have any insights into the murder of Sen-em-iah."

"I know. Me sister's the cook of your family. I told her I got me own ideas." With her thumb, she pointed at an adolescent boy at her side who was earnestly binding flowers to his pole. Already, the crown of a colorful bouquet was forming. "This here's my son."

The lad nodded respectfully but never stopped working.

"So, tell me. Have you seen anything that might help us?" Neferet asked.

The woman glanced around her and lowered her voice. "The master's been really nervous lately—scared, you might say. And the mistress too. Normally, she don't come to the workshop, but she come quite a bit these last few months, and there was a big confab between her and the master, with her hangin' on his shirt and wavin' her hands. Him gettin' mad but his face all worried."

Neferet exchanged significant glances with Bener-ib. *Yahyah! We're getting somewhere.*

"I don't suppose you ever heard what they were saying?"

The woman smiled craftily, baring a well-worn set of gray teeth. "Not me, no, but me daughter works in the master's house as a maid. She's overheard plenty." She paused her work long enough to beckon Neferet closer with a crooked finger and whispered, "She said some o' the priests o' the Hidden One come to the house, and they an' the master was closeted together for a long time. Then they come out and left, an' the poor master was practically peein' hisself with fear. He an' the mistress had a huge fallin' out, with her bawlin' like a baby."

"Priests, you say? Did you hear any names?" Neferet was already planning how to access the servants of the god. With her mother and uncle in his service, it shouldn't be too hard.

"No, me lady. But I'll tell me daughter to keep her ears peeled."

Neferet shook a few colored stone beads she'd brought for the purpose into the woman's palm. The worker tied them around her thick wrist with a twist of fiber and bobbed her head in gratitude.

"There's more for both of you if you hear anything else useful. What's your daughter's name?"

"Thank you, me lady. May Mut the mother of us all bless you. She's called Wabet."

The two *sunet*s zigzagged their way to the edge of the

courtyard. Not far away, a well-dressed man with a whip was eyeing them. He started in their direction.

"I bet that's the workshop foreman, and he's coming to tell us not to distract the bouquet makers," Neferet said from the corner of her mouth. "Do you think we've heard enough for now? I can't imagine anyone else knows anything here on the work floor."

Bener-ib agreed, and the young women scuttled for the entrance. They saluted Pen-buy as they made for the door, but he was in the middle of a conversation and just acknowledged them with a bob of the head.

Out in the street, evening was starting to descend. The wall cast a long purple shadow, even though the sky above it was still luminous. The pair set off at a brisk pace, followed by the cudgel-wielding servant.

"Well, well. That turned out to be interesting. We've actually got our own spy in the household," Neferet said with a feeling of satisfaction as she walked.

"It sounds like the priests scolded Sen-em-iah for something. It would be a terrible loss of status and income if they decided to dismiss him from his post. That would worry anybody." Bener-ib's brow was wrinkled in thought.

"Why, though? Surely they can't object to the quality of the flowers. I've never seen anything as beautiful as those bouquets. They're like pieces of jewelry."

Her companion shrugged. "Anyway, I can't imagine priests would kill him because they didn't like his work."

CHAPTER 7

T HEY WALKED ON IN PENSIVE silence. At last, Neferet said, "Let's stop by Mama and Papa's house. I want to tell Papa what we discovered. He's had lots of experience figuring such things out."

They peeled off inland at the appropriate corner and passed through clustered blocks of houses until the settlement opened out around larger villas skirted with modest dwellings. At Hani's gate, they knocked, and Iuty admitted them with a smile.

"Is Papa home? We'd like to talk to him," Neferet said, already moving toward the house.

"Yes, Lady Neferet. He and the mistress of the house should be in the kiosk."

Leaving their bodyguard with Iuty, the two young women took the graveled path along the side of the house, through lush bushes and shady trees. Evening was already well advanced under the spreading branches of plane and sycamore fig. Above the cicadas' song, voices drifted toward them, and a burst of laughter.

"Mama! Papa!" Neferet called and trotted forward.

"No greeting for Grandfather?" Mery-ra demanded in mock severity. "Cut the ingrate out of your will, Hani, my boy."

Neferet guffawed. "You're so slim you're invisible, Grandfather!"

"Let it not be said any man of our family is insubstantial, young lady." He extended his arms, and both Neferet and Bener-ib embraced first him then Mama and Papa.

Mama called a servant to bring more stools, and the others scooted their chairs aside to make room. Between Papa and Grandfather, there wasn't much space left for the three women. They were, in fact, men of considerable breadth.

"Well, Papa, we just went to talk to Sen-em-iah's workers, and we found out some *very* interesting things. In addition to the dispute with the farmer next door to the flower farm, a couple of priests have been harassing the man. His maid, who's Cook's niece, said he was terrified after they left. And his wife was acting strange, too—following him to work and arguing with him. The maid said they both seemed scared for a good while before he died."

Papa shot his own father a glance then turned back to his daughter. "Surely the priests didn't kill him."

"I thought maybe they didn't think his work was good enough. It may have had nothing to do with his death," said Bener-ib as if in apology.

"Here's my theory—still tentative, of course." Neferet lifted a pedagogical finger and inched her stool closer. "What if Sen-em-iah and his wife were having a row because she'd caught him in an affair with some other woman?

Maybe even the maid Wabet, who seems to know an awful lot about it all. And what if the priests got wind of it? I imagine there are standards of conduct for lay employees of the temple, aren't there, Mama? Maybe the priests came to tell him, 'You'd better toe the line, or we're replacing you as Bearer of Divine Offerings.' That would have shaken him."

"But it doesn't explain who killed him." Papa pursed his lips dubiously.

Neferet plowed on without stopping for breath. "If he told his lady love he was going to leave her, she might have killed him out of jealousy!"

The others stared at one another in silence for a moment. Then Mama said, "You certainly have a good imagination, my love."

Hani reached out and squeezed his daughter's knee affectionately. "Little duckling, all this may turn out to be true, but I don't think the evidence you have at this point can support the hypothesis. Why would this Wabet have told you what she knows if it incriminates her? Told you through her mother, I mean."

"Maybe she's not smart enough to realize it incriminates her," Neferet said in defiance. *Of course, they aren't taking me seriously.* "And it may not be her. I said the idea was tentative, anyway. But it does make sense of everything." She crossed her arms, and her jaw grew stubborn.

"Why don't you ask Uncle Amen-em-hut whether there was dissatisfaction with the florist's work?" suggested Mama, carefully avoiding giving any opinion about Neferet's theory. "He might know or could certainly find out for you."

"I appreciate the constructive contribution, Mama,"

Neferet said pointedly. She eyed her father through narrowed eyes. "I thought maybe Papa could suggest a line of questioning to bring more facts to light, but clearly, he's not interested."

Papa struggled to fight back a grin.

Finally, Grandfather spoke. "If you could find out who the priests were who spoke to your man, perhaps they could shed some light on the cause of the visit, as your mother says. That would either confirm or debunk your theory, my girl."

"If they'll reveal internal temple business like that," Papa said. But when Neferet turned her most chilling expression of disapproval upon him, he made a hasty addendum. "No harm in asking, of course. Or maybe get Amen-em-hut to probe a little. They could hardly refuse to answer the Third Prophet."

That sounded like a serious place to begin. Perhaps Papa was interested after all. Mollified, Neferet said, "All right. Tomorrow we'll go visit Uncle." She rose to her feet, and Bener-ib followed. "We're off, then. Thanks, everyone."

As the two *sunet*s set off down the path, Mama called, "It's almost dark, Neferet dear. Don't you want to use the litter?"

"No, no. We have a burly servant with us. Anyway, surely you trust Mahu to keep us all safe."

⚜

The next morning, Neferet, Bener-ib, and Mut-tuy stood in the elegant vestibule of Lord Amen-em-hut, Third Prophet of Amen-Ra, where the steward had directed them to wait.

The first person to burst from the salon door was Aunt Anuia, all smiles and squeals of pleasure.

"Neferet, my love! And girls! What brings you here? Have you eaten? Do come in and tell us how things are going at the dispensary."

Anuia was as dumpy and comfortable looking as her husband was precise and—even in his midfifties— strikingly handsome. Neferet had always thought they made an unexpected couple, but they seemed devoted to one another. Anuia enveloped each of the young women in a big hug, their faces pressed into her wild, curly hair, then led them into the salon, where the priest was enjoying a pot of beer with his eldest son. Cousin Pen-amen was also a *hem netjer* of the Hidden One and as good-looking as his father. He was tall, besides, in contrast to Uncle, who—for all his manly beauty—was small. Despite the two years between them, Amen-em-hut and Mama resembled one another so closely that they were often taken for twins. Grandfather called them Shu and Tef-nut, like the twin gods of creation.

"Neferet! Ladies! To what do we owe this pleasure?" Amen-em-hut set aside his straw and rose, an expression of delight on his face. "It's not often you grace us with your presence."

Pen-amen gallantly vacated his chair, and Anuia and a servant drew up several others. The young women settled themselves, and Neferet proceeded to describe the murder of Sen-em-iah and how they'd become involved in discovering his killer.

"We paid our respects at his home," said Pen-amen. "Everybody liked him, and his floral offerings were splendid."

"I would have thought so," said Neferet. "But it seems like some of the priests came to visit him at his workshop and left him very upset. What else could it have been but a rebuke of some kind? I wondered if his personal life might have been... irregular."

Uncle frowned pensively. "I've never heard anything to that effect. And it's unlikely they would have upbraided him in public. Perhaps there was some mix-up in an order or something. But surely that wouldn't have had any relationship to his death."

Neferet put on her pleading face—the one she'd perfected by watching hungry puppies. "Uncle, could you find out who those priests were so we could talk to them? If this was about something that couldn't have brought about his death, then we don't want to waste time on it. Otherwise, it may be a clue."

Amen-em-hut stared into his lap, his brow buckled with anxiety. "I suppose I can try, my dear. But I want to warn you—there's still some feeling between the priests who stood firm against that damnable Aten business and those who capitulated." He and Pen-amen exchanged uneasy looks. "One has to be a little careful poking around or seeming to blame anyone's actions. But if they were sent by the First Prophet—as they presumably would have been, were this an official rebuke—I can find out for you."

"Oh, thank you, Uncle. That will be so helpful."

"It's not going to get you girls into difficulty, asking questions and stirring up things, is it?" he asked, a troubled pleat between his eyebrows. He rose and drifted toward the entry, so the others did too. "I don't just mean among the priests. Somebody was willing to commit murder, whatever

111

his motives. Nub-nefer would never forgive me if I led you into danger."

Neferet managed not to heave a loud, weary sigh. How often had she heard this argument? And they had barely begun their investigation. From the corner of her eye, she saw Mut-tuy's look of disgust.

"No, no. We're being very subtle. Papa is helping us."

"Oh, is he? Good. Hani is a force for prudence."

The irony was that Uncle Amen-em-hut was hardly a model of prudence himself. He had been an openly dissenting firebrand for the cause of the Hidden One during the reign of Nefer-khepru-ra, the heretic who had subordinated the king of the gods to the Aten. Uncle had been forced to spend years in hiding from the Atenist persecutors. *Somehow what's heroic for a man is "dangerous" for a woman.*

The three took their leave. Once out on the street, Neferet muttered, "I hope he'll actually ask those priests and not decide he's putting us at risk."

"Why is everybody so protective?" said Mut-tuy. "It's downright suffocating."

Neferet wanted to say to the orphan, "If you think it's bad now, imagine what it would be like if you had a family"—though of course, she didn't. In fact, she felt some scruple for involving the thirteen-year-old in an inquiry she had to admit might carry its share of hazards. But there seemed to be no way to detach the girl. The mere mention of the crime brought a wild, avid light to her eyes. *Maybe, since she couldn't help her own father, she feels that doing something for Sen-em-iah's ba will be the next best thing.*

"We've never talked to the farmer whose cows got into the flower fields," said Bener-ib as they walked.

"Right. That's our next project. Other than mixing ointment for Sit-amen's son's eyelid.

If the children left us any calendula. We have the bat's blood."

"What's calendula?" asked Mut-tuy.

"That golden flower in the bed by the dispensary door. The one your siblings trampled flat."

The girl snorted. "They're worse than a herd of hippopotamuses."

Neferet stopped in her tracks and squinted up at the sun, which, despite the hour, was still high in the heavens. "I think we have time to go downriver and interview that farmer before dinner. We may be a little late getting back, but Mut-tuy, you can run on and tell the cook that we won't—"

"I want to go too," the girl objected loudly.

"I'll tell Cook. No need for us all to go," Bener-ib said. "I can mix up some ointment and have it ready for tomorrow morning."

The tasks thus divided, Neferet and Mut-tuy parted company with Bener-ib, who headed home while the two intrepid investigators turned and made their way toward the embarcadero. *One of these days, one of us needs to put her foot down with this girl.*

But it wasn't going to be *that* day. At the water's edge, Neferet hailed a small boat for hire and directed its boatman north past the glowing flower fields to the first patch of green thereafter. They slid out of the current and bumped against the reed-tufted bank, where she and Mut-tuy scrambled out and up the slope.

"Wait for us, please. We won't be long, and I'll pay you for your time," Neferet called to their boatman.

Then they turned inland and scanned the horizon. A cubical house of mudbrick and a maze of low brick walls were the only signs of habitation. Nowhere did she see any traces of cattle.

"Well, let's see if our man is at home or with his herd someplace," she said. "Maybe his fields are scattered."

They marched up the dusty path to the house, which had the usual yard planted with two doum palms. Neferet could see the farmwife spreading wet laundry on the courtyard wall to dry. But before she came within hailing distance of the woman, a man rose from behind one of the corral-like enclosures that marched alongside the path and called out, "Who are you?"

She turned and considered the person who had spoken. He was close to middle age, sun darkened and wiry, his hair covered with a cloth that looked as if he might have wiped his hands on it. His expression was suspicious and none too welcoming.

"My name is Neferet daughter of Hani and Nub-nefer. My father is appointed by the king to adjudicate between you and your neighbor. You know," she added, seeing his skeptical expression. "That business about your cows getting into Sen-em-iah's flower fields."

"Cows?" He eyed her up and down. "I don't have no cows. Like I could afford cows."

"Well, goats. Sheep. He didn't think to tell me what

they were. But my father wanted me to hear your side of the disagreement. He wants his judgment to be fair."

The man seemed surprised at the idea of a fair judgment. His sour expression softened. "An' he sent you, did he?"

"He thought a woman might be less intimidating. We tend to listen better than men—some men, anyway. This girl is my assistant."

The farmer gave a nod of acknowledgment.

"So, just tell me what happened. Everything you know."

"Well, sometimes my critters gets under the walls and into the flower fields. I know they oughtn't, but how's a fellow to stop 'em? It's their nature, ain't it? I always gets 'em right back as soon as I notice and stop the holes an' all. An' I was properly polite and apologetic an' all. But he gave me the whole talk about how it's the god's fields an' the god's flowers and what have you until you'd think I'd purposely stomped right into the sanctuary an' had sex on the floor. I mean, they're just animals. What do they know?"

He leaned closer and said in a confidential tone, "You tell your father, mistress, that I think that Sen-em-iah's just tryin' to get me off my land. Them priests are probably pressurin' him. This bit o' land is right in the middle of theirs, and I'm the last one not to sell out to them. See? They'd never make so much of it otherwise. How much can a few rabbits even eat?"

"Rabbits?" bleated Mut-tuy.

Neferet's heart picked up its pace. She said in a trembling voice, "Excuse me, my friend. How did rabbits come into the conversation?"

"Why, isn't that what you're askin' about? My rabbits

what got into the flower fields." The man gestured behind the wall between them. "Look at the li'l fellows. How could anybody hate them?"

Neferet craned her neck over the wall, which was about chest high. The ground seethed with furry brown bodies and twitching ears. A row of wooden hutches, concealed from those casually passing down the path, pressed against the base of the wall. *Mut the mother of us all. He raises rabbits.*

"Ah, right. *Those* rabbits. What was your name again, master? My father told me but…"

"Surer," said the farmer. "Be sure an' tell your father about the land."

"Of course. Now, tell me, Surer—how many times did Sen-em-iah confront you about these, er, rabbits?"

"Hmmm. Two or three at least. I kinda lost track. I see him comin', an' I just crouch behind this wall and act like I ain't at home." He grinned, looking both cunning and innocent.

"Did it make you really mad? Would you have considered harming him to get him off your back?"

Surer looked surprised. "Harm him? No. Like I says, I figure somebody else is pushin' him. He's actually a real nice fellow. We've always been on good terms otherwise. He even brung us flowers when my little girl got married."

Maybe I'm gullible, but he surely seems to be telling the truth. From the corner of her vision, Neferet saw Mut-tuy rolling her eyes. Somebody apparently thought Neferet was gullible.

She hesitated. "Were you aware that Sen-em-iah has been murdered?"

"Murdered?" Surer looked genuinely horrified. He sank to his knees and threw dust on his head cloth. "May the Lady of the West receive him! Who done him in?"

"Nobody's sure. Might it have been the priests?"

"Ammit take 'em—they'da been more likely to have killed me than him. I don't know who'da done him in. Not me, for sure." Surer climbed to his feet with admirable agility.

"Well, thank you for your insights, Surer. I'll tell my father what you said. He may come back himself if he needs more information."

"Yes, mistress. Tell him I'm real sorry about Sen-em-iah. We mighta crossed swords now an' then, but I liked him. He was a real fine fellow."

The two made their polite goodbyes and set off down the path toward the River once more. Neferet was reeling.

"He did it. What do you bet? And Sen-em-iah knew who it was." Mut-tuy's eyes were aglow.

"It certainly looks like it. The rabbits are conclusive." Neferet was almost disappointed to have settled the mystery so quickly. And she had ended up rather liking Surer. "Now, what do we do about it? Do we tell the *medjay* who the guilty party is, or do we make them work it out for themselves?"

"We could slip them an anonymous message. You can write, can't you?"

"But it may not have been Surer personally. Could he afford to pay a couple of bravos? We don't want to punish him if there was somebody else spearheading the crime."

Mut-tuy made a dubious noise.

They reached the riverbank, where their boatman dozed

in the bottom of his vessel, a palmetto frond over his face. The late-afternoon shadows had stretched out—evening wouldn't be long in coming.

Neferet emitted a piercing whistle between her teeth, and the fellow jerked upright in confusion.

"Time to head upriver, my man," she said, climbing into the boat. "Leave us at Lord Maya's private dock. I'll show you where."

CHAPTER 8

O N HIS WAY HOME FOR lunch the following day, Hani stopped by Ptah-mes's house. He had a question regarding a treaty with some of the vassals of Kharu that he wanted to run by his sometime superior. Ptah-mes had just closed the weekly morning of audience at his home and was sitting down to table when his steward announced Hani's arrival.

The treasurer looked up with an expression of pleasure. "Hani, my friend. Do join me for lunch."

"I thank you, my lord, but Nub-nefer will be expecting me. I heard rumors of carp on the menu." Nonetheless, Hani seated himself on the stool his host drew up to the small table. "I just had a legal question I wanted to ask you about."

"I'll do my best. Oh, incidentally, your daughter tells me that our old friend Mahu is in town." A note of ice crept into Ptah-mes's voice at the name.

Hani shook his head grimly. "So she said. I don't know if he's here in an official capacity or not, though. The girls apparently just saw him at the police garrison and turned around and left."

"I did a little research after she mentioned him and found out the rest of the story. He's been appointed chief of police in Waset."

"Hidden One protect us," Hani groaned. "Ay must have more dirty deeds for him to carry out, the blackguard. I guess revenge will be on his mind if he knows I got him put out to pasture."

"I'm not sure if Ay is at the root of it or not. He's headquartered in Men-nefer these days, as the vizier of the Lower Land."

"Who, then? Pentju?" Hani accepted the cup of wine Ptah-mes offered him and sipped it with delight. It was a splendid vintage from Djahy. But the idea of Mahu being in a position to curdle all their lives again infused it with a certain bitterness.

"My sources say Har-em-heb."

Hani set down his cup in surprise. "He must not know what sort of a corrupt specimen Mahu is. Otherwise, I can't believe he'd bring him back. Har-em-heb is uprightness in the flesh." The infantry general who had become a mentor to the little king had been a friend of Hani's family for years. He had been a passionate partisan of the Hidden One in the dark days of Nefer-khepru-ra's religious revolution.

Ptah-mes lifted his eyebrows cynically. He was too polite to eat while Hani sat before him without a setting, and his meat, wafting its delicious, complex perfume of coriander and cardamom, was growing cold in the plate.

Hani eyed it apologetically. "Please don't let me keep

you from your meal, my lord. I should be going. I'll call on you at your office."

But Ptah-mes waved him off and poured him some more wine. "We need to warn the ladies to be careful. If Mahu gets wind that they're asking questions around the edge of a police investigation, he'll be livid. It would give him the excuse he needs to do them harm."

"I wish there were some way I could make them stop. But Neferet will do the opposite of anything I tell her. Besides, she's a married woman. I don't really have any authority over her anymore."

"I suppose that should fall to me, then, but our agreement permits her to do as she likes without any commentary on my part."

Hani thought that it was an interesting aspect of his friend's character that despite his reputation at work—and among his children—as a demanding disciplinarian, he seemed uninterested in controlling his wives to the slightest degree. Both Neferet and her predecessor, Lady Apeny, were women of firm, independent will.

As if he'd read his friend's mind, Ptah-mes said smoothly, "I respect your daughter's intelligence, Hani. And her courage. Perhaps if we spoke to Lady Bener-ib, she might exercise a prudent influence over her."

"If she's not afraid to say anything. But it's certainly worth a try. The challenge will be to catch her by herself." The little physician was almost always to be found trailing Neferet, content to remain in her shadow.

Hani upended his cup and drained the last few drops of its content, then he rose. "I thank you for this exceptional wine, my lord. I'll head home now and leave you to your dinner."

"It's always a pleasure, my friend." Ptah-mes got to his feet and graciously accompanied Hani to the door.

As they approached the exit, a three-legged mongrel darted inside, nearly colliding with them, and hotfooted it into the house. Ptah-mes didn't seem at all perturbed by this invasion of his domestic space. At Hani's surprised look, he said with a wry twitch at the corner of his mouth, "One of your daughter's charity cases."

Hani had to smile. The disreputable-looking mutt certainly didn't square with the orderly perfection of his friend's ancestral mansion. He had seen Ptah-mes's hunting dogs, and they were as elegant and purebred as their master. He wondered what they thought of this common new companion.

The men clasped forearms with affection, and Hani made his way into the cicada-blasted summer noon. Some distance down the street, he realized he'd forgotten to ask his question.

The next morning, the doctors arrived at the dispensary at the usual hour, accompanied by the children and their nurse. Neferet carried an enormous basket in her arms, the contents carefully hidden by a cloth. After feeding the resident animals and establishing the little ones in the shade of the courtyard to play, Neferet and Bener-ib, with Mut-tuy at their heels, opened up the house and prepared for the day. With a sense of defiant satisfaction, Neferet finally unveiled the basket's contents, filling the room with the fragrance of toasted sedge nuts and honey. The others stared at her curiously.

"What are all those treats for?" Bener-ib asked.

"They're to distribute to our patients for free. To make it worth their while to come to us. Don't you think children are going to want to come back if they get sweets?"

"But how will they know about them? They have to come first, and nobody does," Mut-tuy said, a sneer sitting ill on her girlish face.

"Because we're going to go around the block and tell all our neighbors and give them a sample. I'll bet Djed-har doesn't do anything like this."

Bener-ib nodded uncertainly.

"Besides," Neferet added in a sinister voice, "we never did find out what Djed-har is telling people about us. Sit-amen will let us know if we ask her directly."

"We don't want to get him mad at us," Bener-ib said.

"Oh yes, we do!" Mut-tuy cried, her eyes lighting up.

Neferet said dryly, "See here, my girl. Are you for or against this?"

"I'm for getting up Djed-har's nose, the jackal turd."

Neferet was amused and gratified by the girl's warrior spirit, but Mut-tuy also needed to remember her place. "Let's wait till you cut off your Haru-lock and grow your maiden braids before we send you into battle, eh? Right now, one of us is going to go door to door, hand out treats to the children, and talk to the parents if they're people we know."

"I'll go," Mut-tuy said. "They won't be shy talking about you if neither of you is there."

"I don't think they're likely to reveal anything at all to

a child, my girl, and as long as you have the lock, you're a child."

"That's not fair!"

"Life isn't fair. The gods have their own rules. They just happen to have created you a mere thirteen years ago."

Mut-tuy stomped out of the room, her face red as a pomegranate. From the former kitchen came sounds of rummaging then silence. A moment later, she reemerged, brandishing her braid, which she'd whacked off close to the scalp. Since the rest of her formerly shaven hair had grown out to about a fingernail's length, she had a singularly scruffy appearance. A wild light of defiance glittered in her eye.

Neferet took in the sight, her jaw agape. Then she burst out laughing. It was so like something she would have done. "Bravo!" she cried despite herself.

Bener-ib looked horrified at first but then joined in the laughter. Such merriment didn't please Mut-tuy, who glared at the two young women, her face aflame. "Well? I don't have the braid anymore," she said in a tone of challenge.

"You look like Faithful." Neferet grinned. The old dog had stiff hair that stuck out in all directions. "I'm not sure you're fit to be seen by anybody now."

Mut-tuy cried in furious anguish, "But you said—"

"I'll go around the neighborhood, and you can come with me—in a scarf. Ibet will man the dispensary. Does that suit everybody?"

The others agreed, and Neferet hoicked her basket and headed to the door. Bener-ib found a linen towel and tied it behind Mut-tuy's nape so that the ends hung down her back. It was a look both men and women affected when doing a dusty job or one in the heat of the sun.

First off, they crossed the lane and stuck their heads in Sit-amen's door. Nobody was home.

"She's working in the dyery," said Neferet. "I wonder where the children are."

Around the corner of the house, the work yard stretched out within the same wall. Five men and women, the latter with their skirts hiked well up, were busy stirring fabric in plastered vats or treading it to keep it under the foul-smelling blue liquid. The odor of urine was almost too acrid to endure, mingled with the smells of the rotting plants that served as dyes.

Sit-amen sweated over a vat, moving the heavy, wet cloth gently around with a long pole. Her blue feet suggested she had already trod it. She looked up at the approach of the visitors, and a weary smile lit her face. Signaling to her husband, she laid down the pole and came to meet them at a distance from the workers, trailed by unpleasant smells.

"Lady Neferet! What brings you here? I'm due a little break, so we can talk a moment."

She stopped in the shade of a big persea tree, and the three squatted on the ground.

"We brought you some treats for the children. Where are they?"

"The eldest is at work, and the others are with my mother. How sweet of you! I haven't had time to bake anything else."

She was a sinewy young woman, not many years older than Neferet, with a broad, good-natured face. Sit-amen had been the first to welcome the doctors to the neighborhood and was always quick with a greeting.

"We're going to be offering free treats to any children who come to the dispensary for treatment. If your little ones enjoy these, you might think about it."

Sit-amen's face froze, and she looked down guiltily.

Neferet grasped her earnestly by the indigo forearm and said in a lower voice, "We know Djed-har has told everybody something about us that makes people afraid to trust us. Won't you please tell me what he's said? It's almost certainly a lie."

The woman looked anguished, gnawing her lip and casting her eyes around as if looking for an escape. Eventually she murmured, "He said that you and Lady Bener-ib were bored rich ladies who didn't really know anything about medicine and were just playing at being doctors. He said your rich husband paid to have the corpses of those who died under your care disposed of."

Neferet felt the heat rising to her cheeks. It blurred her eyesight for a moment with the red veil of anger. She said through a clenched jaw, "That lying hound. And everybody believed him?"

"We didn't know you then. This was before you started practicing. It confused us, you know? It would be so much more convenient to go to you, like we used to go to Khuit. But I just wasn't sure." The dyer's wife looked apologetic.

"Let me tell you the truth of the matter, Sit-amen. Lady Bener-ib was trained at Sau. Her father taught there. I started out apprenticed to Khuit, then we both studied under Lord Pentju and his wife, the palace physicians. We were the late king's personal *sunet*s for more than a year before she died. We're both literate, my friend—we can read the speech of the gods. It's true my husband is rich, and that's why we can afford to do this and not keep working at the palace. We want to help ordinary people. We hardly ask for anything in return. We just want to see people healthier and happier. It's not pleasing to the gods that folks should die just because they can't afford a good doctor."

Sit-amen wiped her nose, looking thoroughly ashamed. "He never said none of that."

"Of course not. But now you know." Neferet stared at her neighbor, willing her to come to her senses. "And what are *his* qualifications? He told us he trained at Sau, but it isn't true. I think he's just a self-taught healer who really has no idea what he's doing. Just like he accused us of being. He's afraid of us."

"My husband says he don't trust women to know what they're doing."

"And you're going to put up with that?" sniffed Mut-tuy.

Neferet said pointedly, "Khuit was a woman. You trusted her."

Sit-amen heaved a sigh. "I'd come to you happily, my lady. I will. I'll bring little Huy to have you look at that stye. It's no better."

Of course not, Neferet thought hotly. *Because Djed-har doesn't know what ointment to use.* "I'll give you something for that. It'll clear it up in no time." She scrambled to her feet, and Mut-tuy and the dyer followed. "You're a good woman, Sit-amen. You put the welfare of your loved ones above the lies of some malicious old hyena."

They picked up their basket and took their leave, heartened by Sit-amen's expression of relief and solidarity.

Neferet slipped a little pile of treats inside the house as they passed the doorway.

This is going to take a while. We probably ought to split up and do the others. But she didn't altogether trust Mut-tuy not to get argumentative.

At the next house, no one answered. Everybody was working, she supposed. At the third house, an old grandmother responded. She didn't seem to hear at all well, and by the time they emerged, Neferet wasn't sure whether the woman had ever quite understood why they had come. The sun was high in the heavens, and Neferet's stomach hinted that lunchtime was nigh.

"Let's go on back. By the time we get the children home, it will be time to eat."

They found Bener-ib mixing potions and organizing supplies in the back room. "How did it go?" she asked eagerly.

Neferet made an ambiguous noise and stuck a sedge-nut treat in her mouth. "At least we've planted a seed of doubt. But it takes so long. We only reached three households."

"Sit-amen has come around," said Mut-tuy. "She's going to bring Huy for you to look at his stye."

"I have the ointment ready." Bener-ib slid a little pot forward. "I made it last evening while you were talking to the rabbit farmer and left it out in the dew overnight. It should be ready to use."

Neferet stroked her arm gratefully. "Thanks for keeping the dispensary going, Ibet. Now that Sen-em-iah's murder is more or less solved, I'll be around more to do my share of the work. I promise."

"But we haven't decided what to do about the murder,"

said Mut-tuy. "Are we going to report it to the *medjay* or not?"

"We should at least tell Pen-buy." Bener-ib folded the towel she'd tied around her as an apron. "Let him decide what to do, perhaps. That way we won't have to go to the police."

"Excellent idea, my girl. We can explain that we have some doubts and let him choose whether to go after Surer."

But Mut-tuy said, "Come on, Lady Neferet! You know it has to be him. Why else would Sen-em-iah's dying word be 'rabbit' if it didn't have to do with his argument over the rabbits?"

"Oh, agreed. But somebody other than Surer might have made the decision to kill the florist. I can't imagine he could afford to pay professional killers."

"Maybe they were his sons or nephews or somebody." The girl wasn't about to give up.

"Unless they were soldiers or assassins by profession, I wouldn't think so. Somebody knew how to handle a knife or sword. They didn't take any chances on him surviving."

"If they really hated him…" Mut-tuy mumbled.

Bener-ib added timidly, "It does make sense of the visits by those priests. They might have been encouraging him to deal with the farmer so they could get his land."

"Then they're the guilty ones." Neferet spread her hands to dramatize the evidence. "That's what's stopping me. I don't want Surer put to death if somebody else was behind it. We need to find out who those priests were."

"Should we go see your uncle again? Maybe he's talked to the high priest by now," said Bener-ib.

Neferet suspected he would drop in on his sister to

communicate the result of his investigation. He would report to Hani, not Neferet. "We need to check with Papa whether Uncle has come—he probably thinks it's really Papa's case. Right after lunch, on our way back. Before Papa's had a chance to get away."

They made their way home in the usual unruly procession. Heads turned in amusement or annoyance at their passage. Once at Ptah-mes's villa, Neferet observed with a pang of conscience that her husband was eating by himself in the salon. Hustling the little ones on into the garden, she resolved that she would eat with Lord Ptah-mes that evening.

She and Bener-ib and Mut-tuy made short work of lunch and charged out, leaving the children at table with their nurse. She waved guiltily at Ptah-mes as they clattered once more through the salon where he still sat. "We're off to see Papa!" she called.

"Salute him on my behalf."

They arrived at Hani's villa in time to find the family still at their meal. Even before they had emerged into the salon, Neferet heard the familiar voices laughing hilariously. Everyone was there—Mama, Papa, Grandfather, with Baket-iset on her couch at Mama's side, and Maya, with his pen case, as usual, over his shoulder even at table. The family looked up as the trio entered and called out their greetings.

"Amen-em-hut was looking for you," said Mama.

"Did he think he'd find me here?" Neferet laughed. "I suspect he was looking for Papa."

Papa lifted his eyebrows in a gesture of guilt. "Yes. He's

under the impression that I'm working on that florist's murder."

"If the Third Prophet of the Hidden One thinks you are, maybe you should be. Although I suspect we've pretty much resolved the mystery. The question now is what to do about it."

Neferet and the others pulled up stools and seated themselves. She leaned over the nearly scraped serving dish and fished out a fingerful of mashed lentil.

"Tell, tell," prompted Grandfather. "Who was the culprit?"

With an appropriate variety of voices and expressions, Neferet summarized their interview with Surer and the connection she'd made with the visits of the priests.

"I thought it was Sen-em-iah's jilted girlfriend that murdered him," said Maya dryly.

"That was just a theory, my boy. This refinement of the theory explains not only the involvement of the priests but also Sen-em-iah's final words."

"So, you think the rabbit farmer killed him." Papa cracked a pistachio with a nail and popped it in his mouth.

"Well, that's the sticky part, Papa. I find it hard to believe Surer literally set the murder in motion. I mean, if somebody had jumped Sen-em-iah on a path among the flower fields, maybe. But it seems a little sophisticated to set hired footpads on him on the streets of Waset. How would Surer have known where he lived?"

Grandfather asked, "Who do you think did it, then, my girl?"

"Maybe the priests. Maybe they were disappointed that he hadn't been able to dislodge the farmer from his lands."

There was a moment of uncomfortable silence, during which Papa, Maya, and Grandfather exchanged meaningful looks. Then Papa said, "Only there seem to have been no priests, my duckling. Amen-em-hut asked the First Prophet whom he had sent to talk to Sen-em-iah, and he said there hadn't been any delegation. Nobody went."

"What?" Neferet and Mut-tuy cried as one.

"But so many people saw them. More than once." Neferet was gobsmacked. Offended, even. "You don't think Pen-buy and the workers were all lying, surely? And Wabet, the maid? Those priests even went to the house."

"How is it they were so sure the men were priests?" asked Maya with his usual skepticism. "They must have been in civilian clothes, just walking around the city like that."

"I don't know," Neferet said defensively. "Maybe they introduced themselves. Maybe the others saw their arms and legs were shaved."

Everyone sat silent, thinking hard.

Finally, Neferet said, "We need to have the witnesses describe these people for us. Then we'll find out which priests fill that description. We'll go talk to them and ask them directly why they were there."

"Neferet, my love," Mama warned gently, "there are nearly nine thousand priests at the Ipet-isut. Don't be disappointed if you can't find the men."

Iyah. So many? Discouragement already lapped at Neferet's resolve. "What else can we do?"

"You should probably tell the dead man's son what you've discovered," said Papa. "If he thinks it's going to lead you to the Hidden One's servants, he may tell you to let things lie."

"I'm afraid he may want revenge on Surer, though."

"Explain your reservations."

Neferet felt thwarted, and it wasn't a feeling she liked. Her brows drawn down, she said stubbornly, "Maybe somebody lower down than the First Prophet sent them. Who was in charge of dealing with Sen-em-iah?"

"Ask his son," said Grandfather. "He's the point of contact now."

Maya said cynically, "Maybe he's the murderer. Maybe he wanted his inheritance."

"Or maybe he's in love with his stepmother!" Mut-tuy's malicious little face had lit up like a torch. "She's a lot younger than her late husband."

Oh no, thought Neferet. *We're back to the beginning.* With a big sigh, she stood up and pushed in her stool. "Come on, people. We have work to do."

CHAPTER 9

THE NEXT MORNING, THE THREE young women stood in a conspiratorial circle in the salon of the dispensary.

"Here's what we have to do," said Neferet. "One: tell Pen-buy what we've discovered and let him decide whether we should dig any deeper." She held up a hand and began folding down one finger at a time.

"But what if he's the murderer?" Mut-tuy objected.

"Come, my girl. If you're going to propose that, it could be anybody. It could be you or me or anybody else with no particular motive. We have to stick with our only lead. It has to do with the rabbits, all right? That means it's either Surer or the priests."

"Maybe we should find out who the priests were first," Bener-ib suggested.

"Right. That's number two." She folded down a second finger.

"What if Pen-buy's the murderer?" Mut-tuy said again.

Neferet rolled her eyes. "I heard you, Mut-tuy. Don't

you think if he were the murderer, he wouldn't have been so generous in helping us investigate?"

The girl shrugged, unconvinced.

"We need a lower-rank priest than Uncle to ask around for us. I doubt if he even knows who's in charge of dealing with the Bearer of Divine Offerings. It would probably be a *hem-netjer*, though. They're higher rank than the *wabu* and likely to be the ones giving orders. There can't be so many thousands of *hemu-netjer*."

"Where are we going to find one of them?" asked Mut-tuy sullenly.

"*Yahyah*, my girl! Lord Ptah-mes's eldest son is a *hem-netjer*! He'll surely know who's in charge of florists!"

"Oh, how smart, Nef'et!" Bener-ib cried, clapping her hands. "That's perfect!"

Mut-tuy pursed her lips dubiously. "Will he do it?"

"Of course he will if his father asks him to. And Lord Ptah-mes will ask him if I beg him to."

"So, is there a three?" the girl asked, eyeing Neferet's hand with two fingers crooked.

"Three: ask Wabet and some of the other servants or workmen who claim to have seen the priests what they looked like. It would help Djehuty-mes if we could narrow down his choices."

"That's the first thing to do, I guess." Bener-ib stooped to pat Mangler, who had ambled in and stood at her feet, tail wagging listlessly.

"Right. We can go at midday, when the workers eat their lunch."

"Lady Neferet," said Mut-tuy in a dark voice "it's clear

you've never been poor. Workers don't eat lunch. If they pause for a drink of water and a nap, they're lucky."

That stopped Neferet cold. She realized with a pang that she'd taken a lot for granted in her comfortable life. She said with a show of lightness, "Well, *we* aren't busy at lunchtime."

"We aren't ever busy," Bener-ib said sadly.

"Then we can send Nurse home with the little ones, and the three of us will head for the florists' workshop. We can grab a bite with Mama and Papa—their house is closer. And this evening, I'll talk to Lord Ptah-mes."

They set about their morning routine—checking supplies, preparing any potions and ointments that didn't have to be used immediately, setting fresh flowers on the shelf of the shrine. Hu-may fed the dogs then disappeared off to work, while the younger children, organized by the nurse, began a noisy game.

Then commenced the depressing daily activity of waiting for patients who never came. But that morning, just as Neferet prepared to sit down on the examining stool, a knock at the gate made her jump to her feet. She rushed ahead of the others to find Sit-amen standing in the street with her Huy and his red eye.

Sit-amen was beaming. "I told my husband I was coming, and he said 'Awright, then. We'll give 'em a chance. If the boy's eye gets better, they're our new healers.'"

Neferet threw her arms around the dyer in delight. "May the gods bless you, Sit-amen! You're a ripe fig among women!"

Bener-ib and Mut-tuy stood in the door of the

dispensary, where they greeted the first patient of the day with warmth.

As soon as Huy had been seated on one of the beds, Bener-ib slipped him a sedge-nut goodie. "There's another one for you when you're finished."

Neferet squatted at the boy's side and pulled down his lower eyelid, staring closely at the red and swollen edge. "I do believe he's got a lash growing into the skin. You rub your eyes, don't you, little man?"

Huy, a solemn lad of eight or nine, nodded.

"This all come up after that big sandstorm," said his mother.

Bener-ib, already knowing what the next step must be, handed Neferet a bronze tweezer.

Neferet delicately took hold of the in-curled lash and gave it a brisk jerk.

Huy let out a yelp.

"All gone. Now, we'll put some of this wonderful-smelling ointment on your lid, and it will bring out the pus. All the soreness should go away in no time." She applied a bit of the ointment with a smooth little stick.

"Don't rub it, though, or you'll get it in your eye, and everything will look blurry," Bener-ib said as the boy automatically lifted his hand. She turned to Sit-amen. "If he can't keep his hand away, we can put a patch on it for a bit."

"I'll see to it he don't rub it."

Pressing the pot of ointment on her, Bener-ib said, "Apply a little every morning. It should be fine, but let us know if the red doesn't seem to be going away."

"Thank you, my ladies. I feel so bad about not coming earlier. Can I bring you some dyed fabric? Grain?"

But Neferet waved her hands. "You don't owe us anything. Just tell your friends."

After loading Huy with more treats, the young women said a grateful goodbye to their neighbor and her son.

The salon empty once more of patients, they faced each other with grins on their faces.

"She'll tell everybody, and little by little, Djed-har's castle will crumble!" crowed Neferet. The three seized hands and shook them triumphantly.

The idea of patients led Neferet's thoughts back to the dead florist. "That reminds me—we can talk to that bodyguard of Sen-em-iah. He'll be able to let us know what the attackers looked like, and maybe he even saw the priests."

"Do we know where he lives?" asked Bener-ib as if reluctant to throw water on the fire of their enthusiasm.

Neferet made a disappointed grunt, but Mut-tuy said, "I do. I watched him after he left here. He entered the door on the corner where we turn to go to your sister's."

"Why don't we go down there this evening?" Neferet said.

Later that morning, as if she'd been conjured up by the mention, Sat-hut-haru appeared with her second born, Mai-her-pri, in tow.

"He burned his finger touching a hot serving dish," she said in a harried voice. "It's always one of them. But Mai-her-pri is old enough not to do things like that."

"How was I to know, Mama?" the victim cried in a

grown-up tone of exasperation. "Hot things look the same as cold things."

"But why did you even touch the dish, my love? Just take a piece of food off with the knife."

"I did, but it fell off." Clearly, the nine-year-old wasn't going to give up his position of innocence easily.

Neferet examined the hand he presented. The outside edge of his little finger was blistered, and she could picture how it might have happened. Mai-her-pri was a dwarf, like his father, Maya, and even at eight, he would have had difficulty reaching high enough above a plate on the table not to graze the pottery as he grabbed for a piece of meat.

"Ibet, get me some of that aloe-and-cat's-hair ointment you made up, please, and we'll put this young gentleman to rights."

"The worst is," the patient continued, "that I can't write 'cause it's my right hand. What's the point of going to school?"

"Is Mama making you go to school?" Neferet exchanged a conspiratorial look with her sister. "I'll bet there are still things you can learn even with a bandaged hand."

"I doubt it."

Sat-hut-haru rolled her eyes. "You're going to be the laziest scribe in the Two Lands, Mai."

"It's 'cause I want to join the army, not be a scribe."

"I'm sure your gamfather could quote you all sorts of maxims why it's better to be a scribe." Neferet laughed and swabbed his small hand with the gelatinous ointment Bener-ib presented.

The latter then wrapped the finger expertly with a

narrow bandage of linen. "Change this when it gets dirty," she told Sat-hut-haru. "And if it should get wet."

Mai-her-pri slid off the bed, ready to go. "If I have to go to school, let's get it over with."

His mother fought down a grin and headed after him. "The captain says it's time for his troops to move out. Thank you, my sisters."

The three waved them off, suppressing smiles. Mut-tuy ran after him with treats, which he accepted eagerly.

"He's adorable," Bener-ib said fondly. "Can't you just see him as a little soldier? A real lion on the battlefield."

"Perhaps we should hire him as a bodyguard," Neferet said with a snicker. "Since everyone says our investigation is so dangerous."

Mut-tuy laughed then quickly repositioned a look of indifference.

The sun was directly overhead and, for a moment at least, no longer streamed through the high, narrow windows. "Let's head to Sen-em-iah's house. I'd like to talk to the maid in person. She seems to know what's going on all the time. And also, maybe we'll see that bodyguard around. What's his name?"

"Tut-em-heb," Bener-ib said.

The children had already left. Neferet shut the gate behind the three, and they set off past the empty properties that adjoined their dispensary. At the corner, she hesitated. "Do you suppose Tut-em-heb might be at home for lunch?"

Just in case, she approached the gate and knocked.

A buxom young woman with her dress strap down and a baby on her hip answered. Her eyes widened at the sight of two women and a girl.

"Is your husband here, by any chance? We're the *sunet*s from down the street, and we wanted to ask him about his late master."

"He is," said the woman, brightening. "We're so grateful for how well you fixed up our daughter's arm. She keeps talking about your one-eyed cat and how he wanted a sling too."

She led the three visitors into the courtyard, where the family sat on masonry benches under the shade of the trees. A loom was upended against the wall, warped with delicate linen thread. The smell of onions frying brought the water to Neferet's mouth.

Tut-em-heb, who was dandling the toddler on his knee, rose as he saw his visitors. "My ladies, what can I do for you?"

After asking about the child, Neferet said in a lower voice, "Did you get any kind of look at the men who attacked your master, Tut-em-heb? How many were there?"

"There were three, Lady Neferet. I didn't see them clearly. It all happened fast. Two of them were definitely Egyptians, one very thickly built. The third was light-skinned. He might have been a man of Kharu or Djahi, or at least from the Lower Kingdom. He had a funny little queue of hair up front but was otherwise half-bald. They all had knives but no other weapons that I was aware of."

"Thank you—that's quite useful. Did you ever see any priests who might have come to visit you master?"

The guard sat back and stared ahead thoughtfully, as if ransacking his memory. "I wouldn't normally have been likely to see visitors to the house, but there were several times when the master had us stand to attention in the salon when he was receiving. I couldn't swear the men were priests—they were dressed like anyone else. No leopard skins, no white sandals." He grinned. "But it seemed to me their forearms were shaved. And they just had that look about them. Real well-dressed. Big gold pectorals. Kind of floated when they walked, or rolled—you know what I mean? There were two who always came together. One was short and fat—not hugely fat but round. Fat around the jowls and maybe fortyish. They both were."

"What did the other one look like?" asked Neferet, her pulse beginning to pound. Here was something really useful.

"Medium height, I'd say, but thin, with a long neck and a big knot here." He flicked his own pharynx. "And big, projecting teeth."

"Sounds like a beauty!"

Tut-em-heb laughed. "They were both full of gold jewelry. It never occurred to me not to take them seriously."

"And Sen-em-iah felt he needed bodyguards against two middle-aged priests? That seems odd."

The man shrugged. "Maybe he just wanted to look impressive. But I think he was scared, yes."

"How often did they come around?"

"I could swear to at least twice. It may have been more times, but maybe at first, he didn't need us. I honestly don't know, my lady."

Neferet shot a burning glance at Bener-ib. "What did they talk about?"

But suddenly Tut-em-heb looked reluctant. "I don't know if I can tell you, my lady. My master expected complete confidentiality."

"He's dead, my man. And we're trying to find out at whose hand to appease his *ba*. Don't you think he'd want you to cooperate? Besides, his son is counting on us."

After gnawing his lip for a moment, a conflicted frown on his face, the guard spoke again in a low voice. "I didn't understand much of what they were talking about. They seemed to rely a lot on people already knowing. 'What we've discussed' and 'the matter that interests us all'—they would say things like that. The buck-toothed man seemed to be in charge. He became pretty aggressive sometimes. He'd say something like, 'Need I remind you that we have written proof of your approval?' and such. I'd say he was threatening the master in a polite way."

"You've been really helpful," Neferet said, almost bouncing with enthusiasm. "If you think of any more details about those priests, let us know."

In a state of excitement, the three young women took their leave.

"*Yahyah!* That was a goldmine!" squealed Mut-tuy once they were standing once more in the street. Her narrow face, under its disheveled thatch, was flushed.

Bener-ib's eyes shifted back and forth uneasily. She seemed to shrink as if to escape notice.

"It sounds like those servants of the Hidden One were really pushing him to get them the rabbit man's land." *Wait till we tell Papa. This is all shaping up so well.* "Do we even need to talk to any other servants? Apparently, no one but the bodyguards were present for these interviews."

"Shouldn't we speak to the widow? If she was and is scared, she must know something about this business." Bener-ib spoke reluctantly, yet she was offering ideas nonetheless. Her first reaction might be fear, but Neferet knew she'd be the first to see *ma'at* done, cost what it might.

"A wonderful idea, Ibet! You're always so thorough. In the meantime, Djehuty-mes should be able to identify these two priests for us."

Neferet set off with jaunty steps, the others scurrying to keep up. Knowledge had suddenly begun to gush out like the waters of the Inundation, sweeping away their ignorance. *This is why Papa loves to investigate*, she thought, exhilarated. *There's nothing like the feeling of the truth starting to fall into place.*

When they arrived at the gate of the Osir Sen-em-iah's house, however, Neferet realized she didn't know where Pen-buy lived. "He mentioned his father's house as if it were no longer his. And to be sure, he's old enough to have a house and family of his own. He must be Pa-kiki's age."

"His stepmother will know," Bener-ib said. "We can talk to her first. We'll have to ask to interview her maid anyhow."

They knocked on the gate and identified themselves as the physicians who had seen Sen-em-iah through to the other world. The gatekeeper bade them enter, and they waited on the front path while he took the news to his mistress. A moment later, she came flying out the door and down the shallow steps of the porch. She was wearing a mourning scarf, but her hair was no longer dirty and disheveled. There was kohl around her eyelids, and she looked considerably younger than Neferet had remembered, although her eyes were huge with fright and her face stiff and anxious.

"Yes? What is it? I'll pay you if that's why you're here," she said bluntly.

"Oh no, mistress," Neferet assured her. "We just wanted to see how you were doing. Your stepson suggested that you might need a calming potion to help you sleep."

"That's kind of you. I'm fine. He needs to mind his own business." She turned as if to go.

But Neferet wasn't so easily shaken off. "Before you go, may I ask you something? We have a report to make to the police, as I mentioned that day in our dispensary, and we thought it might be helpful to talk to some of your servants. Or maybe you could help us if you know anything that might have brought someone's enmity down on your husband. We—"

"By the Hidden One, can't you leave a grieving family alone?" the woman exploded so violently her spittle flew. Her eyes blazed, and her face was scarlet. "No. I don't know anything, and I won't talk to you, and neither will my servants. Just stay away from the police. This is none of your business. Don't bother us again." She spun and clattered up the steps and into the house, the skirts of her caftan fluttering in her wake. The door slammed behind her.

Neferet, her cheeks burning, stared in amazement at Bener-ib. "*Iyah*. Somebody doesn't want to talk to us. She knows who killed her husband, though, I'd bet anything."

"She's terrified," said Bener-ib, gazing in pity at the space the woman had just occupied.

Chilled by the blast of hostility, the three hustled toward the gate. As the keeper pushed back the panel for them, an older man stepped out of the shadow of the shrubbery. It was Sen-em-iah's steward, his face rigid with anxiety.

"Please forgive the mistress, my ladies. I'm sure she didn't mean to be rude. We appreciate your concern." His eyes cut back to the door of the house. "Things are tense at the moment. I'm sure you understand."

"No, I don't think I do," said Neferet slowly. "Grief, yes. But everyone seems scared to death. Doesn't she want to know who killed her husband?"

The steward stiffened. "We must believe her when she says not." He locked eyes with Neferet, but she wasn't sure what his stare meant.

"We'll be going, then." She turned and then wheeled back. "Oh, could you tell me where your late master's son lives?"

"Please, my lady. Leave Pen-buy out of this. He knows nothing."

"So is there something to know?" blurted Mut-tuy.

The steward blanched. Without a word, he bowed and disappeared back into the garden vegetation.

Neferet's neck hairs prickled.

The three young women hurried through the gate, glad to have escaped the strange, taut atmosphere of the house of mourning.

CHAPTER 10

"Τ HAT'S THE STRANGEST REACTION I'VE ever seen. It's as if she's afraid we'll find out what happened to her husband."

"Maybe she's the murderer," Mut-tuy said avidly.

But Bener-ib murmured, "Or maybe she's afraid the murderer will target her next if he thinks she's talked to someone. Us."

Mut-tuy turned to Neferet. "What do we do now? Back off like she wants?"

"Not quite." Neferet gritted her teeth in a stubborn clench. "It's clear our investigation is getting warm, and this isn't the moment to give up." She glared back at the gate behind them—that expressionless gate that seemed to be keeping secrets.

"But we could be bringing danger down on the woman, whatever her name is—I don't even know. She probably has a very good idea of who killed Sen-em-iah." Bener-ib looked troubled.

"We oughtn't to discuss this out here in the street. Let's

find Pen-buy at the workshop and tell him what's going on."

"Oh, Nef'et, we can't." Bener-ib stopped and drew back. "She just told us not to come around."

"Around her house, but we're going to the workshop," said Mut-tuy.

"But it's the same place. You know she meant both. We can't go against the proprietor's command. Besides, she said to keep Pen-buy out of this."

Neferet stared at her, astonished and frankly disappointed. "Ibet, my girl. Are you suggesting we stop our investigation? Because if we back down every time we seem to be getting close to something, we might as well quit."

Bener-ib hung her head and wrung her hands. "But if we poke around against her will, she'll call the police."

So that's it. She'd rather die than fall into the hands of the police again.

"She didn't seem to want the police to get involved either. I think she's the murderer," Mut-tuy said confidently.

"But what about the rabbit man? Why was Sen-em-iah's last word 'rabbit'?" asked Bener-ib.

"Maybe that was his wife's pet name." Neferet shrugged.

She glanced back again at the gate of Sen-em-iah's house, half-afraid someone might be watching them through a crack. Her back tingling, she drew the other two around the corner, where the garden wall would conceal them. Ahead stood the door of the florist workshop, abandoned at the noon hour. *So close...*

"It would be safer to talk to him at his home. But we don't know where he lives, although Djehuty-mes may know. Let's go talk to Lord Ptah-mes and get this line of investigation opened up. If we can't approach the murder from the victim's side, we'll go at it from the side of the priests." Neferet drew her friend by the arm and set off briskly toward the south.

Mut-tuy followed them for a moment then scurried abreast.

Elbow to elbow, sweeping the occasional other pedestrians from the path, they made their way home.

When they arrived, Lord Ptah-mes was rising from the table. "Ah, Neferet, my dear. Ladies," he said courteously, sitting back down. He clapped for a servant, who appeared bearing a basin and towel while another set out stools and a third laid a variety of dishes on the table, clearing those of his master.

"Lord Ptah-mes, I have a favor to ask you," Neferet said with her usual directness. "We need to find out who the priests were who visited the Osir Sen-em-iah. We think their leader was probably a *hem-netjer*, and we wondered if your son would recognize them if we described them for him."

"I suppose he might. But there are thousands of priests, you must realize, and they're on duty in alternate quarters of the year, so it's also possible that he might not know a given person."

"Oh, true." Neferet's assurance drooped. *I should have thought of that. Mama always works for three months at a time and then is off duty.* "But it's worth a try, I suppose. If Djehuty-mes is willing."

"I'm sure he'd be happy to talk to you." Ptah-mes's

coolly pleasant expression grew somber. "I hope you won't find yourselves in danger as a result of this investigation."

"Me too," said Bener-ib with utter sincerity.

"Oh, I'm sure we won't. The police may already have arrested the murderer."

"Do you think so?" Ptah-mes lifted his arched black eyebrows skeptically.

"I don't know." Then, moved by the need to hear her confused ideas out loud, Neferet told her husband what had happened at the bereaved widow's house. "We thought it was the rabbit man, but now I wonder if it wasn't the wife."

"I think she's afraid she'll be next." Bener-ib's face betrayed her own fear.

"So she at least knows who did it. No wonder she doesn't welcome your intervention." Ptah-mes nodded slowly. "Hani's insights would be useful here."

All at once, Neferet's eyes popped wide in excitement, and her heart seemed to clap its hands with glee. "Oh, people! We have a perfect way to get Papa involved. He said he had no jurisdiction unless a foreigner was involved, right? One of the attackers was a man of Kharu!"

Her husband stared at her. "How do you know?"

"A witness was able to describe the three assassins. One was light-skinned. Papa has a duty to investigate now. Oh, I'm so glad I thought of that!"

Ptah-mes looked thoughtful then said seriously, "Just be careful, I beg you. You're all of too much value as healers to throw away your lives on something like this. I'm sorry to have to say that criminals are rarely punished as they should be unless they're poor."

Mut-tuy shook her head with a world-weary air.

Bener-ib looked desolate. Her father's murderer had never been arrested, although Neferet suspected that Papa knew his identity.

After a moment of reflection, Lord Ptah-mes rose, his kilt and shirt, the latter with its pleated sleeves, looking as fresh and unwrinkled as if he had just put them on. "Please forgive me, ladies, but I need to be getting back to the Double House. Djehuty-mes should be at home any morning. I understand he's not in service this quarter."

He took his leave with beautiful courtesy, and the three young women were left staring at one another.

"Well, what are we waiting for, troops?" Neferet set her hands upon her hips. "Let's get going."

"But he said his son would be home in the morning," Bener-ib pointed out.

Neferet made a noise of disappointment. "Right. Back to the dispensary, then. And first thing in the morning— Dejehuty-mes's house."

⸙

Lord Djehuty-mes was surely the living image of his father at the age of forty, if perhaps a little heavier—Neferet had to admit she'd rarely seen such a handsome and distinguished face. He and Lord Ptah-mes had been at odds for years because of all that ridiculous business about whether to resist the Aten or play along, the better to undermine him. At first, Ptah-mes had chosen loyalty to the throne, despite the king's religious policies, while his wife and seven children, almost all of them priests, had been outspoken resisters. Only last year, after the death of Ankhet-khepru-ra and the accession of young Neb-khepru-ra Tut-ankh-aten, had they finally made their peace, to Neferet's relief. She, too, had been the object of the aristocratic family's scorn, but they went out of their way to be nice to her now, and she certainly wasn't one to hold a grudge.

The *hem-netjer* welcomed his young stepmother with cordiality and, no doubt, surprise, although he was too well-bred to show it. "Lady Neferet, to what do I owe this honor?" He bowed to the other two, and Mut-tuy ran her fingers self-consciously through her butchered hair. Her face had grown ferociously scarlet.

A certain young girl is rather smitten by an older man, thought Neferet with a silent snicker.

"We're trying to identify two priests, and your father thought you might be able to help us. I think one of them at least may be a *hem-netjer*, but I'm not even sure of that."

She described the rotund man first, but Djehuty-mes shook his head.

"It could be any number of people," he said apologetically. "Had he no distinguishing characteristics? His voice?"

"Nothing that we've been told," she admitted. "But the second man was pretty distinctive." She proceeded to describe the leader of the two, with his long, bobbly neck and buckteeth.

A dry smile twitched at the corner of Lord Djehuty-mes's lips in a similar expression to the one his father often made. "I know exactly who that is. A *hem-netjer*—you were right about that. He's almost certainly the fellow named Pu-im-ra. He's in charge of—what shall I call it?—the physical aspects of the liturgy. Supplies of incense, lamp oil, flowers, and such things. He has a number of underlings who specialize in the divine garments, seeing to the meals of the god—what have you. It all passes through him."

"So he's a very important person?"

"Oh yes." His smile grew harder. "And he's only too aware of it. Not well liked, for the most part, but competent enough."

"Would he be likely to deal face-to-face with the Bearer of Divine Offerings of Amen? Let's say there was a problem with a delivery, or the flowers weren't fresh or something."

Djehuty-mes nodded thoughtfully. "I suppose he would. Does this have anything to do with the death of the Bearer of Offerings?"

"Everybody knows about that, do they? Yes, it may. Pu-im-ra had visited Sen-em-iah several times recently. But it sounds like that was part of his duty."

"I would say so." He added, "The fat man you mention might be his lieutenant in charge of gold vessels, one Tetiky."

He waited politely for additional questions, but Neferet gave him a heartfelt squeeze of the hands. "Thank you *so* much, Lord Djehuty-mes. You've been so helpful! Say hello to young Amen-mes for us."

Amen-mes, the priest's twelve-year-old son, was a favorite pupil of Papa and the engineer of the family's recent reuniting.

Djehuty-mes accompanied the threesome to the door. "You must dine with us sometime, Lady Neferet. Whenever we invite Father, you know you and Lady Bener-ib are invited too. Amen-mes would be delighted."

They made their way into the lane, Neferet fizzing with excitement. "So now we know their names!"

"Probably," said Bener-ib.

"That's the handsomest man I've ever seen," Mut-tuy said in a dreamy voice.

"He looks just like Lord Ptah-mes. You see him every day."

"But *he's* old."

Neferet grinned wickedly at the adolescent. "Djehuty-mes is married, my girl." She set off briskly toward the dispensary, the others in tow. "I guess we'd better get back before the line of waiting patients gets too long."

To her amazement, there really was a line when they arrived. Four working-class women stood at the gate, with little ones in their arms or at their sides. From within the courtyard, the three dogs barked raggedly.

"Sit-amen told us all about you," said one of the mothers. "I don't like that Djed-har. He gives me a funny look. I'd rather have a woman healer."

Neferet could have cried with joy. *May the Great One bless Sit-amen. There aren't enough sedge-nut treats in the Two Lands to pay her back.* She unlocked the gate, and the little group moved in a block to the door, the dogs following eagerly.

"Who was here first?" asked Bener-ib, all competence. "I'll take her at that first bed."

The woman with a babe in arms peeled off to accompany her.

Neferet drew the second in line to one of the other beds.

154

Mut-tuy hovered around, ready to fetch supplies, but her mind was evidently elsewhere.

The other women and their children settled themselves on the floor by the door.

By the time the sun through the high windows signaled midday, the young patients and their mothers had taken their grateful leave, accompanied by stacks of treats wrapped in fig leaves.

Neferet and Bener-ib shared a triumphant look then fell into one another's arms, laughing and whooping. Seeing Mut-tuy looking abandoned at the edge of their rejoicing, Neferet turned to her and swept her up too.

"At last!" Neferet chortled. "It seems there's been dissatisfaction all along, but that turd Djed-har had poisoned everyone's mind against us. Now they feel free to leave him and come to us."

Bener-ib said with feeling, "That poor baby was going to waste away with diarrhea unless someone did something for him. All he needed was some pomegranate juice or fennel tea, but apparently, Djed-har didn't make use of it. He just said spells over him."

They picked some of the flowers spared by Mut-tuy's siblings and arranged them in a homely offering at their shrine. Neferet even added a couple of sweets. She felt quite buoyant.

"Perhaps our investigation will make progress now too. The gods have smiled on us. We need to give them something."

"And while we're at the temple, we can look up those two priests," said Mut-tuy.

"I don't think it's that simple. But now that we know

that our Pu-im-ra is in charge of... what all he's in charge of, that gives us a way to approach him."

"How so?" Bener-ib asked.

"We can say we want to endow something—some gold vessels or a quantity of oil or perfume or something. I'm sure Lord Ptah-mes won't mind. He was First Prophet himself a long time ago."

"Gold vessels. In-hapy's studio can make them. Maybe our Hu-may can even work on them." Bener-ib seemed almost eager, but then, she was a priest's daughter. "Only..."

"What, Ibet? That's a wonderful idea."

"Only, what are we going to ask when we see him? He's probably not going to reveal to us why he visited Sen-em-iah—that's internal temple business."

"We could tell him we're asking all the florist's associates if they know anybody who might have had a grudge against him." Mut-tuy's eyes were bright with that hunting-dog sparkle again.

"I like it. If he doesn't feel we're singling him out, he won't be so defensive." However, after a moment, Neferet scratched her stubbled scalp. "But what is it we really want to learn from him? We *know* who had a grudge against Sen-em-iah—the rabbit man."

Mut-tuy said impatiently, "We want to know why the priests visited Sen-em-iah."

"Which is what he won't tell us." Bener-ib looked from one to the other with an apologetic lift of the shoulders.

Neferet blew out a big breath of exasperation. "I wish those people wouldn't be so secretive." She looked up at the long beams of afternoon sunlight. "Let's go talk to Papa first and tell him he's involved, like it or not. We can deal with Pu-im-ra later. We'll have to get some cups made anyway."

They fed the dogs and cat, drew the gate shut behind them, and were poised to set off down the street when a man came pelting up from the other direction and stopped, panting, right before them.

"Are you Lady Neferet?" he asked between gasps.

"I am." Curiosity lit a hungry fire in her heart, but she felt a flutter of anxiety too.

"I'm a servant of Master Pen-buy, my lady. He said to tell you that his stepmother was just found dead."

Neferet and Bener-ib exchanged looks of horror.

"Was it natural?" A terrible suspicion had awakened in Neferet.

"Oh, no, my lady. Murder."

CHAPTER 11

"MAY THE LADY OF THE West receive her gently," murmured Bener-ib, sinking to her knees.

Neferet's reaction was rather more profane. "What happened?" she finally said.

The messenger had caught his breath a bit and gasped out, "She was found in the garden. Strangled. The young master wants you to come look at the body before the priests of Inpu arrive."

Neferet forced herself to kneel like Ibet and throw a little dust on her head in a decent gesture of mourning—she didn't want to be vengeful, even though she hadn't liked the woman much—and Mut-tuy followed.

"Lead on, my man." She climbed to her feet.

The servant accompanied them all the way to the florist's house, although they knew the route. Once they had entered the garden, it was clear that something serious had disturbed the morning routine. Servants rushed about, the women weeping. From within the house came children's sobs.

Suddenly, Pen-buy appeared in the door, looking around with wild eyes. Seeing the three young women, he made his way toward them in disjointed haste.

"Dear gods, this is terrible!" he cried in an unsteady voice. "Who will be next?" Then he seemed to remember the demands of courtesy. "Thank you for coming so promptly."

"Where is her body?" Neferet said, all business. They followed the man past the incongruously cheerful beds of flowers and into the shade of a fig tree studded with unripe fruit. The mistress of the house lay on the ground, a group of keening maids squatting around her, their hair undone, their faces clawed and dusty. One fanned away the gathering flies with a trimmed palmetto frond.

Neferet knelt at her left side and Bener-ib at the right, and the servants drew away while the two doctors looked the corpse over. An angry blood-beaded welt ran low around the victim's throat, and the whites of her wide-open, bugged eyes were a horrifying speckled deep red. Her whole face was purplish and swollen, her lips and tongue blue.

Neferet could feel an expression of revulsion curling up her own lip and pleating her brow but was helpless to stop it. She swallowed hard. "Well, she's certainly dead, and she was certainly garroted."

"I guess we need to call the police." Pen-buy mopped his face with a towel. He looked as if he might faint.

"This mark is quite dry," said Bener-ib, indicating the line at the base of the woman's throat. "She was probably strangled last night."

"That's right, master," said one of the younger servants, looking up at Pen-buy. "Just before bed, somebody brought her a message, then she said that she was going out and not to wait up for her. We never saw her again."

"A message?" Neferet's ears picked up. "She could read?"

"No, my lady. It just had one picture on it. Maybe it was writing—I don't know. But she looked scared when she saw it, then she tore it into little pieces and burnt them up in the lamp."

"Did you see the picture?"

"I did, my lady," said another of the serving girls. "It was a rabbit."

A chill ran tingling up Neferet's spine. From Bener-ib's saucer eyes, she suspected the news had affected her the same way.

"Pen-buy, could we speak privately with you for a moment?" Neferet said in a low voice as she got to her feet.

He nodded and led the way through the garden to an enclosed space where vegetables and flowers had been planted together, sheltered by a row of pomegranate bushes. A sickly smell of perfume and onion leaves simmered on the hot air.

Neferet proceeded to tell the florist about the encounter with the rabbit farmer and her speculations about the interventions of the priests. "We think a land dispute is at the root of this."

Pen-buy looked numbly around him as if some clue might be waiting in plain sight. "I have no idea. But my father wouldn't have had any control over purchases of land. It all belongs to the priests of the Ipet-isut. And why Ah-mes? She had nothing whatever to do with the farmer or the land. Hidden One have mercy—am I next?" He scrubbed his face with his hands in a helpless gesture.

"If only the police had done something when Father was killed. But they did nothing, nothing. I hardly have the heart to report this, except they'll probably think I killed her otherwise."

Oh no, not Mahu and his bullyboys, Neferet thought with a sinking stomach.

"She knew something. Pen-buy, don't give up hope. We've found out what the attackers look like, and now my father is going to get involved. He's investigated things for the late king, so the case is as good as solved once he puts his hand to the dough."

"Dough?" asked Pen-buy, confused.

"Like bread dough. Kneading. You know. It's an expression we use in my family." She had the feeling he was so stunned he couldn't think clearly. "What I mean is, hold off on the police. Give us a little longer to work on this. I promise we'll figure it out for you."

"Preferably before whoever it is kills me too." He heaved a sigh that wobbled his jowls. "All right. But if things don't budge pretty soon, I may have to go back on that word. We can't have a killer running around, picking off the family. I have little stepbrothers and sisters who are orphaned now. And children of my own."

"I swear to you on my mother's *ka*. May Sekhmet make curly hair sprout on my elbows if we don't get to the bottom of this."

The florist looked dubious, but he was apparently desperate enough to let her continue. "I'd like to meet your father," he murmured as he turned to exit through the bushes.

"Master," came a whispered voice from the other side. "The servants of Inpu are here for the body."

Pen-buy hustled ahead. When Neferet emerged in his wake, the steward was standing on the path in front of her. He was a small man with a mostly bald head and prominent, expressive eyes. He thrust out his hand, which contained a long, tautly twisted cord of some sort, hard with dried blood.

"One of the maids just found this, my lady. I thought it might be the… the murder weapon."

She took it between two fingertips, fighting down the taste of bile, then passed it to Bener-ib. "Thank you."

But instead of moving on, the steward stared at her, his eyes full of the desire to speak.

"If you know anything, this would be a good time to cough it up," she said sternly.

"It's as much as my life is worth, my lady." He dropped his eyes, looking lugubrious, resigned. "As soon as my mistress was seen speaking to you—"

"But she didn't speak to us. She threw us out." The man's discretion was about to eat up the last of her patience. Her voice rose in exasperation. "Ta-weret's tits, man. If you know who's behind these brutal murders, say something. Tell the police, at least. Tell your master. He could be next."

He shook his head sadly. "No. I'll be next." And he walked away.

✦

Hani looked up as his daughter and her two companions hustled into the salon, where he and Maya were attempting dictation.

"Papa!" said Neferet urgently from the door. "Sen-em-iah's wife has been killed now!"

"Garroted in their garden," added Bener-ib, waving the cord. Young Mut-tuy stared breathlessly, her eyes like plates.

Hani exchanged a look of alarm with his secretary. "My duckling, I think you need to flee far away from this family. Something terrible is going on there, and you endanger yourself by getting involved."

The three drew closer and took seats on the floor with the men. "But, Papa, Pen-buy doesn't trust the police to give him *ma'at*. He's counting on us. On you, too, in fact."

"How so, *me too*?"

"Because one of the assassins was a foreigner, probably a man of Kharu."

Hani fell silent, his stomach sinking. She'd managed to trap him after all. He let out a groan. "How do you know this?"

"One of the bodyguards described him to us. He was light-skinned and half-bald, with a kind of queue up front on his head."

"A Hurrian," said Hani dully. "Ammit take it."

"But the kingdom of Naharin doesn't even exist anymore, my lord," said Maya. "Why would a Hurrian assassin be operating in Kemet? Why would he kill a florist, of all people?"

"Probably one of the innumerable refugees who fled in all directions after the division of the country. I'm sure many of Shuttarna's defeated soldiers hired themselves out as mercenaries and, no doubt, private killers. That shaven head and the little tail of hair on the forehead mark him as part of the former cavalry."

Maya looked quizzical. "I thought it was the Hittite charioteers who shaved their foreheads."

"They do. But they undoubtedly took up the custom from the Hurri at the same time as they took horses and chariots." Hani heaved a huge sigh. *Here we go again. I had hoped I'd finished with this sort of thing.* "Well, then, my girl. Better tell me where you are in your investigations."

Neferet filled him in on the information they'd garnered since their last conversation. Hani, his eyes in his lap, nodded now and then, while Maya watched him intently.

"And then the steward said he was going to be the next victim. Because he knows something, although he won't talk." Neferet, done at last, sat back. "He was the one who he gave us this." She held out the grisly cord.

"Looks like a rawhide bowstring. That seems to confirm our former military connection. I wouldn't even know where to look for a bowstring as a civilian."

Bener-ib said sorrowfully, "If she hadn't been seen speaking to us, Ah-mes might still be alive."

Neferet looked aggrieved, as if she'd had to say this before. "But, Ibet, she didn't tell us a thing. She just got all huffy and forbade us to investigate any further."

"Somebody saw her *seeming* to talk to you, though," Hani said. "There must be a spy in the household."

"And the steward's aware of that. That's why he's sure he'll be the next victim. He knows as much as his late mistress." Maya's jaw took on a grim set. "What a snake pit."

"I'll need to investigate this Hurrian, at any rate. They

no longer have an ambassador, of course, so he could be here without anyone knowing. I should talk to a few people about this. Maybe Mane. He ends up knowing about every son of Naharin who crosses our border." Hani's friend Mane had been the last Egyptian ambassador to Naharin, and he still had an extensive network of contacts.

"So, you're going to get involved in this, Lord Hani?" Maya cocked a dubious eyebrow.

"If I can identify and punish this fellow without getting sucked into the internal affairs of the priests, yes."

Hands on hips, Neferet asked him frankly, "What do you make of it so far, Papa? That message Ah-mes received the night she died seems to confirm the involvement of the rabbit man, doesn't it?"

"There's something funny about that, though," Maya said. "If she was so afraid, why did she charge right outside as soon as she saw that picture? Or"—he turned to Hani— "maybe it really was writing, and they meant a word that started with *oon*…"

"Too much coincidence." Neferet was adamant. "It had to be just a picture of a *sekhat*. It's as if he warned her, 'You know who I am, and I'm watching you. You're next.'"

"Then why did she go outside? It would've been more dangerous out there," Maya said.

"Perhaps she was trying to flee."

Maya could be just as stubborn as Neferet, Hani thought in amusement. But his smile faded. People were dying under the genial mark of a small, furry animal.

He climbed heavily to his feet. "Come on, son. Our letter can wait. I want to talk to Mane, see if he's aware of any Hurrians acting as assassins."

N. L. HOLMES

Neferet shot a triumphant grin at Bener-ib, who looked less than enthusiastic.

"Maybe we should be getting back to the dispensary, just in case," said the little *sunet*.

"Right. Papa can handle this alone." Neferet winked, and the three girls rose with rather more grace than Hani.

"I'll have to get an official mandate from the vizier," Hani warned them. "If we're going to tangle with the *medjay*, I want to be protected."

"Ab-so-lutely. Get one for us too!" Neferet gave a snort of laughter.

After a quick kiss, Hani's daughter and her companions hurried out.

Hani and Maya were left looking at one another.

"That girl knows how to get what she wants," said Maya dryly.

"She well and truly trapped me. I suppose I could delegate this, but I don't know who's had as much experience in such matters as I have."

"Not that we need to fear an international incident. Naharin hasn't even existed independently for several years."

"True, but a certain amount of xenophobia has been reported lately in the bureaucracy, Ptah-mes was telling me. We don't want to give them any excuse to stir up worse feeling against all the innocent refugees."

Hani and Maya made their way out into the broiling midday and turned inland. Mane's residence wasn't too distant, but the farther from the River and its breezes they walked, the hotter it seemed to get. Hani's shirt stuck to his back, and his sides were slick with sweat.

He mopped his brow with a forearm. "Seems early for this weather."

"I guess our flower farmer is happy about it. It must make the blooms open unseasonably early."

Hani suspected the florist wasn't too happy about anything these days, what with a lethal net closing about him, but he said nothing.

Once at Mane's house, the men were directed to the garden kiosk by the former diplomat's gatekeeper. Mane was sprawled in his chair, his feet on a stool, his head leaning back against the cool stone wall. When he saw the pair approaching, he bounced to his feet and cried in delight, "Well, what do I see before me? If it isn't my old brother-in-arms Hani!"

He toddled toward his visitor, and the two embraced affectionately. Mane was perhaps ten years older than his friend, a joyous little ball of a man, who—after a long and distinguished career spent in distant Wasshukanni, the Hurrian capital—had finally retired now that Naharin had been swallowed alive by the Hittites on one side and the Assyrians on the other. He and Hani had once spent long months on the road between the two countries, escorting a Hurrian bride to the late king Neb-ma'at-ra, and had forged bonds as strong as brotherhood.

"I've heard rumors of a Hurrian assassin operating in Waset, so I came to the person who knows the men of Naharin better than anyone in the Two Lands."

Mane gestured his guests to seats and called for his servant to bring three pots of the best beer. "Probably one of Shuttarna's demobilized soldiers."

"That's what I thought. Apparently, this man is former cavalry. He's still wearing his military haircut."

"I think I may know who you're talking about. What's he done now?"

"It seems he and a couple of our countrymen have murdered a high lay official of the Ipet-isut. Then someone killed the man's wife as well, and I would wager it's the same upstanding trio." Hani sipped gratefully from the beer his host offered him. "Delicious, my friend. It's hot as the Lake of Fire out there."

"If this is who I think it is, he's a man named Ullum-tishni."

Maya made a noise of disapprobation. "Bes protect us—those foreign names."

Hani suppressed a smile. He'd often heard those foreigners express the same dismay before the names of his fellow citizens.

"Our friend is wellborn, as you'd expect from a cavalryman, but completely without conscience. Like many of the men who fought against the partition of his country, he fled to Kemet to escape reprisals. On and off, I hear he's fighting with one of our mercenary units, but more often, he seems to be hobnobbing with the underworld. Remorseless killers are never without employment, it seems."

"That certainly sounds like our man. Where would I find him, do you reckon?"

Mane looked at him seriously, the habitual twinkle in his eye extinguished. "Are you sure you want to find him, Hani? He's bad business."

The hairs on Hani's neck rose. His little duckling had been about to get herself involved with this sinister specimen. "I really want to find the man who's paying him, but I'm not sure how else to do that except through Ullum-tishni."

For a moment, they were both silent, troubled. At last, Mane said reluctantly, "I think I can put you in touch with him. The Hurrians in the Two Lands tend to keep an eye on each other. One of my contacts can probably make it known that you're looking for him. But, Hani..."

"What, my friend?"

"You're not going to tell him you think he's killed this man, are you? He might..."

"I'll say I'm looking to hire an assassin," Hani said with a bleak grin. Maya, at his side, was goggle-eyed.

They quickly changed to other subjects—pleasanter ones. After a while, Hani rose and stretched.

"I need to be getting back to the real world, Mane. It's been a pleasure to see you again and share your excellent brew. Come see me. We don't live that far apart."

"I'll do that," Mane said, beaming, as he accompanied his guests to the door. "We're going down to the farm for the summer in the hopes it might be cooler, but after the Inundation, I promise I'll come around."

"Sounds like I just caught you in time. Thanks for your help." Hani clapped his friend on the shoulder.

Mane's smile faded. "I hope you have reason to thank me. Be careful, Hani." He gave Hani's hand a quick squeeze.

Once the two scribes were again in the lane, Maya caught his father-in-law's eye. His brow was wrinkled in concern. "Are you sure you really want to contact this man, my lord? The girls have amassed quite a few clues. There may be less dangerous ways of getting at the mastermind."

Hani's secretary had courage to spare, but he was a family man now, with five small children to consider.

"Of course, we'll pursue any leads we come upon. But if Mane can put us in touch with this fellow, he could be the best resource we have. I just don't want Neferet and the others getting involved with him. Anyway, Mane may not even be able to find a contact who has access."

Maya raised a skeptical eyebrow and said nothing.

The courtyards of the House of Royal Correspondence were like braziers between the reflecting mudbrick walls of the buildings. Rather than heading directly back to the precinct of the foreign office, Hani led the way to the chancery in case the vizier should be receiving. The gods were good—Lord Pentju had just returned from lunch and admitted Hani immediately. He was seated in his chair of office, the scepter of authority, in the crook of his arm, dwarfed by his size.

"Hani. What brings you here this time?" the vizier said.

Hani knew his words were not as disapproving as they sounded. For all that he was a physician and might have been expected to have a smoother bedside manner, the vizier of the Upper Kingdom was a big, intimidating man with a resonant voice and brusque demeanor. And he could be a ruthless partisan. It was best to remain in his good graces.

"I'm not aware if you've heard about the recent murder of the Bearer of Divine Offerings of Amen, my lord," Hani began tentatively. He could see from Pentju's lifted eyebrows that he had not. "Only yesterday, the man's wife, too, was murdered in her own home."

"Scandalous. But it would seem to be a matter for the police, not the chancery. Or indeed, the temple police."

"True. Although I'm not certain our illustrious new police chief is pursuing it with much zeal." *Say no more, my boy,* Hani warned himself. *You don't know what Pentju thinks of Mahu.* "What makes it relevant to the foreign service is this—witnesses describe one of the killers as a Hurrian."

The vizier pursed his lips in disapproval. He shifted in his chair. "They're getting quite a reputation for themselves. For refugees, they aren't acting very grateful. We need to shake this man hard, Hani, and show Shuttarna's offscourings that we're not endlessly patient."

"That brings me to my request, my lord. Have I your permission to pursue this investigation? The *medjay* will almost certainly challenge me. Understandably, I suppose." He left out any mention of his daughter's involvement.

"Most certainly. To be frank, I have considerably more confidence in your investigative skills than in those of our esteemed police. They're excellent for chasing criminals across rooftops, but I'm not sure about their acuity." The vizier stood up and, in a bronze voice, called to his secretary in the interior office, who presented himself with a bow. "Take dictation on a good sheet of papyrus, and we'll seal it officially."

Hani was flooded with relief. This part of his mission had been easier than foreseen.

Pentju proceeded to warn whomever it concerned that the king's loyal servant Hani son of Mery-ra had full powers to investigate, pursue, and see to the punishment of any foreign nationals involved in the death of Sen-em-iah and his wife. That local law enforcement was to cooperate to the fullest extent with this mandate, which was in the name of the exalted sun god Neb-khepru-ra Tut-ankh-aten, life, prosperity and health to him.

The secretary concluded his feverish dictation with a flourish, and Pentju sealed it with the heavy gold ring on his finger. He folded the document up and sealed it again on the outside then handed the packet to Hani.

"How are your daughter and that friend of hers doing? Djefat-nebty is always asking after them."

"They're very well, my lord," said Hani with a smile. But a small trill of unease tickled his stomach. *Is Pentju aware that the girls are involved in the very investigation we've been discussing?* "They're quite happy serving their neighborhood as healers."

The vizier shook his head in incomprehension. "Seems like a waste. They should be at court." But to Hani's relief, he pursued it no further. Pentju reseated himself, and Hani backed from his presence in a bow.

Maya was waiting in the reception hall. "Was he receptive, my lord?" he asked eagerly.

"Very." Hani waved the packet of papyrus. "I'm now charged with a royal mandate to take down this Ullumtishni. And of course, that implies that we find out who paid him to kill the florist, right?" He slipped Maya a wink.

But Maya looked more worried than amused.

CHAPTER 12

N EFERET, HER FACE TO THE wind, breathed deeply
of the summer air. Here on the River, it was as moist
and full of rich, living smells as the desert air was arid and
lifeless. She understood why Papa so loved to pole through
the marshes on his little reed raft. At the moment, she and
Mut-tuy were perched on the spray-dampened seat of a
hired boat, heading downriver to the flower farm of the
Hidden One.

"Why are we going back here?" Mut-tuy's bony frame
swayed to the rhythm of the boatman's paddle.

"I want to talk to that rabbit farmer again. He seemed
pretty open. Perhaps he'd tell us more about his dispute
with the florist and the priests. Maybe he's seen those two
hemu-netjer."

They slid in among the towering papyrus and cattails.
The morning's fierce white sun grew shimmering green
through the fronds, while reflections of the water flashed
over the slender forest of stalks. Around the hull of their
craft, the stream curled and gurgled as they bumped against

the bank. The boatman tugged his painter through the ring of stone, and the two young women scrambled up the bank by way of the steep steps.

"Wait for us," Neferet called back down.

They set off along the path toward the farmhouse. Around them, the peaceful flowers sunned themselves, untouched by the enmities of men. Neferet snuffed deeply. It even smelled beautiful—delicate and heady. The men and women who gathered the blooms were spread out through the colorful fields, tiny dots of red, white, and black. Somewhere out there was the pompous foreman.

"Why did we come here, then? The rabbit man is farther north." Mut-tuy didn't miss much.

Neferet was annoyed at the question because, in fact, she had directed the boatman to the wrong point of disembarkation by accident—by force of habit, having reached him the first time after a visit to the flower farm. "I want to look around while nobody is here."

They pushed open the low gate into the farmyard. A dismal sight met Neferet's eyes. The carcasses of twenty or thirty rabbits lay piled in the corner, in the shade of the waist-high wall. Already, a cloud of flies hummed around them.

"*Yahyah!* Somebody's been hunting," murmured Mut-tuy, suppressing a gag.

But Neferet's reaction was more explosive. "This is disgusting! They've wantonly slaughtered Surer's poor little animals. And if they leave them out in the sun, they're not even going to be able to eat them." Her face burning with indignation, she crouched next to the pile and poked about. "Look. They've been clubbed. They must have been penned up somewhere—no self-respecting rabbit would have let a person come that close unless it couldn't get away."

A chilly male voice said, "What are you doing here?"

Neferet jumped to her feet and whirled.

Imi-seba, the foreman, stood in the gateway, his long nose lifted, his eyes suspicious. In his hand, a whip twitched as if it couldn't wait to taste the young women's flesh.

"We came to talk to you, but I had forgotten you'd be out in the fields. And what did we find but a great pile of slaughtered rabbits."

"So you did."

"These belonged to your neighbor, I assume. What happened? Did they get into the fields, and you clubbed them?" Neferet put a bit of sarcastic frost into her voice. She knew that hadn't been the case. The animals could have escaped easily through the flowers.

"Exactly. Now, what did you want to ask me?"

"Why, I've quite—"

At a shout from the path, everyone turned.

The rabbit farmer was stalking toward them, waving his arms, a hoe in his hand. His face was congested with fury.

"Where are my rabbits, you rotten bastard?" he cried in a breaking voice that Neferet judged might well count as a shriek.

And then he saw the pile. His eyes started from his head, and a howl of mingled sorrow and fury escaped him. Brandishing the hoe, he threw himself at the foreman, who retreated into the farmhouse, an expression of terror on his face, and bolted the door behind him.

Surer turned to the young women. "Do you have anything to do with this?"

"No, Surer. We're as mad as you are. I just came looking for you, in fact, and this is what I found."

His anger melted, and bowed down with sorrow, he approached the pile of corpses. He knelt beside it and lifted one of the rabbits by the ears. "I gotta take these back. I'm not lettin' that fat florist get rich on their hides." He stood up, tears in his eyes. "My poor harmless little children. That jackal turd has ruined me."

That was undoubtedly true. Even given what he could make from bartering the hides, if this had been his whole population, it would be a while before he could replace their numbers. *And if he's ruined, he might be willing to sell his land. Yahyah!*

"We'll help you." The carcasses were a bit bloody, but doctors were used to blood. She gathered as many ears as she could in both hands, and Mut-tuy did the same. It was a sad task, and the flies followed in a ghoulish cloud.

Surer pulled a ball of twine from his waistband and tied the remaining corpses by the ears along the handle of his hoe. Thus burdened, the three of them set off along one of the paths through the fields.

The pickers looked up as they passed, curious or uneasy, from their pools of red and gold.

Neferet herself felt considerable uneasiness. Her sympathies lay with Surer, but he'd shown himself to be capable of violence. She didn't want to think of what might have become of Imi-seba if he hadn't managed to lock himself inside. It seemed their war had escalated.

At the rabbit farm, Surer called out to his wife, "Put these in the cellar where it's cool an' start skinnin' 'em."

The woman gave a cry of outrage at the sight of the slaughtered animals, but she took them and ferried them into the farmhouse. He poured out some water from a big jug under the shade of the reed arbor, and they were able to wash their hands.

Neferet shook hers dry with a sigh of relief.

"What's happened here, Surer? The rabbits were killed on your property, weren't they?"

"Aye, mistress. Them blisterin' florists've crossed the line." He closed his eyes as if silently uttering a curse. "The wife an' I had gone to Waset to do our marketin'. When we got back, all the rabbits was gone. Pens empty, hutches wide open. I knew it was them. I could kill 'em with my bare teeth. That fat young fellow what took over from his papa. His old man wasn't a bad sort, but this..." He gestured hopelessly at the house, where the rabbits had been taken, and a broken cry of frustration escaped him.

"Had the rabbits gotten into the fields again lately?"

"So what? Only a few, an' they didn't eat much. This was just plain spite. They're after my land, I tell you."

"Report this to the local magistrate, Surer. They had no right to kill them all," Neferet said fiercely.

But the farmer gave a snort of bitter laughter. "Pardon, mistress, but I don't think you're quite clear on how little magistrates care about poor folks like me when we're up against rich folks like them."

Neferet and Mut-tuy exchanged looks of sorrow. The adolescent gave a lift of the eyebrow that hinted at *I told you so*.

"But you don't want to take things into your own hands, my friend. It will just end up with you getting your nose and ears cut off, if not worse. Besides, I suspect that Pen-buy has nothing to do with this. He's got, er, family troubles at the moment. I bet that Imi-seba did this on his own."

"An' them priests. They think they can do whatever they please." He gazed darkly to the south, where, somewhere out of sight, the Ipet-isut stood. "Not that I don't respect the Hidden One, mind, but sometime them priests is actin' for theirselves, not for him."

Neferet considered the man thoughtfully. It was hard to view him as a brutal killer, but he had provocation and probably the passion to kill in a moment of rage. She couldn't scratch him off the list of suspects yet just because he had shed tears over dead rabbits.

"Do you know a priest named Pu-im-ra, by any chance? He's the florists' superior."

Surer looked blank and shrugged.

"Skinny? Buckteeth?" Neferet asked.

But the rabbit farmer showed no sign of recognition. "Fact is, mistress, they don't come around here. It's always the florist we see. But I know they're pushin' him. They're just waiting to grab my land, soon as it's up for sale."

Not wanting to get him into a fresh state of excitement, the two young women bade Surer goodbye and headed off between the low stone-walled pens that hadn't saved their helpless inhabitants.

"I wonder how many rabbits he'd have to have to stay in business," Neferet mused as she walked. "Lord Ptah-mes would never miss a little gold if we helped him."

"But what if he's the killer?"

Neferet gnawed her lip. "True. There's that chance. He doesn't seem to be a friend of Pen-buy. But in fairness, it's hard to believe he killed Sen-em-iah. He sounded fairly admiring."

"You can never tell with these criminals," said Mut-tuy sententiously as if she knew any number of criminals.

Neferet shot her a wry look. "We've still got this problem: how did he manage to hire three killers? If the loss of twenty rabbits wiped him out, he mustn't have much."

"Maybe he's in cahoots with somebody else, somebody more powerful. Somebody who purposely got him riled up so he'd try to kill Sen-em-iah and it would take suspicion away from the real killer."

"Mut-tuy, my girl, I thought you were arguing for Surer's conviction. Now you say somebody else is using him as a front."

The adolescent shrugged. "It's just a theory."

Recognizing her own words, Neferet burst out laughing. "You're a quick study. If you ever spent any time at the dispensary, you'd be a healer in no time." Then she realized their boat was waiting for them back at the flower farm—another long walk, this time in the midday sun—and groaned. "Let's get moving, or everyone will have gone home by the time we get back to the dispensary."

They followed a path along the riverbank, hoping to avoid the foreman, who wouldn't be in a good mood. Several men were cutting reeds for bouquet poles and for their ferny young greens, but otherwise, the way was clear. They found the boatman snoozing in the bottom of his vessel, shaded by the forest of papyrus overhead. Neferet called loudly, and he jumped upright. Before long, they were out on the glittering waters of the River, springing ahead against the current.

Sure enough, when Neferet and Mut-tuy finally arrived, the streets were empty, everyone already gathered for lunch in their respective homes. The nurse and children had left, but Bener-ib appeared in the doorway.

"Oh, you're back. Thanks be to Sekhmet. I was starting to worry!" the little *sunet* cried, her face brightening. "Did you find out anything?"

"Yes, but it only confuses things the more," Neferet said. "Let's go to Mama and Papa's house—it's closer—and I'll tell you what happened."

With her usual scrupulosity, Bener-ib checked the animals' water, and the three of them set off through the quiet lanes. Neferet filled her in with an exciting description of the morning's drama, complete with varied voices and an imitation of the irate farmer waving a hoe as the foreman hotfooted it to safety.

"Imi-seba killed all those innocent rabbits?"

"I'm pretty sure—or someone he sent. And poor Surer is afraid to take him to law for it."

"Do you think Surer killed Sen-em-iah and his wife in revenge for killing other rabbits, then?" Bener-ib asked, nibbling a pensive fingernail.

"I don't know, though he surely had a motive. He loved those rabbits."

"But didn't he sell them to people to eat?" Mut-tuy asked.

"Yes," Neferet said, "but this wiped him out financially, in addition to murdering his 'children,' as he called them. And hostilities seem to have stepped up since Pen-buy took over. I'll bet anything there's an attempt on him next."

Bener-ib trudged along for a while before she said, "We can't protect him, Nef'et. He... He needs to call the police."

"He probably already has. But if that's so, our involvement is ended. Or else we have to sneak around behind their back. Because we do *not* want to come to the attention of Mahu." Neferet snorted darkly. "What I'd really like to do is sic him on Imi-seba. They deserve each other."

Silence descended once more except for the dull thumping of their bare feet on the packed earth street, Bener-ib looking pensive. Then she said, "What do we do next?"

"Well, we update Papa and see if he has any ideas. And then, I think, we go see that bucktoothed priest. About our donation of gold vessels, I mean." She grinned wickedly.

By the time they arrived at Neferet's childhood home, the family had disbanded. Only Papa, Maya, and Grandfather were still sitting together, talking.

"Well, if it isn't our trio of investigators," said Grandfather in a jolly voice. "What's happening to the sick of the neighborhood in your absence, ladies?"

"It's lunchtime, Grandfather. People don't get sick at lunchtime." Neferet plopped herself down on a stool and scooted closer to the men. The other young women followed suit. "Is there anything left for us to eat?" She eyed the cleared tables.

Papa called out for his wife, who appeared in the

doorway in a billowing egret-white caftan and her best long wig.

She said in delight, "Ah, Neferet, my love. Girls. I'm sorry I won't be able to visit with you. I'm on duty at the temple this afternoon."

"Before you go, could you ask cook to heat up something for our girls' lunch, my dove?" Papa asked with a big, heart-melting grin.

"With pleasure." Mama smiled affectionately. "There's plenty left."

Before she could disappear, Neferet said, "Mama, if you were going to make a big dedication of gold vessels to the temple, where would you go to talk to someone about it?"

Mama's painted eyes grew round in admiration and approval. "Why, how nice, my love. Is this for Lord Ptahmes, or is the idea yours?"

"My idea, but he'll be paying for it." The girl snickered. "We wanted to thank the Hidden One that our business has gotten *very* good all of a sudden."

"So you worked something out with that Djed-har, eh?" Maya nodded.

"No, not that hyena. We started bribing people to come to us. What little boy with a broken arm could resist a pile of sweets?"

The family burst out laughing.

"That's our girl!" Grandfather said proudly.

Mama said, "In answer to your question, see the priest called Pu-im-ra. His offices open to the outside of the sacred complex, so you can find him."

Neferet shot Bener-ib a look, bright-eyed with

satisfaction. "Ah, so you know him, too, Mama. Someone else gave us his name, but I wasn't sure how to reach him."

"You might have known the priests would be available if you wanted to give them gold," said Grandfather with a chuckle.

"I don't know him, no, just his name. Let me talk to cook. I need to be going. I'm so glad you feel free to drop in on us, girls. You're always welcome." Mama blew a kiss and disappeared into the dark corridor in a swirl of pleated linen.

Papa fixed Neferet with a shrewd and amused look. "What are you up to now, my duckling?"

"War is openly declared, Papa." She described the slaughter of the rabbits. "On Surer's own property too. There's no way they could have clubbed those rabbits in the open fields!" Then she told the story of how the irate farmer had appeared ready to shed a little blood of his own.

At the end of the recital, Maya gave an appreciative whistle. "War, indeed. I hope that Pen-buy has hired some extra bodyguards."

"Maybe you three should do the same." Papa seemed quite serious.

That's perhaps true, thought Neferet. *Lord Ptah-mes certainly wouldn't mind assigning one of his men to our service.* But then she decided it was a wasted precaution. The watchdogs were always on duty at the dispensary, and certainly, Ptah-mes's villa was guarded as zealously as the Double House. Besides, she felt sure that Surer considered them allies.

"I talked to the vizier. First off, Lady Djefat-nebty has asked about you," Papa said.

"We've thought of her a lot," said Bener-ib. In addition to being the great *sunet*'s student, like Neferet, she had been a family friend.

"And he gave me a written mandate to arrest and punish that Hurrian. His name is probably Ullum-tishni, a former cavalryman who's sometimes a mercenary and sometimes an assassin."

"Sounds like you're the one who needs a bodyguard, Papa. You still have that amulet we gave you, I hope."

Grandfather raised his eyebrows as if to say, "I told you so," but carefully avoided looking at his son.

Papa drew the amulet through the neck of his shirt. "She never leaves me. If I can apprehend this ruffian, your family of florists may be able to breathe easier for a bit. The villain behind this may have to find some other henchmen, at least."

A servant arrived with a platter of fried vegetables and a spicy sauce of mashed chickpeas, while another brought beer for everyone.

Neferet and the others fell in with a will.

"We want to feel out that Pu-im-ra—see if he knows anything about a plan to scare the rabbit farmer off his land. And of course, we *will* donate those gold vessels."

"I suspected there was more to that act of piety than met the eye," said Grandfather wryly.

Papa began, "Just be—"

"Careful," Neferet finished in unison with him. "I know, Papa, I know." She rolled her eyes. Would she ever be so old that her parents didn't treat her like an infant? "Tell me about something else. How are the brothers doing?"

That was an inspired request. Papa proudly launched

into an account of Pa-kiki's new post as chief scribe of the Waset garrison. He was still secretary to General Har-em-heb, the young king's confidant. Aha was getting rich as Overseer of the Cattle of Amen, and his wife was expecting their sixth child.

There's a man who can tell me about Pu-im-ra, Neferet thought. *He and Aha must know each other.*

By the time the conversation had wrapped up with a report on the grandchildren, the young women had concluded their lunch.

"We're back to the dispensary, people," Neferet said, rising. "Keep us informed, Papa. If you get what's-his-name locked up, I want to spit on him!"

CHAPTER 13

EVEN BEFORE THEY REACHED THEIR gate, the three young women heard the wild barking of dogs they recognized as their own. Neferet turned an alarmed face to Bener-ib, who looked petrified. "Come on, people! Something's up," Neferet said.

They pelted the remaining half block to their house, past empty lots and tumbledown walls. The gate was shut, but the ruction from within made it clear that all was not well. Neferet threw open the panel, and the dogs almost fell out, sounding off in hysterical menace that grew friendlier as soon as they recognized their mistresses. They circled and jumped and whined and yapped as if everyone wanted to tell the story at once.

"What happened, boys? Did something scare you?" Neferet squatted and rubbed their muzzles, while Bener-ib approached the house door cautiously, Mut-tuy at her tail.

A moment later, Bener-ib let out a wail of horror, and Neferet streaked to her side. There she saw what had happened. Someone had broken into the dispensary in their absence. The furniture was overturned, the herbs and dried fruits and berries strewn around the floor as if a madman had been at them. Pots lay broken, chests upended, bandages unrolled and draped everywhere. The slime of goose fat and their carefully confected unguents was smeared on the walls and cushions. Precious bronze instruments were bent and broken. That had taken some effort. This damage wasn't casual. The only mercy was that their priceless casebook scrolls, which had been set on high shelves, had been overlooked.

Neferet's first reaction was disbelief. Her second reaction was fury. She could feel it rolling up inside her in a bitter wave, like the first irresistible tide of the River's flood and just as red. Hardly able to come up with words, she put a protective arm around the shoulders of Bener-ib, who had begun to weep, her face in her hands. Mut-tuy goggled as if she still couldn't interpret what she saw.

"May Ammit the Devourer crack the bones of whoever did this and suck out their marrow. May they roast forever in the Lake of Fire," Neferet growled. "And if I find them, they'll beg for the Lake of Fire, because what I'll inflict on them will be *so* much worse."

"Who would do something so horrible, Nef'et?" Bener-ib sobbed. "After we've worked so hard."

Mut-tuy said in a grim voice, "Djed-har, that's who."

Neferet locked eyes with the girl. They both saw it clearly. Their envious rival, angered by the breaking of his stranglehold on the neighbors, had done this, hoping it would discourage them and send them packing.

The preparation room was, if anything, worse. And on the table lay a big potsherd, drawn all over in red ink.

The sketches weren't too artistic, but they clearly depicted snakes, spears, scorpions, and three females—and the dreadfully personal things that would happen to them if the artist had his way.

"Somebody's put a curse on us," Neferet said in a flat voice. This was even worse than the vague threats the rest of the damage represented. Here was real malice. "We've got to have this lifted. And *then* I'll dismember Djed-har, the foul animal."

"We should take this to the Ipet-isut with us. Somebody there will know how to lift it." Mut-tuy's cheeks were as flushed as pomegranates.

"Right you are, my girl. And the sooner we go, the better."

"We'll have to clean this up first…" Bener-ib stared hopelessly around, sniffing.

"No, Ibet. That would just be an invitation to mess it up again until we can hire a guard. Let's get this curse off us first, then we can take our time with the cleanup. And let all the neighbors know what's been done to us.

"But before we leave, let's give our watchdogs something nice. They probably kept anything worse from happening." In truth, Neferet couldn't think of what worse act might have been perpetrated, except to kill the dogs.

She picked up a few of the sedge-nut treats scattered around the room and offered them to the eager trio of guardians. Mangler, formidable as he might once have been, was old and gray bearded now. Faithful could hardly hobble and had big patches out of his bristly fur, while Hedgehog was so low-slung and fat that he couldn't have run after any invader bigger than a baby bird.

We need a more redoubtable watchdog, she thought reluctantly. She didn't want the oldsters to feel their mistresses didn't appreciate them, though, and slipped them all a second treat.

The young women marched in silence down the lane, each sunk in her own grim thoughts. After a block or two, Bener-ib said, "What will Nurse do when she brings the children back after their nap? She may think we've been kidnapped."

"Good point. It won't be out of our way to stop by home and leave a message."

When the immense wall of the Greatest of Shrines loomed into sight, with its towering parapets and red banners flapping over the pylon, the young women kept going. At Lord Ptah-mes's gate, Neferet left a message with the gateman. Then they reversed course.

It was a little past midday, and the temple shimmered with the shadowless heat of the sun. Lord Ra was at home, drenching all in his burning rays. They walked around the perimeter, feeling more and more dwarfed by the magnitude of this sacred place. Above the wall, the golden pinnacles of obelisks winked in the dancing air. Even Neferet was losing her confidence fast.

"Great Hidden One, help us, please," she murmured then raised her voice. "Where do you suppose the door to Pu-im-ra's office is? There's only one door per side, as far as I've seen, and they have big, long, ram-lined approaches, like entrances to the temple itself."

"We'll have to ask," Mut-tuy said with a thirteen-year-old's blissful ignorance of the complexities of the religious hierarchy.

But Neferet preferred to explore a little before asking some man for directions. They trudged around to the inland side of the temple complex. Across the road, the cluster of buildings the late king Nefer-khepru-ra had built even before he took the throne alone still stood, but they had a derelict air. Papa had described the bizarre and disturbing sculpture that decorated the Gem-pa-aten, the first of the temples that had foreshadowed the heretic's revolution. It gave Neferet a sense of satisfaction to see them falling already into ruin, while under their nose, the Ipet-isut glowed with divine health.

"Look, there's a smallish door," Bener-ib said.

And none too soon. It seemed they'd been circling the wall for hours. With Neferet in the lead, the three drew up to the door, which looked big enough at close range. Other people, mostly male, came and went. The three women attracted some stares.

At the gate stood a pair of temple police, while a majordomo of some sort took down the names of the visitors and ushered them inside or set them to wait. He finally turned his haughty attention to the *sunet*s. Neferet knew she needed to pull rank on him. *It was a mistake not to have dressed better.*

"I am Lady Neferet, the wife of Lord Maya, Master of the Double House of Silver and Gold. My uncle Amen-em-hut is the Third Prophet. I want to make a substantial donation of gold vessels. Is Pu-im-ra available?"

"I'm sure he will be, my lady," the man said, eyeing her dusty bare feet with more than a little skepticism.

She added loftily, "I'm in disguise. There have been robberies on the street lately."

The majordomo bowed and retreated into the shadows. A moment later, he returned and bowed the three young women inside the gate. Following him, they found themselves in an open-ended corridor that seemed all the blacker for the square of blinding sunlight at the end. At either side were doors leading into what she assumed were offices. Beyond, the vista might have been that of a village—narrow unpaved streets with mudbrick walls crowding up to either side. She remembered Mama saying that some of the *wab* priests lived on-site while they were serving their three-month shift.

The majordomo led them to the second door and, still without a word, gestured them to enter. The reception room looked like that of any of the chancery offices Neferet had entered in search of her father over the course of her life— there was certainly none of the splendor of the liturgical areas of the great temple. A secretary sat cross-legged on the floor with a papyrus across his knees, ready for dictation, and on the chair of office sat a shaven-headed man she assumed was Pu-im-ra. A great stack of tall, braided wax candles filled the corner.

"My lady, to what do we owe the pleasure of this visit?" he asked with a cool, haughty lift of the nose. He had some sort of speech impediment, and every *r* came out blurry, like a little child's.

Pu-im-ra—or *Pu-im-wa*, as he would have identified himself—was strikingly thin and gangly with goggle eyes, a long neck, and a receding chin. As she'd been warned, he had big buckteeth that refused to stay hidden in his mouth. Neferet suspected that this man had been mercilessly teased as a child. She could think of some apt nicknames herself but managed to hold them back and maintain her seriousness.

"My husband and I and my fellow physicians, here, want to dedicate a nice set of gold vessels for the Hidden One. We aren't sure what pieces would be most pleasing to him, so I haven't commissioned them yet. I wanted to talk to you first."

"My lady has done well." He uncrossed and recrossed his legs, and she saw that his toenails were hennaed in the most fashionable manner. "Some people would tell you to talk to the treasurer of the temple first, but I am, of course, overseer of cult objects, since you already know that's what you want to dedicate. How much were you intending to spend?" He looked down at her from the height of his dais with a lift of the eyebrows.

Neferet was so galled by his supercilious attitude that she said carelessly, "Oh, price is no object. Tell me what you need, and we'll have it made."

His eyes slid over her working-class shift and unsandaled feet. "Are you willing to dedicate a complete set of golden dining vessels for the Lord of the Heavens? Of course, if you prefer, even a few pieces would be pleasing to the god."

"Oh, let's do a complete set." She hoped Lord Ptah-mes wouldn't be shocked by her generosity with his resources. That would be a good many *deben*s of gold. "This is a thank-offering, and in addition, somebody has put a curse on us three. We need to lift it and assure the Hidden One of our goodwill."

"You're writing this down, aren't you?" the priest said sharply to his secretary. Then he turned to Neferet a face that was both arrogant and complaisant. "Since you are such a generous donor, I can see to this exorcism, my lady. Do you have the doll or text with you? I'll give it to the proper authorities."

"Why, yes. Thank you."

Bener-ib presented the vile potsherd, and the priest's bulging gaze skidded around over it. "My, my. Somebody doesn't like you."

And I don't like you, my boy. She particularly didn't like the greedy way his eyes lit up at the graphic imagery.

"This will be a particularly complicated matter, to undo such a curse. Perhaps for a small gold cup, I can have the exorcist expedite it."

Neferet stared at him caustically. "I thought our status as generous donors was worth something."

"Oh, indeed, my lady. And the esteem we bear your husband, who was once First Prophet. Needless to say, this isn't for me. It will enrich the coffers of the god. Such is the tradition."

"Needless to say." She was eager to be off now. "Well, do you need anything else from me?"

"No, no. When do you anticipate having the gifts ready?"

"That depends on the availability of the artisan. For sure, before the Inundation." Neferet edged toward the door. Then she thought of something else. "Oh, we also wanted to endow some bouquets for, er, a week."

"Very well, my lady. What magnanimity."

"But maybe you're not the one to talk to about flowers…"

"Oh, yes. Everything to do with the sacred liturgy."

He smirked with what was perhaps meant to look like a humble expression.

"From that Sen-em-iah fellow. He makes the nicest ones. Or is he the man who died?"

"Unfortunately, yes. His son continues the Osir's work, however."

Neferet tried to think of a way to prod him into some kind of admission. "I don't suppose you've ever had any problem with his flowers? Freshness? Always delivered on time?"

"No. I'm sure you'll be pleased with the workmanship."

"Never had to talk to him or anything? About problems with the neighbors, for example?"

The priest started to look at her askance. "His workshop is worthy of the service of the Hidden One, you may reassure your husband, my lady."

Finally, as if to put an end to this strange line of inquisition, Pu-im-ra rose and stepped down from his dais, and her stomach lurched at the wave of perfume that blew out to envelope her. He drew back his lips, all ingratiation, and she could have sworn he looked like a malevolent hare. She didn't even listen as he babbled his flatteries. The three visitors were out the door and through the gate without drawing a breath.

"*Iyah*," said Mut-tuy as if expelling him from her lungs.

"I'm glad I know lots of nice priests, because otherwise I'd certainly have a bad impression of them." Neferet snorted. "I was just waiting for his nose to twitch, and I'd have laughed out loud. We should bring carrots the next time we come."

Mut-tuy sprayed a raucous laugh, but Bener-ib looked

serious. "Nef'et, do you know how much a whole set of gold vessels is going to cost? Not to mention a week's worth of flowers. That's hundreds of bouquets. I hope Lord Ptah-mes won't be mad."

"He can afford it," Neferet said confidently. They made their way through the back streets toward the dispensary, and as they walked, her thoughts were churning. "Did we learn anything useful?"

"That priest's a dog turd," said Mut-tuy. "I wouldn't believe a thing he says."

"So, do we accept that he never chewed up Sen-em-iah?"

"Dog turd."

"Just as I thought. What do you think, Ibet?"

"I don't think he'd tell us internal business like that. He's trying to get you to pay for flowers, anyway. Of course, he'll say they're perfect."

"Did you hear the way he talked to his secretary?" Mut-tuy's nose wrinkled with disgust. "Typical."

"So, if we go by the principle that whatever Pu-im-ra tells us is a lie, I guess this just confirms what the bodyguard told us. He probably *has* visited Sen-em-iah. I didn't think to mention that fat priest."

"Tetiky? It's probably better. Pu-im-ra would wonder how you knew his name." Bener-ib had, of course, remembered it.

Neferet grinned wickedly. "Why, we got it from Uncle Amen-em-hut, of course."

Mut-tuy looked ready to smash foreheads. "What do we do now?"

"We go serve the sick and injured of the neighborhood, my girl. And this evening, we pay a visit to In-hapy."

CHAPTER 14

NEFERET HAD FORGOTTEN THAT BEFORE they could go back to being physicians, they had a lot of cleaning up to do. One glance inside the dispensary reminded her, and her heart dropped to her feet.

Bener-ib, at her side, looked hopeless but tucked up her skirt and began to pick up the unwound bandages.

Mut-tuy got the broom.

"Djed-har had better stay out of my sight for a while," Neferet said grimly. "I can't answer for what I'd do to him. It makes me almost wish we could go to the police about this and have them bastinado the wretch."

"Maybe we could send somebody else so he doesn't realize we were involved." Bener-ib looked up from where she crouched, picking up broken crockery. "I'll bet Sit-amen would go for us."

Neferet gave a skeptical hum. "And when he came and saw it was us?"

"But the chief wouldn't come himself, would he? Just one of those *medjay* with a baboon to sniff around."

Iyah, *she really seems to want to get them involved*, thought Neferet in surprise.

As she so often did, Bener-ib seemed to read her mind. "If nobody punishes Djed-har, he may try something like this again. We'll never feel safe."

But Mut-tuy spoke up excitedly. "What if it's not Djed-har?"

The two young doctors stared at her. "Who else would do something like this?" Neferet asked.

The girl shrugged, but her eyes were sparkling. "Maybe it has something to do with our murder case."

That stopped the conversation dead. Neferet stared at the floor, her thoughts churning. "But who among all those people is aware we're involved? Pen-buy? The foreman? The rabbit farmer? None of them even knows where we are."

"Pen-buy's steward does. The bodyguards..." Mut-tuy shrugged again. "Your father thought there was a spy in Sen-em-iah's household."

"This is scaring me," murmured Bener-ib, seeming to shrink.

Even Neferet had to admit to a chill running up her neck. "We need to get a guard for the night right away. Maybe that muscular servant Lord Ptah-mes sent with us the other day."

"This wasn't done at night, Nef'et. It was while we were gone for lunch. We could have walked in on them."

"Didn't anybody hear the dogs barking? I'm surprised none of the neighbors came running over." Neferet stared around as if someone might appear in the doorway with an answer. But the only sounds from outside were the blare of the cicadas and the clopping hoofbeats of a passing donkey.

"What if the children had been here?" Bener-ib shivered.

"All right, now, people," said Neferet firmly. "We're just frightening ourselves with this talk. It's Djed-har. I'm going to go talk to him."

"Oh, Nef'et, don't. He'll only lie to you anyway."

"Of course—everything he says is a lie. But I think I'll get a sense of that. Grandfather always says to trust your gut. If, somehow, he were genuinely shocked, that would tell me something."

Mut-tuy said eagerly, "I want to go with you."

But Neferet held up a hand. "No, my girl. You need to run home and tell the steward we have to have that servant and maybe another one to guard this place night and day for a while. We can't go through this over and over."

"He won't pay any attention to me."

"Yes, he will." She picked up a sherd of one of the pots that had been smashed on the floor and found a block of ink and a reed brush then plopped to the ground and crossed her legs. A moment later, she had written out her instructions and handed them to the girl. "Flee like the wind. Maybe you'll be back before Nurse brings the children."

With a look of resentment, Mut-tuy shot away. They heard the gate slam behind her and the sound of fleet footsteps disappearing down the lane.

Neferet climbed to her feet, dusting down the seat of her skirt.

Bener-ib stared pleadingly at her friend. "You're going to leave me here alone?"

Neferet's heart melted, and she put an arm around the little *sunet*'s shoulders. "Poor Ibet. No. Come with me.

Didn't we promise we'd always be together? Afterward, we'll drop in on In-hapy and commission those gold vessels. You know better than I do what pieces we should have." She kissed her on the cheek.

As they left, Neferet tied a piece of twine around the gate latch and sealed it with a ball of mud. That way, they'd know if anybody had entered in their absence.

⸙

The next morning, Hani was standing at the kitchen door, dunking a stale flatbread in his bowl of milk and listening to the twitter of the birds in the garden, when the steward appeared.

"Lord Hani," he said. "There's a man here to see you. He says he's here on behalf of Lord Mane."

Hani set down his breakfast and stumped after the servant. "Excellent. I'm expecting him. Show him into the salon."

Hani had on no shirt or sandals, and only his own curly, close-cropped graying hair adorned his scalp, but no matter. Mane had come through for him. Hani's heart stepped up its pace, and a chill rippled along his spine.

The messenger entered almost simultaneously with the master of the house and bowed. "Lord Mane has a message for you which he desires me to repeat, my lord. He wants you to know that the person you seek is to be found in an empty-appearing house in the small neighborhood off the southeast corner of the temple of Montu. There is a very large fig tree that overhangs the gate, and a beggar habitually sits there in the shade. The beggar is really a guard, however."

Hani didn't like what he heard. The place was probably guarded inside and out. If Ullum-tishni weren't convinced by what Hani had to say, Hani might never emerge alive. "Thank your master for me, my friend. And wish him a pleasurable stay in the country."

Once the messenger had departed, Hani was left standing in the middle of the salon, staring, his peaceful morning suddenly grown darker. He heard the thudding footsteps of someone heavy descending the stairs, and his father said, "What is it, my boy? You look like one of those realistic statues Bak carves."

Hani turned and managed a smile. "If it isn't my favorite father! There's some stale bread in the kitchen that's good enough to dunk."

Mery-ra toddled toward him, his little eyes sharp under the bushy line of his brows. "I was referring to your rigidity, son, not that of the bread. Did I hear someone talking to you?"

"Mane's messenger. He's located that Hurrian bullyboy I need to talk to."

"Talk to or arrest?"

Hani blew out a deep, troubled breath through his nose. "I can't arrest him unless I can convict him of some crime."

"And you think he's going to confess to you that he killed that florist? I grant you're persuasive, but that may be expecting too much." His father clapped him on the arm. "Have you eaten?"

"Yes, but I'll join you while you eat."

They made their way to the kitchen, where the cook was already at work on the day's fresh loaves. Mery-ra pulled a couple of flatbreads from the pile of old ones, and after a moment's hesitation, Hani did the same. They both ladled milk, still warm and foaming, out of the jug and headed for the garden with their cups.

"Decided on a second breakfast?" Mery-ra asked with a grin as the two men mounted the step of the kiosk.

"Anything to delay doing what I have to do today." Hani settled upon his low-backed chair while his father took the one with a back and arms.

"If you have a bad feeling about this, son, perhaps you shouldn't do it. Send a soldier to play the spy."

"I wonder if Baket-iset has any instinct about it," Hani said thoughtfully. "That girl is a real oracle." His eldest daughter, paralyzed since her fourteenth year, seemed to have been given alternative gifts by the pitying gods. "I'll ask her when she's up."

They sat in silence, eating the leathery bread, while Hani's thoughts labored over his coming task.

"Is this for Neferet's investigation?" asked Mery-ra after a while.

"Yes and no. Pentju told me to make an example of this foreigner who had broken the king's laws, but for Neferet's sake, what I'd really like to do is find out who paid him for that murder. I'm afraid she's going to hang onto this case like a terrier with a rat otherwise. It's too damned dangerous for the girls. And they've dragged that orphan child into it." Hani stopped to down a swallow of milk. "I can't talk any sense into the duckling."

Mery-ra chuckled. "She's seen you catching malefactors all her life, even though you weren't a policeman. You know how she loves and admires you. It doesn't surprise me at all that she wants to emulate you, Hani."

"If only she wanted to obey me instead."

"This is Neferet we're talking about."

"Ptah-mes suggested we get Bener-ib on our side and have her tell Neferet." Hani tried, without success, to imagine the timid girl from Sau standing up to his forceful daughter. "No, the only way to disengage her from the case is to solve it."

Feeling fortified after his second breakfast, Hani decided to discharge his duty with no further delay. Nub-nefer was sitting at her dressing table, painting her eyes, when he returned to the bedchamber to get a shirt and wig.

"Good morning, my dove," he said, leaning over her and giving her a kiss on her freshly rouged lips. "Are you in service at the temple today?"

"I am, dearest. Did I tell you we have a new *weret khener*?"

The *weret khener*—the Great One of the Musicians— was the administrator of the entire musical body of the cult of Amen-Ra, hundreds of men and women. Ptah-mes's first wife had held the office for years.

"No. The position hasn't been empty since Lady Apeny's death, surely?"

"Oh, some nonentity has kept things together, but I'm very hopeful about our new *weret* if she has half her mother's talent."

"Her mother? You mean one of Apeny and Ptah-mes's daughters?"

"Yes, that beautiful Mut-em-wia. She'll keep the men

in line, no fear." Nub-nefer lifted a beaded *weshket*-collar to her throat. "Can you fasten this please, Hani?"

Well, well. Hani knew from painful experience how direct and masterful the beautiful Mut-em-wia could be. "I'm sure her father will be proud."

He unfolded a clean shirt and tugged it over his head then tucked the tails lumpily into his kilt. With a smile, Nub-nefer rose and straightened it out where it caught over his belly.

"You don't want to look like you slept in it, my love." She concluded her ministrations with a kiss. "Are you headed to the office so early?"

"No. I have a little mission to perform."

"Oh?" She inserted an earring into her lobe and screwed it tighter. "And what is your mission?"

Hani winked at her. "I need to hire an assassin."

"You're sure you want to come along, son?" Hani asked Maya. "This is very likely going to be dangerous."

The two scribes were striding along the road that edged the temple of Montu on the south. They'd had to go considerably out of the way inland, because the street they had followed northward had ended at a boat channel and basin that enabled ships to supply discreetly the service of the war god. Somewhere between the channel, the River, and the wall of the sacred enclosure lay the enclave that harbored a certain tumbledown house.

Maya looked worried, but he said stoutly, "Of course, my lord. I belong at your side."

Hani respected the little man's courage. It had to make

a fellow feel vulnerable, knowing he was only about half the mass of anyone likely to be coming at him with intent to harm.

After what seemed like an endless walk in the increasingly warm sun of midmorning, the men entered the grove of palms that shaded this forgotten corner of the City of the Scepter. There was something sleepy and neglected about the walls around them. No one was in the street—no sounds of workmen or children playing disturbed the lethargic air. The houses and their ill-kempt gardens were widely spaced beneath the trees, rather as if a tiny village had been transported into the heart of the great capital. Ahead, Hani saw the black-green mass of an immense sycamore fig, its ancient branches spreading almost as long as the block, sweeping the ground with intense shade. Clearly, no one had trimmed the venerable tree in more years than a donkey lived.

The fig appeared to be growing from the walled garden of an empty house, perhaps right through the crumbling brick. Beside the unpainted gate hanging half-open from a tottering pivot pole, a beggar squatted, his head down. Hani's stomach began to flutter.

"I think this is it," he murmured from the corner of his mouth. "Say a prayer."

With Maya on his heels, he marched up to the gate and knocked. The beggar was watching now, his face impassive. But even after the passage of a good long space of time, no reply came.

Hani pushed the sagging panel back and called, "Anybody there?"

Silence was the only reply. His heart hammering, he

squeezed into the ruined courtyard, overgrown with weeds and straggling tufts of shrubbery. There might have been footprints in the dry earth, but it was so hard packed that it was difficult to tell if they were really there, let alone whether they were recent.

"Hello?"

No one emerged from the weathered door ahead of him. Hani knocked and was rewarded only by his own echo. With a gingerly finger, he pushed the door, and it swung open with a dismal creak.

"Hello? Is anyone—"

Out of the shadows to either side of the doorway sprang two beefy men, who grabbed him by the arms and jerked him tight between them. Gasping with the impact of the attack, he forced himself not to struggle.

"Who're you, mate?" growled one of them. He turned to Maya. "And you, half mate—better not try nothing, 'cause we've got your friend here." They shoved the secretary forward.

"My name doesn't matter," said Hani as steadily as he was able. "I'm here to look for another man with no name. A Hurrian. My sources tell me he'll do most anything for enough gold."

"'Zat so?" The door had swung shut, reducing the vestibule to musty near darkness, but Hani could see that both his captors were Egyptian. One was almost as broad and thick armed as he was.

"That's so. I was told he could be found here."

"An' who told you that?" The thickset man's white grin was visible in the shadow. It didn't look friendly.

"Another man without a name. A Hurrian as well. He was afraid to identify himself."

The man gave a laugh like the crunch of rocks upon bones. He tossed his head sideways in a gesture of mission and said to his fellow, "See if he's here."

Both of his captors let go of Hani's arms. Then the slimmer of the two disappeared into the darkness. Hani straightened his shirt.

"So, who's the little fellow? Your bodyguard?" asked the remaining man.

Fingering his writing case, Maya drew himself up. "I'm his secretary."

They waited there in tense silence until the return of the second captor. "Bring him in."

"Don't try nothing," warned the bigger one, "or we'll have to tie you up."

The small salon, lit by high windows, was somewhat lighter than the vestibule had been. A cobwebby twilight reigned, pungent with the smell of mice. There was no furniture, just the masonry couches built into the room and the platform of a birthing bower in the corner. A crudely painted wooden column supported the ceiling, which had begun to hang down in places in a moldy curtain of reeds and plaster. A man stood in front of it, his back to the fading wood. He was tall and light-skinned with pale-brown hair shaved bald across the front except for a tuft tied into a sprightly queue. His sturdy body was encased in a short woolen tunic, and a mean-looking straight sword hung at his hip.

He observed the approach of his associates and their prisoners, a watchful expression upon his face. A collar of beard set off his strong jaw. Hani would have put him in his midthirties. He was not handsome but impressive. Hard.

"Who are you, and why are you here?" the man of Naharin said in a gravelly accented voice.

"My name is not important," replied Hani in Hurrian. "I have a job for you if you're interested."

The man's eyebrows rose. "You speak the language of a country which is no more, yet I see you are an Egyptian."

"I have spent many years in the foreign service. Your people and their culture have earned my respect. Your soldiers have earned my respect—there are none better."

The Hurrian considered Hani. "What do you need done?"

"I need a man sent to the Mountains of the West."

"You Egyptians!" The fellow laughed unpleasantly. "Always so poetic. We of a country that is no more are not afraid to speak of death. You want a man killed, do you? Who?"

Hani's stomach was fluttering like a flock of sparrows descending on a tree full of ripe figs. "The man who paid you to kill Sen-em-iah."

There was a moment of silence so profound that Hani would have sworn he could hear the whisper of dust motes floating through the air.

"What makes you think I killed anybody by that name?"

Hani shrugged deprecatingly. "That's what my source said. If it wasn't you, I'll make my goodbyes and keep looking for the one who did. He was a master of the art. I thought he must be Hurrian."

Ullum-tishni was no doubt smart enough to know he was being flattered, but Hani had a feeling he didn't much care. A slow, frightening smile spread across his pale face. "He pays me well for my loyalty."

"I'll pay you better for your disloyalty."

"And what is this man's name?"

You tell me. Hani shrugged. "As long as you know, I don't have to. I'm a respectable personage. It's better I don't know."

But the Hurrian wasn't so easily satisfied. "What do you have against a man with no name, Egyptian? You don't even know the fellow, and you want him dead?"

"I am the father of daughters."

Ullum-tishni nodded, to all appearances convinced. "Twice what he paid me." He named an extravagant amount in silver *deben*s.

"Show me his corpse, and it's yours."

"Half before, half afterward. I'll have expenses. Bring it tomorrow at the same time."

"As you will." Hani spat into his palm and extended the hand, which the Hurrian grasped in a fist of bronze. *Gods help me—you see this oath is not sincere. Don't hold me to it, I beg you, Great Ones.*

"Show him out," the assassin said in Egyptian.

His two henchmen hustled Hani around and all but pushed him toward the door. They stumbled through the dark vestibule and out into the courtyard, with Maya herded on ahead. The guards fell back and disappeared, and the two scribes squeezed through the rotting gate, Hani's heart soaring with relief.

A loud voice cried, "You're under arrest!"

CHAPTER 15

HANI STARED ABOUT HIM IN shock, but it was too late to defend himself. Multiple sturdy bodies flung themselves upon him. He struggled wildly to throw them off, but they had hold of his arms and legs. They pulled him down hard onto his face in the street and proceeded to tie his hands behind his back.

"*Hai*, what's the meaning of this?" he shouted, dragging his captors as he struggled to get to his feet. One of them clouted him angrily across the cheekbone, and he fell back in pain. His heart was thundering, and his cheeks burned with outrage. "What's going on?" Through a swelling eye, he stared up, to see in disbelief a horribly familiar barrel-shaped figure standing over him. "Mahu! You? What's this all about?"

His shock could have been no greater than that he saw on the police chief's crimson face. But that soon gave way to a spreading grin of malicious satisfaction. "Well, if it isn't Hani. How is it I always find you at the scene of the crime?"

He gestured to his men to haul the prisoner upright, which they did as ungently as possible. Somebody clapped Hani's wig back on his head so that it almost blocked his sight. Hani's first instinct was to invoke his mandate from the vizier, which certainly ranked him above the local government of Waset and its municipal *medjay*. But he was conscious of the so-called beggar crouched against the wall behind him, no doubt drinking in the whole scene to report to his master. The last thing Hani wanted was to identify himself as a royal investigator.

"Why am I being treated like this? I've committed no crime." He tasted blood on his lips.

"Seen emerging from a house where we've come to make an arrest. A house known to be the lair of a notorious assassin. An assassin whose latest killing we happen to be investigating. Is that a coincidence, Hani?"

"It most certainly is. And if you were trying to arrest this assassin, you've undoubtedly missed him now, having spent all your time falling upon an innocent citizen." Hani tossed his head, trying to settle the wig. "Where is Maya?"

"Probably ran away. Don't worry. We can always find him." Mahu's surprise had given way to a gourmet's delight. The thing he most loved in the world—dealing pain and humiliation to Hani—had dropped into his lap. He couldn't seem to rid his jowly face of the grin that split it.

Get me away from this place, Hani thought wearily, *so I can show you my mandate and explain why I was here*. But of course, he hadn't brought the mandate with him, for fear the assassins would search him. He hoped Maya had run for help and that he would think to bring the sealed document to the police garrison. Lord Ptah-mes would wither Mahu and his men under the flames of his wrath. For that matter, so would Nub-nefer. Neither of them was afraid to use their class as a bludgeon when needed.

At last, Mahu ordered the bulk of his men to enter the house, armed to the teeth, while a pair of *medjay* hustled Hani off to the police garrison in the chief's wake.

As Hani was marched away, he glanced over his shoulder and saw that the beggar was no longer there. He would have bet good silver that the policemen who stormed the house would find it empty.

Neferet and Bener-ib tramped shoulder to shoulder through the streets, heading to the River. Neferet's hands were doubled into fists, swinging at her sides, and her face steamed with righteous indignation. "All the work we have to redo. All the supplies we have to buy again. *Grrr.*"

"It'll be all right, Nef'et. We don't want to be confrontational."

"Oh, yes, we do! We want to be *very* confrontational. We want to pop this jackal turd in the mouth and knock out his teeth. We want to twist his nose until his eyeballs rotate. We want—"

"I don't. I just want him to leave us alone so we don't have to go through all this again." Bener-ib looked wrung out. "I don't understand why people are so mean."

Neferet's voice softened. "Because, my Sweet Heart, they're mean people. You, who are a kind person, don't understand. Like that Mahu beast, remember? He enjoyed inflicting pain. So does this abominable Djed-har."

"But he's a healer." Bener-ib seemed unable to

comprehend the contradiction. "How could he heal if he enjoys pain?"

"As it happens, he heals badly. From what the neighbors have been telling us, his cure rate isn't much better than if people did nothing about their ills."

Bener-ib fell silent. The streets began to fill as siesta hour ended, and the traffic around the royal magazines was, as always, congested. The young women maneuvered carefully between the ox carts and donkey trains until they saw the leaning palm tree that marked the house of Djed-har.

"This mansion is it, Ibet. I would have preferred to think he had a rotten place to live, the rotten man."

They approached the brightly painted gate, and Neferet retracted her hand to knock. At that exact moment, the gate flew open, and the old servant started through it. He drew back with a squeak of alarm at the proximity of Neferet's fist to his nose.

"Where is Djed-har? We've come to see him. And none of that manure about his being with a patient." Neferet was not in a mood for the niceties.

"He's... He's in bed. I'm sorry—he can't see you."

"What's the slug in bed for at this hour of day? Tell him we want to have a word with him."

The servant didn't seem so haughty this time. His expression was, rather, one of distress. Perhaps he imagined Neferet dealing out to him whatever she intended to inflict on his master.

"No, I mean he's sick. He's been sick for days. Unable to leave his bed."

Neferet and Bener-ib exchanged looks of confusion

and—in Neferet's case—suspicion. "You mean he's really sick or just pretending to be so he doesn't have to face us?"

"No, no, my lady. He's really sick. Even doctors can get sick, you know."

"Then we should take a look at him," said Bener-ib. "Maybe there's something we can do for him."

"Do for him?" squawked Neferet. "Don't you mean 'do *to* him'?"

Bener-ib dropped her voice and said earnestly, "Think, Nef'et. If he's been sick for days, it can't be him."

Neferet had to admit that Bener-ib was right. Little as she liked the old fraud, they had sworn to heal. "Whatever you think," she said reluctantly, hoping that her expression would convince Djed-har that she, at least, wasn't taken in by his supposed alibi.

The aged servant led the way into the gaudy salon crammed to the cornice with herbs, lamps, boxes, bowls, and sacks. Dust sat heavily on everything, reducing it all to a dingy gray.

Just what you'd expect of one old man keeping house for another. Why doesn't he hire more servants if he's so prosperous?

The servant tapped on a closed door. "My master, the two *sunet*s are here to see you." An ill-tempered rumble from within seemed to convey some meaning to the servant, who said, "I didn't summon them, master. They just showed up. They thought perhaps they could help you."

He stepped aside, and the two young women squeezed into the dark, malodorous little room.

Neferet found herself holding her breath against the sickroom fug.

Djed-har lay in bed, his sharp face gaunt and a hideous

dark yellow. The feverish eyes he turned on them were bloodshot.

"Oh, he has jaundice," murmured Bener-ib. "Do you have any licorice root or milk thistle in the house, Djed-har?"

The healer shook his head feebly. His eyes flickered around at the various persons assembled at his bedside. He looked like a man who wanted to express anger and suspicion but was simply too weak.

"Don't worry. We aren't going to take our revenge on you," said Neferet dryly.

"We'll have to go back to get the proper herbs and amulets." Bener-ib was nodding over the bedside as one might do to a patient who didn't comprehend too well. She turned to her companion. "Come on, Nef'et. Let's see if we can find what we need."

"You'll notice she says, '*If* we can find.' Since someone completely ransacked our dispensary this afternoon, we may not find it, in which case you could die." Neferet turned and followed Bener-ib. Without another word, they made their way into the street and set off at a good clip inland.

"Serve him right if he died," she muttered as they strode elbow to elbow down the street.

"But it couldn't be him, Nef'et. He's genuinely sick."

Neferet waved her hands angrily. "He could have sent that servant of his or somebody else, my girl. That doesn't exculpate him." She blew out a frustrated breath. "If you had heard that 'little lady' speech of his, you might not be so quick to make excuses for the old vulture. Off*en*sive."

"We're healers," said Bener-ib simply as if that answered every objection.

There was no arguing with her. Neferet supposed it was the way she'd been brought up, since her father had been a *sunu* and a priest of Sekhmet and all.

When they reached the dispensary, they found Mut-tuy and two strapping servants standing in the courtyard. The nurse had brought the children back, as well, and they were shouting and screaming under the trees as they played, while the dogs barked joyously. Cheetah sat on the wall above the gate, literally and figuratively above the fray. Bener-ib hustled into the preparation room to search among the dried herbs strewn around, but Neferet stopped in the courtyard, where Mut-tuy and the two stalwarts dawdled, waiting for instructions.

"They came, I see," she said to Mut-tuy. "You people are going to need to guard this house day and night for a while. You can take turns if you want. But there should be at least one of you here at all times. We'll bring meals for you."

"Should we be armed, my lady?" asked one of the men.

"Probably. Somebody ransacked our dispensary while we were away at lunch. I don't know that you'll have to fight, but the sight of a man with a stave might give them second thoughts if they try it again."

"Should we call for the watchmen if something happens at night?" the second man said.

That gave Neferet pause. The watchmen would report to the police. "No, I don't think so. We're not keen for the *medjay* to get involved. But I'll tell the neighbors to be on the alert and run to the rescue if they hear any commotion."

Having resolved that protocol, Neferet was on her way into the house when Bener-ib came flying from the doorway, a scroll under her arm and a sack in her hand—one that both clattered and rustled.

"I have the volume about the liver," she said breathlessly. "And some licorice and the milk thistles. I started the tisanes steeping so they would be ready to administer by the time we get there. There's something strange about Djed-har's eyes, though, and I'm not sure what it means. There're hardly any pupils."

"Ibet, my girl," Neferet said uncomfortably. "Do you mind going alone? I just can't see myself palpating that man's liver. I still think he's responsible for this act of malice."

"Oh. Of... of course. If you can't treat him in good conscience..."

"Don't think less of me." She stroked her partner's cheek. "But I'm not as forgiving as you."

"That's all right, Nef'et. Somebody needs to be here anyway, in case more patients come."

How have I deserved this girl? "Then go on, and may the Powerful One guide your hand. I'll put ointment on the neighborhood sties while you're gone."

Bener-ib assured her that it was perfectly all right. She wasn't afraid to go alone, and yes, she could find the place. Then she was off.

Pensive, Neferet watched her patter rapidly out of sight down the dusty lane. *Could she be right about Djed-har? What if he didn't wreck our dispensary? But who else would want to?*

The rest of the afternoon passed slowly. A man came in with his donkey, which had run into a guyline and sliced a big piece of flesh out of its neck.

Neferet cleaned it and stuck down the flap of skin with resin, since she had no needles large enough to pierce leather, then bandaged the poor creature.

Its owner gratefully left a cluster of dates.

Mostly, with the help of Mut-tuy and the guard who had remained, she just cleaned up, throwing away anything too spoiled to make use of—all the crockery and anything in it. The potions and unguents. Many of the dried plants, animal parts, and pieces of crocodile dung, ground to dirty powder underfoot. They would have to buy new furniture. It was depressing, and she wasn't feeling very fraternal toward Djed-har by the time Bener-ib returned. But the salon and preparation room were clean and swept.

"How is our student of the Shepherd of the Anus?" Neferet said snidely as the three led the procession of children home that evening.

"He's quite sick. And unbelievably constipated. I suspect he drinks a lot."

"Oh, by all means, cure him, then. We really need a drunken healer pouring things into people."

After a moment, Bener-ib asked, "Who might have done it if it wasn't Djed-har?"

"It's somebody trying to scare us off our case, I tell you," Mut-tuy insisted.

"But who, my girl?" Neferet asked. "Even granting that they were able to find out where we were, who would want us to back off it? The wife did, but she's dead."

"Pen-buy. I bet he's the murderer."

Neferet snorted despite herself. "You've accused everybody we've spoken to. I still think it's the rabbit man, little as I want him to be guilty. Remember that mysterious picture that lured Ah-mes outside to her death."

"Maybe Djed-har killed them," said Bener-ib, her eyes lowered.

Neferet gaped at her, not sure if she was serious—yet Bener-ib was always serious. The girl's face was flushed with something that might have been embarrassment, and her lips were pressed tightly together.

"Are you being sarcastic? Ibet! I'm proud of you!" Neferet gave a whoop of delighted laughter. "I knew you could do it!"

Bener-ib, getting redder and redder, could hardly suppress a smile.

The young women spent the next morning purchasing supplies. Neferet, who had yet to keep her resolve to eat with her husband, left the children to lunch with their nurse in the rear garden while she and Bener-ib joined Lord Ptah-mes in his garden pavilion. He seemed pleased to have their company, and she felt a pang of guilt.

"We thought we'd dedicate a set of gold vessels to the Hidden One," she said, watching him sidelong to see how he reacted. "And a week of floral offerings."

"Excellent," he said, lifting a meatball to his lips. "Perhaps he'll reward you with even more clientele."

The expense didn't seem to trouble him in the least. Neferet heaved a silent sigh of relief. "I don't know if we're in a position to take patients for the moment, though. I forgot to tell you what happened yesterday while we were gone to lunch." And with her usual animation, she recounted the story of the vandalized dispensary.

As she spoke, Ptah-mes's face became graver and graver. He fixed her with an obsidian eye. "My dear, this could be extremely serious. You need to post a guard. And you should have a guard accompany you to and from the place."

"We have now. I borrowed a couple of your servants to watch in shifts."

"You did well. Does this have anything to do with the murders of those florists, do you think?"

Neferet shot Bener-ib a glance. "Maybe. We thought at first it was that healer who tried to ruin our business by spreading lies about us."

"But he was sick in bed," Bener-ib said.

"In either case, it makes me very uneasy to know that someone is targeting you ladies for violence. Under normal circumstances"—his mouth curled sardonically—"I would advise you to notify the police."

"But we have enough problems without Mahu jumping in, swinging his fists," Neferet finished with a nod of agreement.

There was a stretch of pensive silence, during which everyone turned their attention to the food. Then Ptah-mes said, "I just bought a new watchdog for the farm, but I'm going to give him to you. Leave him there at the dispensary. People will think twice before they try to get in with this fellow snapping at their heels. He's highly trained."

He excused himself from the table and disappeared into the rear part of the garden. A moment later, he emerged from the gate, leading an enormous brown creature by a leash. At a command, the dog settled himself with a whump on the porch of the kiosk, and Ptah-mes took his seat once more.

Neferet stared at the creature, agape with admiration. He was the size of a small donkey, massively built, with a close, brindled coat and a leonine head and impressively wrinkled. His drooling jaws could have sucked down a baby, but his expression, while watchful, was mild.

"*Iyah!* What a beautiful dog! I hope he won't do any harm to the others. They'd barely make a mouthful for him, even Mangler."

"Introduce him to them. Once he knows they're friends, he'll defend them."

Neferet offered the beast a meatball. He looked questioningly at his superior officer then rose and stood patiently at Neferet's side until she had poked the ball into his slobbery mouth. His curled-up tail gave a restrained wag of approval. Bener-ib drew back timidly.

"What's his name?"

"Brute, I'm told. Evidently, that's part of his mystique."

"*Hai*, Brute, old man. We're going to be friends, aren't we? Give me your paw. That's a good fellow. Now, kiss Aunt Bener-ib."

As if he understood perfectly, Brute turned to the cringing girl and gave her an enormous, dripping swipe of the tongue, while her face expressed the most stoic agony.

Neferet beamed. "See? He loves you, Ibet."

She had just aimed another meatball at the mastiff's mouth when the steward appeared in the doorway.

His brow was pleated with anxiety. "My lord, Master Maya is here to see you. He says it's urgent."

The smile dropped from Ptah-mes's face, and he shot

to his feet. Before he could reach the door, Maya burst in, winded and disheveled. A bad feeling sparkled in Neferet's middle.

"Forgive me for interrupting, my lord," the secretary panted, "but the *medjay* have Lord Hani."

Ptah-mes seemed charged with a sudden bristling energy as if an eel had shocked him. He spun on his heel and shouted for a servant to harness up his chariot. "Come, Maya. We'll head to the garrison. When did this happen?"

"A short while ago, my lord. I ran back to his house to notify Lady Nub-nefer, but she wasn't home—apparently, she and Baket-iset are at Sati's. Lord Mery-ra said to take them this." He pulled a folded and sealed papyrus from his waistband. "He's on his way directly from Hani's house."

"What's this?" Ptah-mes cast a quick eye over the document, taking in the seal.

"It's Lord Hani's mandate from the vizier, my lord. He's not under the jurisdiction of the municipal police."

"Let's go."

"Wait, we want to go too." Neferet stormed to the door after them.

"I'm afraid the chariot only accommodates two people, my dear."

"Then I should be one of them. This Hani everybody's talking about happens to be my father."

Ptah-mes looked indecisive.

Maya roared in an authoritative patriarchal baritone, "Neferet! You're holding us up." He turned to follow Ptah-mes, but Neferet rushed ahead of him.

"Stand back, my boy. Blood wins this one. Besides, I'm bigger than you if you want to fight about it." It wasn't a very nice thing to say, but her dander was up. Her beloved Papa Duck was in the hands of that foul Mahu.

She and Ptah-mes rushed into the street, where the chariot and two fine horses awaited, shivering and stamping with eagerness. He pulled on the red leather driving gloves his groom handed him then jumped into the box and helped Neferet up. Behind them in the gateway stood Maya, hands on hips, looking apoplectic, and Bener-ib holding Brute's leash. As Ptah-mes yelled to the horses, Neferet saw her friend slip the leash off the dog's collar, and the chariot took off in a thunder of hoofbeats and a cloud of dust, Brute following them at a flying gallop. She supposed the two humans would make their way to the garrison on foot.

Neferet had never ridden in a chariot before. It was a frightening experience. *How haven't I noticed how flimsy they are? It's as if somebody tied a basket to the tail of a running horse.* She felt wildly off balance in the swaying, bumping vehicle and hung onto the rail for all she was worth as they plowed unapologetically through the few pedestrians on the street at high noon.

Ptah-mes said nothing except an occasional shout at the horses. Stony-faced, he was as fixed on his task as a hawk dropping from the sky onto its prey. When, from time to time, Neferet dared to glance behind them, she saw Brute charging along tirelessly in their wake, his tongue streaming.

Neferet scarcely noticed their route except to mark when the majestic bulk of the temples flew past on their right. With a flurry of curvets and tossing heads, Ptah-mes drew the team sharply to the left, and they pounded down the narrower street that harbored the police tower, Neferet clutching the rail, her heart in her mouth.

They pulled up before the building, and Ptah-mes tied the reins inside the box. He sprang to the ground with the same tense energy as the thoroughbreds and gave Neferet a hand down, like the gentleman he was. Together, they marched past the guard and through the open door, radiating frost. At their side, Brute swaggered, his panting like a drum cadence.

In the reception hall, a group of men was gathered to confabulate, Mahu among them. Ignoring the others, Lord Ptah-mes strode up to him, thrust out the mandate, and said in a voice of flint, "Free him, Mahu."

The chief of *medjay* turned slowly and eyed Ptah-mes up and down his grand height. Mahu smirked with studied insolence. "Well, well, my lord. I do believe I'm reliving the past. It seems to me this same scene occurred some ten years ago."

"Hani is acting on orders of the vizier, and that means the king," Ptah-mes said relentlessly. "His authority is far higher than yours, and you have no legal right to interfere. You may already have cost him the success of his mission, and if so, you will answer to the Lord of the Two Lands— life, prosperity, and health be his."

Neferet, who was planted at her husband's shoulder, breathing truculence, half expected Mahu to make some sort of disparaging remark about the king, because a sneer already twitched at the corner of his mouth. But he didn't. His gaze flickered toward her and grew colder, hateful.

"You're legally obliged to let my father go," she said defiantly.

But Mahu had apparently decided to ignore her. "What was he doing in the secret lair of a notorious murderer, Ptah-mes? How is it he's always underfoot when the police have a capture to perform? Just because a man is employed by the king doesn't mean he can't be crooked. Isn't that right... *my lord*?" The nasty tone in which he pronounced the honorific made it a title of shame.

Lord Ptah-mes, who had stripped off his gloves with a jerk, looked as if he'd been turned to icy and dangerous stone. He slapped the gloves against his leg, like a lion lashing its tail, and his black eyes bored holes into the coarse-featured face before him. "You might want to consider watching your words, Mahu. There are laws against insulting a nobleman. I rank just below the vizier."

"Ma'at can't be intimidated, Lord Grandee." Mahu smirked.

Ptah-mes's quivering intensity seemed to dissipate, and he said lightly, "I shall enjoy breaking you, you carbuncle on the honor of our kingdom." He turned to the other *medjay*, who were watching in an uncertainty bordering on fear, and shook the mandate at them. "Do you know who I am? The Master of the Double House, and I speak for our Sun God. One of you, set Hani free by order of the vizier or face the ruin of your career. If you're reluctant, a platoon of soldiers may change your mind."

Several of the men edged nervously toward the interior of the room.

Rather than see his orders disobeyed, Mahu gave a snort and growled, "Let him out. He's learned his lesson."

Neferet, her face flaming, thought she'd never so generously hated any other human being in her life. The feeling burned like an acid in her heart. The hatred she bore Isfet—Chaos—and the Apep Serpent that slimed the world with the malice of his filthy coils was cool and abstract beside the burning lava of her contempt for this walking wart who had troubled her family for much of her lifetime. *I'll see you go down. For what you've done to Papa and to Ibet and to Lord Ptah-mes. And to me. I swear it by Mama's* ka.

Brute echoed her thoughts with a low rumble of warning.

A quiet commotion in the doorway made her turn, and she saw Maya, Bener-ib, and Grandfather clustered, red faced and steaming, on the threshold.

Mahu's eyes flickered over the new arrivals, and he said in a nasty tone, "I see the rest of the family has come to make scary noises at the servants of the law. Where's that fat brother of Hani's and his fire-breathing wife?"

"If you insult my family again, you'll be sorry," snarled Neferet, no longer able to control her fury.

Lord Ptah-mes cautioned her to discretion with a gesture of his hand.

By this time, a pair of the policemen had returned from the bowels of the garrison, with Papa between them. He had a purple bruise across one cheek that had swelled up his eye, and his arm was scraped, his sleeve torn. But he was walking without much difficulty.

"Papa!" Neferet cried in an ecstasy of relief. She threw herself into his arms, and he hugged her tight.

When they separated, his eyes met Ptah-mes's and the others', and a grateful smile lit his face. He turned to Mahu and asked frigidly, "Am I free to go?"

"For the moment. But the next time you obstruct the investigation of the police…"

"The next time *you* obstruct the investigations of the crown…" Ptah-mes skewered the police chief with a look and turned his back.

Papa's little party trooped out in triumph.

CHAPTER 16

PAPA AND LORD PTAH-MES RODE together in the chariot so they could talk, but the horses were kept back to a walking pace, allowing the others, who thronged around them on foot, to keep up. They moved in a victorious knot through the streets toward Papa's house, to the jingle of harnesses. Maya, at Neferet's side, flashed her a cold eyeball, but she, her anger dissipated—or rather, off-loaded onto Mahu—was cheerful to the toes.

"Sorry to pull rank, Maya, but I hate it when you do that father-of-the-family voice. I was the next of kin. Now, if Grandfather had been there, I would have had to yield."

"Think nothing of it," her brother-in-law said with bad grace.

Bener-ib suppressed a smile. Brute seemed to have taken a liking to her and padded at her side like a placid shadow. She scratched his nape without even bending.

Neferet turned to her and lowered her voice. "What do we do next, my girl?"

"Perhaps we should wait until we hear what your father learned this morning."

"True. But one thing is sure. We don't have to spend energy considering whether to share our discoveries with the *medjay*. They're on their own. And no asking them to investigate who wrecked our dispensary."

Bener-ib, bowing to the evidence, nodded reluctantly. "It seems Lord Hani is the official investigator at this point, doesn't it?"

"Why, so it does! We can be his deputies. Our mandate comes from Lord Pentju, if anyone should ask."

By the time they reached the house, Mama and Baket-iset were back. The little group trooped into the garden, where the mistress of the house directed the servants to set out pots of beer that had been chilled in the well.

"Hani, my love!" she cried in horror at the sight of her husband's discolored face. "What happened?"

"In a word—Mahu. He's back, and I wandered into his investigation while pursuing my own."

"That corrupt jackal," she spat. "I'll kill him if he harms my family again."

"You'll have to stand in line, Mama," Neferet said fervently. "We all feel the same way."

"Apart from Mahu's interruption, how did the morning go? Did you meet the assassin?" Mery-ra drew in a big draft of beer through his straw and gave a belch of pleasure.

"I did. I know who he is—a Hurrian sellsword named Ullum-tishni. He essentially admitted to having killed Sen-em-iah. He wouldn't tell me who paid him, but I hired him to kill the man"—the three women gasped—"and was to have given him his silver tomorrow. I was going to have some of Menna's soldiers follow him and find out whom he tried to kill." He looked around. "Hopefully, we would be able to save the victim from death when arresting the assassin in the act."

"Why would you want to save him? Isn't the king going to execute him anyway for murder?" Neferet said.

"He has information we need, my duckling. Why did he kill Sen-em-iah? Did he also kill the wife? Does he have accomplices? You see what I mean."

Of course, she thought. *Learn at the knee of a master, my girl.*

"I suppose," Hani said with a broad grin that bared the gap between his teeth, "the vizier will reimburse the silver I'll have to pay this fellow."

Lord Ptah-mes smiled grimly. "As the treasurer, I can promise that he will. But won't your Hurrian have fled now, after the police's untimely irruption?"

"You can be sure of it." Mery-ra snorted. "Maybe Mahu is in cahoots with him."

"I don't know about that, but Mahu certainly ruined my plans. The only positive part is that the guard witnessed my arrest, which makes me look like exactly the private citizen bent on vengeance I claimed to be."

"Good," Ptah-mes said. "I think it would become extremely dangerous if this Ullum-tishni suspected you of tracking him."

"I dare not return to his lair tomorrow. Mahu may have a net of surveillance laid. I hope the Hurrian tries to contact me somehow. Otherwise, this may have queered my whole attempt to hire him."

A sudden magnificent idea bloomed in Neferet's

heart. "You could send somebody innocent looking to feel around. He may show up, knowing you're supposed to pay him. And if it were somebody the *medjay* wouldn't suspect of being your representative, you could at least set another rendezvous."

"But who?" said Maya. "The *medjay* know me."

"Me—that's who." She smiled, pleased with herself.

Mama immediately cried out in protest. Papa and Ptah-mes exchanged uneasy looks.

"The medjay know you, too, my girl," Grandfather said.

"Wrong. Mahu knows me, but the average policeman who'd be watching the place wouldn't. They'd just see a harmless young woman."

Maya said tartly, "And what would be your excuse for hanging around an abandoned house known to have been the hiding place of desperados?"

Neferet's smile widened into a triumphant grin. "I'm a *sunet*. Our dispensary has been ruined, and I'm looking for a certain herb to replace our supply. Right, Ibet?"

Bener-ib, despite an expression of reluctance, nodded. "If they check your story, it's all true."

But Papa shook his head. "If they check your story, they find out you're my daughter."

"So what? You're the one who told me you saw this herb growing there in the yard."

Everyone fell silent, digesting this, although Neferet could feel each of them bursting with the desire to say no. She finally rose and said, satisfied, "Well, then, that's settled."

Papa sprang up, too, as if to stop her from leaving.

"Wait a minute, my duckling. You don't seem to realize how dangerous this is. Either side could do you harm."

She didn't respond but, fizzy with eagerness, beckoned to Bener-ib with a sideways tip of the head. "Come, Ibet. We have a lot of work ahead to get that dispensary restocked."

The others, stunned speechless, watched them leave.

Once in the street, Neferet found that Brute had followed them out. "They forgot about you, eh, boy? You'll protect me." She scratched him around the wrinkly jowls.

Bener-ib's eyes were as big as *deben* rings. "You're not really going to do this, Nef'et?"

"Well, of course. This is the only way to find out who paid the assassins to kill Sen-em-iah and his wife—to follow this Hurrian and see who he's preparing to kill. But first, Papa's got to pay him."

"Why couldn't your father just send a servant?"

That stopped Neferet momentarily. "Let's get going before one of them thinks of that."

They set off toward the north with hasty steps, the mastiff padding alongside.

To the rhythm of their paces, she explained, "I'm going because I'm the one who is looking for clues. Maybe I'll even have an opportunity to ask the man point-blank who paid him. Maybe I'll remind him of his little daughter who died in the war in Naharin, and he'll soften up completely."

"Did he have a little daughter?"

"Probably. Maybe that's why he went bad. The loss of his family embittered him, and he abandoned all his morals because it's a cruel world."

Bener-ib stared at her as if she completely failed to

follow, but that was all right. She'd come around. She was a smart girl.

It was clear from the volume of squeals and shouts and barks that filled the neighborhood that Nurse had brought the children back to the dispensary.

"Let's see how Brute and the other boys get along." If Brute didn't like the three old dogs and lunged at them, not even both girls together could hold him back. But Neferet was in a buoyant mood, and that prospect didn't fill her with the anxiety it might otherwise have done.

He turned out to be the well-trained gentleman Lord Ptah-mes had promised. They led him into the courtyard, where he stood with a modest wagging of his curled tail, while Mangler, Faithful, and Hedgehog gaped incredulously at his size and finally began to wag as well. There was mutual sniffing, and the oldsters passed in and out under his belly while Brute looked on with a small, benevolent eye. The children were properly awestruck.

"Ride! Ride!" Tiry begged, her arms around the creature's neck.

"All right. Once. But you boys are too big. He's the size of a donkey, but he's not built the same." Neferet wondered if there weren't some sort of little cart he could pull, though. Even goats did that.

Once inside the bare dispensary, other, somber thoughts chased out the good mood. *Where do we start? Beds and stools. Pots and boxes. Then replace the medicines. Oh no. We should have instruments remade first—that will take time.*

"Where is Mut-tuy?" Bener-ib asked.

Neferet looked up. Only then did it strike her that

the girl hadn't been among the other children. "Mut the mother of us all! I don't know. Ask the nurse."

But the rustle of the fly mat being pushed aside made the two young women turn, and their question was answered. Mut-tuy stood in the doorway, her short hair sticking up like Faithful's, her fists on her narrow hips.

"Where were you people?" she said angrily. "Lord Ptah-mes's servants said you'd all charged out at once, and nobody told us *anything*. That was hours ago. I've been looking all over."

"It's been quite a morning, my girl. We'll tell you all about it."

They sat in a circle on the floor, and Neferet began the account eagerly. But her audience didn't warm. Mut-tuy's face was as hard and red as a pomegranate, her eyes narrowed in fury. It took Neferet aback. She'd expected the girl to get excited about the advance in their investigation, but the thirteen-year-old looked ready to commit murder herself.

"You could have told me. I could have gone with you," she shouted.

It occurred to Neferet that this was a girl whose mother had abandoned the family—run away with a man she thought loved her. The little ones had accepted the idea that the woman was dead, but Mut-tuy had been old enough to suspect the truth. No wonder she had a particular fear of being left behind.

"You're right. We should have," Neferet said contritely. "Everything just happened so fast. We charged off on Lord Ptah-mes's chariot—"

"A chariot! That's the limit! You got to ride a chariot

while I didn't even know what was going on. You treat me like a child." Her voice was rattling with tears of rage.

"That's how the men treated us," said Bener-ib comfortingly. "They wouldn't let us do anything."

"But we do have a plan to carry things forward, even though Papa dare not show up again to pay the man."

Mut-tuy refused to ask about the plan and sat, arms folded, in disgruntled silence.

"I'm going instead," Neferet finished.

"Then take me with you." A coal glowed in Mut-tuy's tear-rouged eyes.

Neferet and Bener-ib looked at one another, caught between reluctance and the hope of a quick cure for the girl's snit.

"All right," Neferet said slowly. "But you've got to do exactly as I say."

⚜

The next morning, Neferet and Mut-tuy set off toward the temple of Montu, having only a general idea of their destination. Neferet had loaded the required number of silver *deben*s into a chest, which a servant carried. She'd had, of course, to alert Lord Ptah-mes that she was taking a substantial sum from his strongbox. He looked troubled— seemed to want to say something—then bit back his words.

"Don't tell Papa what we're doing," she said.

But while he'd agreed in a vague way, he hadn't exactly promised. At least, he hadn't forbidden her the silver or locked her in the house.

Now Neferet and the girl stood in front of a tumbledown dwelling overhung by a massive sycamore fig. The cicadas pulsed under a sun like electrum, but it wasn't the heat that made Neferet's scalp run with perspiration. The risks of her plan had begun to penetrate. She was starting to hope that no one had dared return to the place.

"You can set that chest just inside the door and leave," she told the servant. He seemed eager to be gone, and in a heartbeat, the two young women stood alone, facing the sagging door panel. Mut-tuy swallowed hard, then Neferet did the same.

"Anybody in here?" Neferet called. "I've brought your silver."

The silent darkness answered them. A rustle that set Neferet's hairs on end turned out to be a rat.

"I guess they're not here," she said in disappointment and turned to go.

But at that moment, two men emerged from the shadows and took hold of an arm of each. They marched Neferet and Mut-tuy wordlessly into the twilight of the interior.

Neferet fought back the lump of her heart that seemed to want to pop out of her mouth. This was what she'd hoped for, but it was fraught with the possibility of disaster.

In the salon, a faint ray of sun stretched diagonally across the upper part of the room, leaving the lower part in twilight. A man was sitting on the low platform of the birthing bower, his face in shadow. Neferet could see the little tail of hair that garnished his shaven forehead.

"Who are you?" said the man in heavily accented Egyptian.

"I'm the daughter of the man who engaged you yesterday. The police arrested him as he was leaving, so he couldn't come back in person to pay you. He told me to bring your silver. He wasn't even sure you'd show up after the police raid."

The man stood, and he was tall and formidably built. "Give it to me and leave. My men have distracted the *medjay* for the moment, but they're encircling the house. We dare not stay around."

"It's in that chest. I can't pick it up. It's too heavy."

The Hurrian gave orders to one of his men to get the chest and check the contents. The clank of metal rings echoed dully. From the vestibule, the fellow called, "It's all here, Chief."

"Go," said the chief tersely. "Tell your father he'll receive the corpse in due time."

"Before we leave, could you answer one question for me, please? Who is this man?"

The assassin laughed, a hard clatter of stones. "A jackal on two legs. I won't be sorry to see that bastard go." He squinted at her closely. "Are you the daughters who've suffered at his hands? Then I needn't tell you the sort of man he is."

Papa didn't say anything about this. Neferet felt a great hollow pit open in her stomach, as if she'd fallen off a ledge. *Dear gods, what's the story here?* "Uh, yes. He's ruined our lives, and we want to see him punished."

"Yes," said Mut-tuy with convincing savagery.

All at once, the man jerked as if he'd heard something. "Get them out," he said to his guards. He melted into the shadows, and they heard his footsteps disappear into the darkness.

The two henchmen stepped out of the shadows and

half guided, half frog-marched the young women toward the door and the light.

"He never told us the human jackal's name," Neferet complained to her captor.

The big man rumbled with a sinister chuckle. "They call him Sekhat. Rabbit."

Neferet shaded her eyes, blinded by the sunlight. "Let's get out of here before the police get back."

They hustled along the street until a shout made Neferet stop. Someone had called her name. She turned and saw Papa and Maya appearing from around the corner.

They hurried toward Neferet and Mut-tuy and swept them inland, away from the dead end of a neighborhood.

"What are you doing here?" she asked in surprise.

"Lord Ptah-mes said he wanted you protected, and we came in case there was trouble."

"I thought you were afraid of encountering the police."

"There didn't seem to be any." Papa set a brisk pace, and the others kept abreast with difficulty. "Neferet, I know everything turned out all right, but that was incredibly foolhardy."

Her sense of triumph was tinged with annoyance. "Or you could say, 'It was foolhardy, but everything turned out all right. Congratulations, Neferet. Brilliant work.' We gave him the silver, and we got out safe. He had somehow distracted the *medjay* from the area. And"—she turned to her father with sparkling eyes—"we found out something *very* interesting about the man who had Sen-em-iah killed."

"What's that?" Maya asked dutifully.

"His name is Rabbit."

The two men stopped abruptly and stared at her.

"Rabbit is his *name*? I've never heard anybody called Sekhat." Maya looked skeptical.

"Nickname—whatever. It's what the Hurrian calls him. He seems to think he's quite a low beast." Neferet beamed back and forth at the men. "Which means our florist *was* saying his killer's name with his final breath. He wanted us to find and punish the man."

Papa frowned, deep in thought, Maya looked dubious, while Mut-tuy's face was lit by wild fires.

"And the sight of his name made that woman run out into the garden to flee, where she was killed," Neferet crowed. Nobody could remember the florist's wife's name except Bener-ib. But at least her nickname wasn't Rabbit, as Neferet had once considered.

"I guess we'll go home for a bit and reassure Lord Ptahmes that everything is all right. You owe him a number of silver *deben*s, Papa. I raided his strongbox."

Neferet parted company with her father and brother-in-law, Mut-tuy trailing along.

"Actually," said Neferet after the men were out of sight, "I want to reassure Ibet first. Let's go back to the dispensary."

The servant who had deposited the chest was already back on duty in the garden. On the path to the house, Brute sat like a lion-bodied statue of the king, keeping watch over his new domain, while the three oldsters slept in the shade. The children seemed to be in a fight, with much loud name-calling.

Neferet rolled her eyes. "We should sic your brothers

and sister on this murderer. That should scare him into embracing the path of virtue."

"They're worse than animals," Mut-tuy said pitilessly.

Bener-ib appeared in the doorway, clearly on tenterhooks. "Oh, thanks be to the Great One, you're home safe! I was so worried." She threw her arms around Neferet, who reciprocated joyously. Mut-tuy watched with narrowed eyes.

"You won't believe what we found out!" Neferet proceeded to describe the meeting and how the identity of the killer had been revealed. "Now we just have to locate him."

"And convict him," Bener-ib said.

"But he's already going to be executed, isn't he? Isn't your father going to pounce on him when the assassins try to kill him?" Mut-tuy said.

"But consider, my girl. It will make it a lot easier to watch and follow the Hurrian if they know who Rabbit is. There's a little service we can perform."

Bener-ib had spent the morning most fruitfully. Several stools had been restored to the salon, three beds were ordered, and pots of all sizes sat stacked in the preparation room. Freshly cut herbs even hung from the rafters.

"This is marvelous, Ibet. You've gotten so much done. How is Djed-har coming along?"

"Much better. But I don't know how well he's ever going to get. At least he won't die right away—which he would have without us."

"I hope he's grateful."

Bener-ib stuck out her lip in consideration. "I'm not sure he is. His pride has been hurt, I think."

"Saved from death by women, you mean?" sniffed Mut-tuy. "Let him die if he doesn't like it."

"Behold real life," said Neferet, world-weary. "We have to prove ourselves every moment."

She had just about decided to put an end to the day and take the children home for the rest of the afternoon when two dust-whitened workmen came shuffling in, supporting a third between them on the saddle of their hands. His foot was dripping blood, despite a greasy rag bound around it. The poor man's face was so anguished it tore the heart.

"What happened to you, my friend?" Neferet asked as she directed them to seat him on a stool and propped his foot up on another.

"We're stonecutters, mistress. A big stone fell on his foot."

Her heart sank. He would almost certainly be crippled by the accident.

She had the men lift their companion onto the scrubbed worktable, and Bener-ib carefully unwrapped the injured foot. It wasn't an encouraging sight. The bones were crushed and mingled with the flesh in a bloody, shapeless mass. There was no way to clean it. If they just bandaged it, it would surely putrefy. Neferet, the sweat breaking out on her forehead, caught Bener-ib's eye. They looked hopelessly at one another.

"Do we have a saw?" she mouthed.

Bener-ib nodded.

"We're going to have to amputate." The thought made her shudder. She'd watched Lady Djefat-nebty cut off limbs, but she herself had never done it. "How much *sepen* do we have?"

"Enough."

The poppy juice, which was imported from somewhere across the Great Green, was as dear as gold, and only the rich could afford it, mixed with white wine and saffron. Of course, their precious bottle, with its bulbous shape and long neck that recalled the shape of a poppy seed capsule, had been destroyed in the sacking of their supplies. But either Ibet had managed to salvage some, or she had replaced it.

Thanking Sekhmet that Ibet's shopping trip had replenished their supplies, Neferet sent Mut-tuy after clean cloths, wine, an obsidian scalpel, and a bone saw. "And a cauterizing iron. Do we have one?"

Bener-ib shook her head. She was biting her lip and looking distinctly pale.

We'll have to sew. Ibet would do a neater job with this, but I don't think she has the strength to saw through a bone.

Bener-ib dosed the man with the poppy-juice tincture, and soon, his screams and moans subsided.

"Give him as much as you dare, Ibet. We don't want him waking up too soon." Neferet dashed the sweat from her face with the back of an unsteady hand. "You men hold onto him just in case he comes to."

She poured a libation of wine over the ankle and over her scalpel and, with a heartfelt prayer to Sekhmet and Im-hotep, started cutting. Bener-ib stuffed cloths against the bleeding surface. Neferet's hand was trembling, her heart hammering in her chest until she felt faint. But her surgery had only just begun. She left a longer flap of skin and muscle in the rear with which to close the stump. Now only the bones held the foot to its leg. She reached out for the saw, and Mut-tuy passed it to her. It was still dripping with wine. She began to saw.

The bones were both hard and spongy—like wet wood. Severing them seemed to take forever.

Mut-tuy and one of the men held the leg down tight.

Neferet's face was afire with effort, and her nerves buzzed with the pitiless *zip* of the blade going back and forth. At last, the saw fell through, and she stepped back, limp, wiping her forehead, while Bener-ib tamponed the blood with cloth after cloth.

Mut-tuy handed her the needle threaded with a long strand of gut.

"Ibet, can you sew? I'm done for."

Bener-ib was showing remarkable fortitude. Despite her pallor, the hand with which she took the needle was firm. She had the capacity to push everything out of her mind except the task of the moment.

After an apparently endless time hunched over the patient's ankle, she straightened up. "It's finished. You'll have to leave him here overnight, at least, and probably for several days. We want to be sure this doesn't start to bleed too much."

CHAPTER 17

T HE MEN, WHO WERE EVIDENTLY shaken, babbled their thanks. "Can we have his wife come?"

"Of course."

As Neferet showed them out, Bener-ib bandaged the stump into a great bundle full of wadding. "Oh, Ibet, that was the most horrible moment of my life. I'm not meant to be a surgeon."

"You did a splendid job, Nef'et. Those bones were so clean—I never could have done it myself. Djefat-nebty would be very proud of you."

The two young doctors fell into each other's arms, emotionally exhausted.

Mut-tuy, looking shaken, watched them from under her brows.

"I guess we won't be going home tonight, eh? And we don't have any beds here, not even for this poor fellow. He'll have to stay on the worktable."

"We'll use up all our *sepen* if we have to, and he won't even know what he's lying on. It's apparently being grown around here now and isn't as expensive as it used to be," Bener-ib said.

"That's good news." Neferet turned to Mut-tuy. "Go ahead and take the children home, my girl. I'd like to keep it quiet around here for the rest of the evening. And tell Lord Ptah-mes what's happened. He's still waiting to know how the meeting with the Hurrian turned out."

But the girl's reaction was swift and firm. "No. I want to stay."

Neferet glared at her, not in the mood to fight. "Normally, you can't wait to get away from the dispensary, and now nobody can pry you away. Could you just once do what you're asked?"

"That's because it's normally as boring as can be. Nothing but little twerps with boo-boos on their fingers."

Neferet heaved a martyred sigh. "Oh, all right. Tell Nurse to take them home, then. You can throw all the bloody cloths in a pile to take to the laundrymen."

"What do we do with this pitiful foot?" Bener-ib prodded the severed object.

"Throw it to the dogs, I guess."

But the little *sunet* looked dubious. "Do we want them to get a taste for human flesh?"

"Wrap it up and toss it in the River when we take the laundry." *Where we're giving the crocodiles a taste for human flesh.*

The two young women busied themselves tidying up the room and scrubbing out the stains. Flies had already begun to gather. The smell was stomach churning in the heat.

Neferet looked down at her bloodstained shift in

disgust and said to Mut-tuy, "It would certainly be nice if somebody ran home and brought us clean clothes."

The girl considered the request. "I can do that."

"Would you be so gracious, then, my lady? Anything else we need, Ibet?"

"Something for dinner," Bener-ib said.

"Something for dinner, my girl."

With a suspicious look, as if she feared they would bar the door after her to prevent her returning, Mut-tuy shot off, leaving the nurse to organize her own exodus. Once the noise of children on the march had faded, the two *sunet*s sank to the stools. The patient slept on the table, talking and groaning from time to time. From out in the yard came the rhythmic thump of one of the dogs scratching himself and the buzz of flies circling the pile of bloody rags.

"Tell me we'll never have to do this again."

Bener-ib smiled wanly. "I don't know. Lady Djefat-nebty did several amputations while we were her students, and she wasn't treating stonecutters and such."

They fell silent.

"What I don't know is what I'd ever do without you," Neferet said after a moment. She took Bener-ib's hand but dropped it an instant later as two people pushed their way through the gate and made straight for the door.

"Is this the house of the surgeons who just operated on Pa-iry?" said the man, his face stretched with concern.

"Yes," said Neferet, rising, "if this gentleman is Pa-iry."

The woman at his side gave a cry and threw herself on the patient, who moaned and stirred feebly but didn't wake. "My brother! Oh, thank all the gods you're alive!"

"This is his wife," said the man. "I'm his work foreman. The others told me how you saved his life."

"Well, we'll see about that. But we're hopeful." Neferet hoped, as well, that the wife and foreman wouldn't be too shocked by the bloody bundle where his left foot had been.

"I don't know what they owe you, but she wanted me to offer you this. It's an heirloom and should be worth something." He held out a gilded bracelet with enamel animals laid into it. "Our boss gave it to her because Pa-iry was injured on the job. But she wanted you to have it."

"That's very generous of you, mistress," Neferet said. *There's not enough gold under the light of Ra to make me enjoy what we've just done for you.* "He needs to stay here for at least the night. If there's no bleeding by tomorrow, you may be able to take him home."

"I'll have to go to work, but my grandmother can look after him during the day. Mother works nights, so she'll need to sleep."

"Oh? You don't work at home?" Bener-ib asked in a conversational tone. Neferet knew she was trying to distract the poor soul.

"No, I'm a housemaid for a rich man. That's why I talk nice. They trained us all. In fact, he and the mistress just died, so I guess I work for their son now. That is, the master's son."

Something tinkled in the back of Neferet's thoughts like a little bell on a pack saddle. "How sad," she said, tingling. "What was the rich man's name?"

"Sen-em-iah," said the woman, stroking her husband's arm. "A wonderful master. We'll all miss him. Not so much his wife. I don't know the son very well, so I'm afraid to ask him for some days off. But there are holidays coming, at least."

Neferet saw Bener-ib's head snap up, and she felt like her own was suddenly bounding up on its stalk like a newly sprung wild onion. "Does your mother, by any chance, work in the florist shop?"

The woman looked astonished. "Why, yes."

"And your aunt is Lord Hani's cook?"

Her eyes grew round in superstitious fear. "Yes. How do you know?"

"Your name is Wabet," said Bener-ib with a big smile.

"Y-Yes."

Neferet threw back her head and laughed. "Don't be alarmed. I'm Neferet, Lord Hani's daughter. We're working to find the murderer of Sen-em-iah, and your recollections have been very helpful to us."

Wabet gave a huge cry of relief and delight. "It's you, then. Mother told me two women had interviewed her, but she gave me no names. I'll tell you anything and everything I know, my lady. I owe you Pa-iry's life."

The foreman made his excuses and left the three women.

They immediately seated themselves on the stools, and Neferet clasped Wabet's hand. "You know, your husband is going to be lame. We had to take off his foot. But he can still cut stone, can't he? Try to keep him cheerful about that. He may be down in the mouth. You know how men are."

"I will, my lady. I don't care what's missing—he's still alive. The children still have their father, and I still have my husband."

Neferet pressed the bracelet on her. "I'm sure you can

find a use for this, my friend. If you have any recollections about conversations your late master might have had, that would be payment enough. Was there any talk about buying out a farmer's land? Was he ever visited by priests?"

"Any mention of a man named Rabbit?" Bener-ib popped up and returned a moment later with the jug of wine and some small bowls. She proceeded to pour out a measure for each of them.

Wabet stared at the ruby liquid with astonishment. No doubt it was well outside her modest budget.

"Here's to the recovery of Pa-iry." Neferet lifted her cup, and the others followed. Together, they swallowed down their libation.

After that, things got jolly. Unaccustomed to the force of wine and giddy with relief that her husband seemed to be saved, Wabet grew quite voluble. She was a pretty, fresh-faced woman, rather younger than the two *sunet*s, and observant.

"I'll say there was talk of Rabbit. I was never actually sure of who he was, but the master talked to the mistress about him. The very thought appeared to scare them. Hard as it is to believe, he seemed to be involved in something illegal with him. I mean, I don't want to slander the master's *ka*, but that's what it sounded like. The master and mistress were really scared. I think Rabbit threatened to expose them."

Neferet pondered this. "What could it have been? Flowers don't seem like something you could steal or counterfeit. There wouldn't have been taxes to pay on them, anyway, since the Hidden One isn't taxed."

At that moment, a clatter at the gate proclaimed the

return of Mut-tuy with the night guard. They carried an assortment of baskets and pots with towels tied around them.

"There's our dinner. Please share it with us," said Bener-ib.

The servant, his eyes flickering to the sleeping man on the table, set down his basket and retreated to the yard, while Mut-tuy unpacked. She glanced around her with suspicious eyes at the cups of wine and pulled up the empty stool, her expression accusing. "The party has already started?"

Neferet chose to ignore her. "Did you bring clean dresses?"

After a sullen nod from the thirteen-year-old, Neferet held up one of the garments and decided it was hers. She extended the other one to Bener-ib. "I wouldn't mind a bath, but we forgot a bathing room when we designed this place."

"You can go first," said Bener-ib with a meaningful look.

Neferet understood. *We shouldn't leave Mut-tuy alone with our witness. Gods know what the girl would say.*

Neferet retreated to the preparation room and pulled off her blood-crusted shift. Her hands and arms were still dark with it and sticky with the wine she'd poured over them in offering. The mingled smell made her stomach churn. She ladled a liberal flood from the big water jug and scrubbed herself with the clean back of her old dress, taking a dash at her face too. It wouldn't have surprised her to find she had been splattered all over. Eventually, feeling cleaner in the fresh shift, she returned to the salon.

Bener-ib left to take her turn at the ablutions. "Tell her what you just told me, Wabet," she called over her shoulder.

The young woman had grown quite uninhibited. She leaned toward Neferet and whispered loudly, "I think the master tried to pull out of whatever he was involved in. One time, he had visitors, and I was cleaning in the vestibule just outside the salon. I heard somebody say, 'Don't think you can just turn your back and act as if you aren't part of this. You're in it as deep as anybody.' And the master said, 'But they check my books. I can't keep doing this.' And the man said, '*I* check your books. Don't panic and ruin everything.' Or something like that." She stared at Neferet with sparkling eyes, eager to please.

I'm glad she's not my housemaid, thought Neferet. *She listens at doors.* "Did you see this person? Was he Rabbit?"

"I didn't, my lady. But he had a funny voice. He couldn't pronounce his *R*s. For example, he would call you Nefewet. He would call my husband Pa-iwy." Wabet giggled, almost spraying wine out her nose.

The cold leg of guinea fowl all but dropped from Neferet's hand. *Pu-im-ra! He's Rabbit! Of course!*

"Did you ever see a skinny priest with a big knob in his throat and buckteeth? You might not have known he was a priest. There might have been another short, fat one with him."

"I seen those men, but I didn't know they were priests, no. I should have, though, the way they paraded around, all decked in fancy jewelry, with fans in their hands. The master fell all over himself when they came. And there were other men that came, too, but not all dressed up like those." She helped herself to a big chunk of warm bread and swiped at the chickpea paste.

Bener-ib rejoined them, clean and freshly dressed.

Mut-tuy blurted excitedly, "Pu-im-ra is Rabbit!"

The little doctor's jaw dropped open. "But of course!" Her eyes were bright as comprehending stars.

"Wabet described him and that fat one as frequent visitors to the house. Now we're getting somewhere." Neferet grinned eagerly. "You say there were others?"

The housemaid seemed pleased to be the center of such rapt attention. "Yes, three of them. They would come at night, though, so I just saw them enter. I didn't overhear—uh, hear—their conversations."

Behind them, Pa-iry mumbled and stirred.

Bener-ib quietly rose and rubbed a bit more of the *sepen* on his lips, which he mechanically licked. He subsided once more into unconsciousness.

"What's that awful-smelling stuff?" his wife asked.

Bener-ib held up the pot. "Poppy juice, white wine, and saffron. It will make him sleep and dull the pain. We'll give you some to take home with you."

"What did these three men look like?" Neferet couldn't wait to bring the conversation back to the subject.

"Rough fellows, big and muscular. One was built like a wrestler. One was a foreigner with light skin and hair."

Iyah! Neferet could have shouted. *Everything is coming together.*

"Ooh, look. It's getting dark," said Bener-ib. The twilight had imperceptibly settled upon them, leaving the salon in shadow. "We need to make some sort of arrangements for sleeping. Normally, we have beds, Wabet, but some bad person smashed everything up."

"Maybe I should go home to the children after all, my lady," said the housemaid apologetically. "I'm putting you out. Now that I see what good care you're taking of Pa-iry, I'm not afraid to leave him for a few hours. I'll be back at dawn, all right?" She rose, unsteady on her feet, and tottered over to her husband, upon whose dozing face she planted a kiss. "Sleep, my brother." She waggled her fingers in goodbye to the women and tiptoed elaborately through the door and away.

Neferet lit a couple of linseed oil lamps. "Where can we go to talk? I don't want to disturb our patient's sleep, but the guard is outside in the yard."

"We can walk around the block," suggested Bener-ib. "It's not fully dark outside."

"Brute can go with us." Mut-tuy's bad mood seemed to have fallen away.

"Not a bad idea," Neferet said.

They told the guard they would be back soon, and whistling the mastiff to their side, they started out the gate. Mangler and the other grandfathers stood up eagerly, wagging their tails, and Neferet didn't have the heart to refuse them. Together, the three humans and four dogs ambled down the darkening street, past the empty lots with their broken-down walls and unkempt trees. Across the lane, lights shone through the high windows of houses as families finished their dinners or washed up. Childish laughter drifted from the dyer's yard.

"Have you ever heard of such marvelous luck? The

Hidden One must like the idea of our offering!" Neferet cried enthusiastically.

"It confirms our suspicions about that slimy Pu-im-ra. He's as corrupt as he can be." Mut-tuy was all but lashing her tail.

"Is he really the one who killed Sen-em-iah and his wife, though?" asked Bener-ib.

"If he's Rabbit, yes. One of the assassins said Rabbit was the man who had paid them. We can tell Papa we've identified his murderer."

But Bener-ib seemed hesitant. "Is an overheard conversation sufficient evidence? Doesn't he have to be caught in the act?"

Neferet fell silent, miffed at this cold water thrown on her triumph. "I don't know. With any luck, the Hurrian will assassinate him, and we won't have that problem anymore." She turned to Mut-tuy, who had missed a goodly part of Wabet's exposition. "Pu-im-ra and Sen-em-iah were doing something illegal together. Apparently, Sen-em-iah wanted to back out of it."

"We need to tell your father right away, Nef'et. He can have Pu-im-ra followed so if the three ruffians try anything, the soldiers can catch them red-handed."

"You mean tonight?" Neferet wasn't keen on marching across town at this hour. She was exhausted by the surgery, and the well-irrigated picnic had left her eyes almost falling shut.

Bener-ib turned an earnest gaze upon her. She would never omit any duty just because she was tired. "Don't you think?"

"Oh, all right," Neferet said, wishing she could assign

the chore to a servant. She heaved herself to her feet. "It would be nice if we had a carrying chair."

But she herself had refused Lord Ptah-mes's many offers for a chair or a litter. So picking up an oil lamp, she let herself out the gate and into the darkened street and headed off with rapid steps.

CHAPTER 18

THE FRESHER AIR OF EVENING helped wake Neferet. Everything was different at night—the human component of the city fell gradually silent, and the animal part came to life. Light still glowed orange from the high windows of many houses, but the crickets' rhythmic chant replaced the cries of street vendors and muleteers. Frogs blared from private gardens, and an owl swooped soundlessly overhead, taking advantage of the endless twilight of summer to mount his hunt. Somewhere, an amorous cat yowled.

Neferet walked as rapidly as she dared by the tiny light of her lamp. Her thoughts were simmering just as quickly. They needed to tail Pu-im-ra until the Hurrian made his move. But how to implicate Pu-im-ra himself? She wasn't sure the word of a hired assassin would be sufficient. They had to find proof that Rabbit had masterminded the murders of Sen-em-iah and his wife. *Perhaps the fat priest could be turned against him by an offer to save his own skin.*

At the red gate so familiar to her, Neferet knocked and

waited. And waited. "Iuty!" she finally called. "It's me. Open up."

She heard the sounds of unbarring then the gate swung open. Papa stood there, shirtless and wigless.

"My duckling," he said, his thick eyebrows rising in surprise. "Is everything all right? What are you doing here at this hour?" He made way for her to enter, and they embraced.

"We've found out who the man who killed the florist and his wife is! It's Rabbit—I mean Pu-im-ra, that smarmy priest. If you'd ever seen him, you'd know why they call him Rabbit. He and Sen-em-iah were up to some kind of corruption together, and—"

But Papa held up a hand. "Easy, my girl. Come inside and go over this more slowly."

They sat knee to knee in the dark salon like a pair of conspirators while one of the servants set lamps on the lampstands, and Neferet told her father everything they had learned from Wabet.

"So now you just need to lay hands on that Hurrian before he can kill Rabbit." She sat back in satisfaction.

"Bravo, my girl! You've given us the bait we needed for our trap." Papa clapped her on the shoulder. He called out for the servant to bring him his writing case and a piece of papyrus. "I want to get a message to Menna right away. The sooner we can put a tail on your bucktoothed priest, the less likely this Ullum-tishni is to get away."

"And we need to get some evidence on Rabbit, too, Papa. He's cheating the Hidden One somehow."

"He may confess if he finds himself in the Hurrian's clutches."

The servant returned, and Papa took a seat on the floor and crossed his legs, spreading his kilt taut. Upon it, he unrolled the bit of papyrus. He wet his block of ink and chewed the end of the reed pen. "Let's see. 'Regarding the case we've talked about, the time has come to set a couple of men to watch the priest—'"

"He's a *hem-netjer* and in charge of everything to do with the divine cult," Neferet interrupted. "His assistant is Tetiky. You should watch him too. They're both involved."

"'The *hem-netjer* Pu-im-ra, known as Sekhat, who is in charge of articles for the divine cult.' You don't happen to know where he lives, I suppose?"

"No, but I'll certainly find out. Djehuty-mes will know, I bet anything."

"What Djehuty-mes?"

"Lord Ptah-mes's son. He put us onto the man from the start."

Papa nodded. He looked serious and focused. "Find out for me, can you, duckling?" He resumed writing. "'Also keep an eye out for the priest Tetiky, who is Pu-im-ra's subordinate.' I hope there won't be any problem with soldiers trailing a servant of the god. I don't know what the jurisdiction is here."

Neferet snorted. "They didn't seem to have any scruples when they executed Lord Mai and the resisters."

As soon as Papa had completed his letter, he folded it up and sealed it. He called the servant over. "Take this to battalion commander Menna at the garrison, will you, please? Don't let them put you off. If anyone tries to deflect you, tell them it's by order of the vizier."

The man shot off into the night, and Neferet rose

to her feet. She was all tingly with excitement and could hardly bear to go back to the dispensary and go to sleep. "I amputated a man's foot today, Papa."

"You seem cheerful for a woman who's just cut off a man's foot," he said with a grin.

"It saved his life, I hope. He would have died for sure if we hadn't. Ibet sewed it up afterward. I was *done* for. So we have to stay there all night to take care of him."

"You seem to have revived." He chuckled then grew more serious. "Neferet, my duckling, please take the litter back. I'd like to think there were four sturdy fellows with you on the way home. We're involved with some rough characters."

"Or I could stay here overnight," she said, feeling a pitter-patter of guilt up her neck. Weariness had just started to replace fizzy energy, and the thought of a real bed was almost too sublime to be refused. "We don't have any beds yet. The patient is on the only table."

"What about Bener-ib? Where's she sleeping?"

That did it. Guilt had her firmly by the throat. "She's on the floor. All right. I'll go back."

"Why don't you take a mattress back with you, at least?" Papa suggested, repressing a grin.

"Excellent idea." She hugged her father. "You're full of excellent ideas, Papa Duck. Maybe two mattresses. Mut-tuy is there too."

He disappeared into the guest bedroom and emerged with a sack of straw, filling the room with its fresh, herby scent. "Here's one. Do you need sheets?"

"Probably." She hadn't even thought of that.

"I'll send an extra servant along to carry all this. You'd

better get back before it's too late. There'll still be people awake, so it won't be too dangerous."

Neferet would have to admit that she dozed off during the trip back to the dispensary—the close heat, the darkness, and the silence were too tempting a combination. The swaying of the litter, coordinated with the tramp of the bearers' feet, was like a cradle rocking. Only when the motion stopped did she come groggily back to herself. They were at the gate of the dispensary. Not a noise greeted them.

"I'll take that bedding in," she said, relieving the servant of the straw sacks and linen. "You all can go on home. Thank you."

"You sure you don't want us to carry it in for you, my lady?" asked one of the men.

Neferet had a suspicion that Bener-ib and Mut-tuy might have gone to bed completely undressed, since they had no additional clothing. The injured man was deep under the influence of the poppy juice and certainly wouldn't be peeking. "No, that's all right."

They set down the big roll and the folded sheets, turned the litter, and marched away into the silence.

Silence. As she pushed open the gate, it struck her how abnormal that was. *Why don't the dogs bark? Are they asleep?* She peeked around in the darkness. There was no moon at this hour, and the courtyard was swallowed up in the darkness of the fig tree. She could see a lighter patch that had to be the kilt of the sleeping guard. Of the dogs, there was no sign. Her heart leaped into her throat. Something was wrong.

"Ibet? Mut-tuy?" she called softly. "Are you awake?"

No answer. She tiptoed to the door of the building, which stood open.

"Ibet?"

The interior was black as charcoal. The little fire in the brazier had burned down. No lamp was lit. She heard a kind of rhythmic growl from the back room and groped her way there. The patient was tossing and groaning on his table.

Time for another dose of sepen. *Why hasn't Ibet given him any more?* Her heart was walloping her chest by this time. Something was badly wrong.

With trembling fingers, she felt around for a lamp and a bow drill. She could hardly still her shaking enough to get an ember alight and ignite the lampwick. A tiny orange flame blazed out, filling the room with monstrous shadows.

"Ibet? Mut-tuy?" she cried again, louder.

Great One, protect us—where are they? Neferet tottered into the salon. By the light of the lamp, it was terribly clear that there had been a struggle—the stools were overturned, baskets of bandages lay on the floor. Bener-ib and the orphan were nowhere to be seen.

"Dear gods! Has someone abducted them?"

But the dogs. The guard.

She rushed into the courtyard, tripping over the mattresses. "Brute! Mangler! Faithful! Where are you, boys?"

An examination of the perimeter revealed their four bodies stretched out around a pile of juicy bones.

"Oh no! Somebody's poisoned them!" she screeched, and knelt at their sides, tears flooding down her cheeks.

But to her enormous relief, all of them were breathing.

Brute was even stirring a little as if coming back to consciousness. *Drugged.*

Against the other wall, the guard was slumped, his legs extended before him. He, too, was alive, snoring roughly, but she could see a big lump rising on his bare scalp.

A chill of fear tingled up her neck. *What happened?* Someone had drugged the dogs and overpowered the guard. And then they'd taken Bener-ib and Mut-tuy. *Were they looking for me?*

She blew out the lamp, afraid that its light made her a target, and stared around her into the moonless blackness with owl eyes. One of the attackers could still be lurking on the property, ready to pounce on her from any dark corner of the house. Every instinct warned her to run—run to a neighbor's, run home. Yet she couldn't abandon Pa-iry, lying alone, injured, and unconscious.

Neferet pressed herself into an angle of the courtyard wall, hidden beneath the spreading branches of the fig. Nobody could see or sneak up on her there. She needed to think. First of all, who had done this? It struck her as unexpected that the Hurrian assassin had so carefully knocked out the guard and drugged the dogs. He seemed more like the sort who would kill them outright.

But who else could it have been? Undoubtedly the same person who had ransacked their dispensary, whoever that was. When that failed to scare them off, the unknown enemy had returned and abducted Bener-ib and Mut-tuy. She would have sworn that was Djed-har, but he had an alibi. *And would he have taken Bener-ib, who saved his life?*

Oh, Ibet. Gods knew where she was or what kind of danger she was in. *And that little girl I'm responsible for. If it had something to do with the murder of Sen-em-iah, they were probably after me, but I wasn't here.* Neferet buried her face in her hands, guilt washing over her in a stinging wave. *Mut the mother of us all, protect them. What's going on? Who has done this?*

A sharp silver wash of moonlight had begun to bleed over the trees, whitening the court. The dogs were getting groggily to their feet, shaking their heads and nearly knocking themselves down again. They toddled to her, not appearing to be concerned by the presence of any unwanted visitors, which reassured Neferet that the attackers had departed. She wanted to rush off and alert Papa or Lord Ptah-mes to send out servants to look for Ibet, but she dared not leave until Wabet arrived at dawn to take her husband home.

Emboldened by the dogs' nonchalance, she ventured into the house again, laboriously relit her lamp, and started up the coals in the brazier. Pa-iry needed tending. Neferet felt his forehead—no sign of fever. She gave him another dose of *sepen* and changed his bandages, which didn't betray any undue leakage. This all must have happened recently since the guard was still unconscious. Her thoughts were fractured, jumping from observation to observation, always coming up against an impatience to be off in search of Ibet, though she had no idea where to start looking.

She sat down on the floor and cradled the heads of the dogs, who snuffled and nudged her in embarrassment. All at once, it struck her that Brute could follow Ibet's scent. But she couldn't go anywhere while the injured man lay untended on the table.

"Hullo?" a blurry voice murmured from the doorway.

Looking up, she saw the silhouette of the guard, rubbing his skull in confusion.

"You're awake! Somebody hit you over the head." Neferet scrambled to her feet and rushed to the man. He needed to sit down. She led him to a stool. "Do you remember anything about what happened?"

"All I remember is hearing a rustling and thinking it must not be anything serious because the dogs never barked. I got up to look anyway, and all at once, things went black."

"When was this?"

"Can't have been much after sundown. You hadn't been gone too long. I… I'm awful sorry, my lady."

"What could you do? They gave the dogs meat with some drug on it. They were sound asleep until just now." *Who would have known where to get poppy juice like that? Does this point us back to Djed-har?*

"Did they steal anything?" he asked.

"I don't think so. But Lady Bener-ib and Mut-tuy have disappeared."

CHAPTER 19

THE MAN STIFFENED WITH HORROR then tried to fall to his knees. "Oh no! Oh, my lady, I've failed you. The master will be furious."

But Neferet had an idea, and she didn't relish wasting time on the servant's blame. "What I want of you is to sit by this patient's side until his wife comes. She'll be here at dawn. He's doing all right, so just watch that he doesn't roll off the table or something. I'm going to track down Lady Bener-ib."

The man nodded slowly, still fuddled.

"And your replacement will be coming at about the same time. When he comes, I want you to run home and tell Lord Ptah-mes what's happened and where I've gone."

"Yes, my lady. Where *have* you gone?"

"To look for Bener-ib." She hoped he would remember. He didn't seem to be at his sharpest.

Itching with the desire to be off, Neferet found Brute's leash and tied it around his collar. He knew he was at work now. She let him thrust his nose into Ibet's dirty shift, hoping her scent and not that of Pa-iry's blood would captivate the dog's interest.

Once he had snuffed his fill, she said urgently, "Find! Find Ibet!"

With his nose glued to the floor, the mastiff began sniffing frantically, and in no time, he charged out the door and across the courtyard to the gate.

Neferet unbarred it, and the animal lunged down the street, pulling her after him. The trail of Ibet seemed to be beckoning him.

Neferet asked herself whether this meant Bener-ib was on her own feet or if she could be carried and still leave such a recognizable spoor. She clung to anything that might be construed as good news. Her heart was hammering. *Let her be all right.*

She'd charged out without a lamp, but the moon was high, and the narrow canyons between garden walls were alternately deep in purple shade and bright as day. Her shadow and that of Brute snaked along the lanes, rippling over every rock and pothole. Rats scuttled against the walls, but the dog never lifted his head. He was profoundly focused on his mission.

Neferet, her gaze locked on Brute, was hardly aware of what neighborhoods they were passing through until she saw the undulating wall of a temple rise up ahead of her. It wasn't the Ipet-isut, but then, many gods received the worship of the people of Waset. Brute took a hard left, and she followed, hanging onto the leash, as they passed alongside a stone-lined channel. A few boats bobbed at anchor. The terrain looked familiar, but everything was so altered by moonlight that she couldn't place it. Houses were scattered. Palm groves shaded the open spaces as if this were deep in the countryside.

I've seen this before.

It dawned on her at last. *The abandoned house where the three assassins holed up. But surely they aren't still here after the police raided them.* The thought of those ruthless criminals with Bener-ib and Mut-tuy in their clutches sent a wild flush of fear up her cheeks.

Yet Brute tunneled on, his nose working systematically, never lifting from the earthen street. Eventually he snuffled down a long wall that had to enclose some good-sized estate and busied himself back and forth at the gate. Finally, he raised his head as if to say this was as far as he could go.

As usual, the owner's name and titles were written over the gateway, but they were in the formal signs of the speech of the gods, and Neferet had never learned to read them. She normally had need only of the priestly cursive in which all but the most important of manuscripts were written. Now she cursed her ignorance.

She gave a gingerly push, but of course, the gate was barred in the middle of the night and there would be a gatekeeper at a house of this importance. *How can I get in?* If only she dared turn to the *medjay* for help, but clearly, that wasn't an option. The thought that Bener-ib might be held just inside that wall was enough to drive her frantic.

Neferet passed feverishly up and down the outside of the wall, hoping to find a breach or an overhanging branch—some way to mount its formidable height. Sure enough, just around the corner, where a spreading tree blocked the moonlight, a cart was tipped against the wall, its traces standing upright. A box had been placed on top of what had originally been the outside front of the vehicle. *Steps.* It was there precisely to be climbed.

Her heart pounding like a pestle in a mortar full of grain, the young woman approached the cart.

Brute seemed interested in it, giving everything a thorough sniff.

She turned quickly to the dog and, squatting, untied his leash.

"Go get help, boy," she whispered. "Go home. Get master. Home."

She didn't know if he was trained to such a command, but his small eyes met hers with intelligent comprehension, and he loped off into the darkness of the lane. *Please the gods he knows what I asked and will do it*, she thought, a cold sweat bathing her temples. She rolled the leash up—it might be useful—and put her foot into the cart. It rocked but didn't overturn. With the aid of the wheels, she hoisted herself onto the front, which rested against the wall, and since it supported her weight, she climbed carefully onto the box. There was nothing to hold onto but the two shafts into which a donkey would be harnessed. She pressed herself against the wall and rose shakily to her full height. To her surprise, she was head and shoulders above the top of the wall, which was studded here and there with sharp stones. She pulled herself up until she was perched on its edge, hiked up her skirts, and stretched a leg across the surface. It was impossible to avoid the rocks. She gritted her teeth against the pain as they scraped her legs. They would slow her down but not stop her.

Still, she wasn't sure she dared drop down to the other side without being able to see what she was landing on.

The result could be a huge crash, or worse, she could turn an ankle. At last, she knotted the leather leash around one of the projecting stones and lowered herself over the inner side of the wall, sliding down while buffering herself against the surface with her feet. The ground seemed to be uncultivated, strewn with branches, probably of the fig tree. She eased her weight carefully over them to avoid crackling. *Please don't let there be dogs or geese around.*

She was inside someone's garden, but she could make out nothing much. Patches of moonlight reflected between the shade of branches. Ahead, it shone silvery on the walls of a large house. Everything was dark and silent. A hunting nightjar rattled overhead, a desolate sound. Toward the house, she could see the skeletal white of gravel paths and a large rectangle of sparkling darkness that must have been a pool.

If only I knew where I was going. Her pulse thundered so loudly in her ears she feared it was audible all around.

As she drew near to the house, a faint murmur of voices stopped her in her tracks. She melted back into the shadows of the trees and held her breath. Two men were speaking in a volume barely above a whisper. They seemed to be standing on a porch—she could see only a block of darkness with occasional flashes of movement within.

"So, have you hidden everything?" said one.

"Same as always," the other said in an exasperated tone.

"Ah, but it's not the same as always," the first man said. "People are watching us now. You must be extra careful." He couldn't pronounce his *R*s.

Had Neferet had any hair, it would have stood on end. *Rabbit! So that's whose house it is.*

"We need to restructure completely now that Sen-em-iah is out. His son won't come along, and I don't want any of us compromised by soliciting him."

"How much do you think he's told anybody?"

"Other than to his wife and what the steward overheard? I don't know. I don't think the son knows anything, or he would have squawked."

"He's notified the *medjay* and those damned females. And I told you, Ullum-tishni said some man came to him with a suspicious commission. He thinks he should go to ground."

Rabbit's voice rose peevishly. "*He* thinks? What about his contract with me? I have work for him to do."

Silence greeted this remark. Neferet pictured the other man shrugging.

After a pause, the second man said, "We should draw back from Sen-em-iah's family. It will start to look strange if one after another of his household dies violently."

"Naturally. There isn't anyone left who can identify us. We'll just have to find another man on the ground. Someone who deals in commodities that are easy to fill with contraband."

In the darkness, Neferet's eyes widened. The summer night seemed suddenly chill. *Contraband?* The florist everybody loved and had nothing but kind words for was part of a gang passing contraband. And even worse, priests of the Hidden One were involved. These men had shown how desperate they were to keep their identities hidden—and they had Bener-ib and Mut-tuy. She shrank into the shadowy branches. Her eyes had become accustomed to the blackness, and she could make out patches of lighter darkness on the shadowed porch that must be the caftans of the speakers. She could only hope her own dress was not equally visible.

The voices grew fainter as if the men had moved away. "How safe are our contacts in the *medjay*? If there's an investigation, are they going to be found out?"

"As long as we pay them, they're safe. But I told you, the new chief is trying to horn in on their share. It's possible Mahu might turn them in if he doesn't get a cut for himself."

Neferet strained her ears and heard muffled curses.

"If he doesn't back off these raids, we need to do more than pay him off," said Rabbit grimly. "We don't want all this attention turned to us. He's playing a double game, mark my words."

The voices dropped again, and the girl edged gently into the bushes to slide closer. A branch cracked beneath her feet, and she froze.

"What was that?"

"I heard nothing."

After a suspicious silence, during which Neferet held her pose with banging heart, Rabbit said, "We have to do something about those women. Ullum-tishni said they were involved in trying to engage him, and they've been sniffing around the flower farm."

"The ones who came to you?"

"Yes. The men said they escaped from the dispensary this afternoon."

Neferet almost emitted a cry of relief. *Escaped! Great One be praised!* But then how was it Brute had followed

Ibet's spoor to this address? She shifted, and the leaves rustled.

"I tell you, I heard something."

Footsteps descended the porch steps. Neferet didn't breathe. She heard the crunch of sandals on the gravel approaching and tried to shrink back into the darkness. A second pair of steps hustled up. Her pulse throbbed in her temples. *Keep moving. Keep moving.* She squeezed shut her eyes so their gleam wouldn't betray her.

All at once, a hand snaked out and grabbed her roughly by the arm.

"I thought so," Rabbit said in triumph.

He jerked her out of the shadows. She pulled back, hoping to break loose, but a fat little man had blocked her escape. They both took hold of her and wrestled her toward the house. As soon as she had room to move, Neferet began to kick and writhe.

"Help! Watchman!" she shouted, digging in her feet so the two priests had to drag her. She had almost managed to detach her arms from their grip when a pair of servants came running and manhandled her into the house. They dumped her on the floor, where she crouched, panting and wary.

Rabbit stood over her, narrow eyed, like a malevolent hare, while his chubby colleague crossed his arms.

"It's the other one," said the latter.

"The wife of Lord Maya, or so she says."

"I am. And you'd better not hurt me, or he'll have the king call out the army on you." Neferet's stomach was aflutter with fear, but she confronted the men with bravado. Surely they wouldn't dare do anything to her. As long as Ibet and Mut-tuy weren't in the power of these men, she was untouchable.

"I'm afraid they'll have no idea where you've disappeared to, my dear. By the time the crocodiles are finished with you, you could be anybody."

"*Yahyah*, they know exactly where I am. My father is bringing troops right now, and our dog will lead them right to you." She tossed her head defiantly.

Rabbit and his companion exchanged uneasy looks.

"Where are our friends?" the skinny priest asked under his breath. "We should clear out of here."

The fat man waved his hands. "How would I know? They come and go as they will. I've never liked his degree of independence."

The *hem-netjer* turned to Neferet, staring down at her with a curled lip of contempt. "I'm not sure what the purpose of your meddling was, but it will bring you to a bad end."

"Was it you who wrecked our dispensary the first time?"

"I have better things to do than wreck dispensaries. It was probably that Djed-har."

Neferet's jaw dropped. "You know Djed-har?"

"He's a useful contact," Rabbit said smugly. "But I didn't tell him to do anything to your dispensary."

The girl didn't know what to think. It had never crossed her mind that the unlettered neighborhood healer had any connections in high places—crooked though they might be.

"One sometimes needs his drugs to knock people out temporarily. Or more permanently. Some jobs require a subtler hand than those of our friends."

Does he know his "friend" is in the pay of someone else with instructions to kill him? Neferet's heart was bursting with questions, but Pu-im-ra's patience seemed to have come to an end.

"Tie the girl up, you two. We'll take her with us when we go, and she can have an accident on the River." He turned and clip-clopped off into the dark recesses of the house. After staring at her consideringly, the fat man followed.

"Tetiky," she called after him softly.

He spun, seeming surprised to hear his name on her lips.

"Why did you want to get mixed up with that fellow? You're so much smarter than he is."

His eyes widened, then he took himself off in his companion's wake.

The two servants had brought a rope and wasted no time in trussing Neferet up, hands and feet. They left her only enough length to hobble but certainly not to run. She wasn't as hopeless as she might have been, however, because she counted on Papa to bring those troops. Lord Ptah-mes would act, too, as soon as Brute came back to him. If only he thought to follow the dog. If only Brute understood her directions to lead Ptah-mes here. If only the criminals wouldn't have gotten away by then. Upon the River, they would be out of reach of even Brute's powerful nose. And they would have her overboard as expeditiously as possible, she didn't doubt. She prayed her little inspiration to sow discord might bear fruit.

They left her on her face on the salon floor in the dark. She pulled herself to her knees and then, with the aid of a stool, to her feet. Shuffling even a few cubits was extremely laborious, but she made the effort nonetheless, hoping no one would come for her until she could hide in the garden. Perhaps they wouldn't have time to look for her when they vacated the premises. Inside, out of the moonlight, it was profoundly dark, and she wasn't even sure she was heading for the door.

All at once, a low voice whispered, "Nef'et!"

Neferet froze, unsure of her senses. She would have sworn Ibet had called to her. "Hullo?" she murmured.

Out of the shadow slid Bener-ib and Mut-tuy, staring about them nervously.

"Ibet!"

Her friend laid a finger across her mouth. "Hold still. We'll cut these ropes."

She produced a pruning hook or some sort of garden tool and, crouching, began to saw the bonds at Neferet's ankles. Next, she severed the shackles at her wrists. Neferet rubbed her arms in an ecstasy of relief. She was bursting with questions, but haste and silence were more important. The two hustled her soundlessly to the garden doorway, where they stumbled down the porch steps and out onto the moonlit gravel of the path. It wasn't comfortable going on bare feet, but the three were strongly motivated. They ran quietly back into the shadowy trees that fringed the wall.

"There's a leash hanging down the wall somewhere so we can climb up more easily," she whispered into Bener-ib's ear. "The cart is on the outside."

They groped along the wall for the hanging leather strap. Behind them, in the house, Neferet heard a shout. *Oh no. They've discovered I've gone.*

Sure enough, the orange light of torches flared near the residence. She could hear men running, orders shouted.

"Hurry! Hurry!" Neferet said.

"Here it is," hissed Mut-tuy.

"You go up first." Neferet practically picked her up bodily.

The girl hung onto the leash and swam her way upward to the top of the wall. She cried aloud in pain as she encountered the stones, but a moment later, a thud announced she had landed on the cart.

"You now, Ibet." Neferet shouldered her up with the strength of desperation. The little *sunet* was wiry as a monkey and shinnied her way, gasping for breath, over the top.

Neferet was left staring at the height of the wall. There was no one there to boost her as she had boosted them.

Bener-ib leaned down. "Hurry!"

Behind Neferet, the torches had dispersed throughout the garden. The sound of running footsteps approached. Neferet wrapped the leash around her waist and began to walk up the wall, but it was too hard to change grip. She clung to the strap with both hands and hauled herself up. Ibet tried to pull from above, but Neferet outweighed her. *Mut the Mother of us all!* Neferet puffed, terror crackling up her spine. *I can't believe this!*

The footsteps were getting closer. "Here she is!" someone shouted. A spearpoint bounced against the wall.

With a surge of desperate energy, she heaved herself across the top, ignoring the sharp rocks ripping at her. Something struck her on the buttocks, but hands dragged her down into the street. As soon as she scrambled to her feet, the three were running for their lives.

CHAPTER 20

W ELL BEHIND THEM, NEFERET COULD hear the gate swing open and the thunder of feet in the road. She had no idea which way led them out of the cul-de-sac, but she set off away from their pursuers, stumbling and flailing. Bener-ib and Mut-tuy, better built for speed, pounded at her side. As if by agreement, they all turned at the next intersection and then again at a gap in the walls, where a date grove waved. Once they were completely hidden in the shadows of the trees, their pace slackened and finally stopped. Neferet bent over and sucked in welcome drafts of air. Far behind them, their pursuers hammered on down the street.

Only then did she dare to whisper, "Thank you, people! Nobody's ever been such a welcome sight! Where did you come from?"

"We hid when the men came and ransacked the dispensary."

"It looked like there had been a fight. I was sure they'd taken you."

"No. But they tore up everything, looking for us."

"We hid on the high shelves with the casebooks," Mut-tuy said excitedly. "Because nobody had looked up there before, you know."

"We followed them when they left," Bener-ib continued. "I worried about leaving Pa-iry, but I knew you'd be back soon."

Neferet thought about how close she had come to sleeping at her parents' house, and it sent a cold wash of shame up her cheeks. "When I got back, I found the dogs drugged and the guard knocked out. I was sure you had been kidnapped. But Brute led me to you. That was Pu-im-ra's house, wasn't it?"

"I think so. We sneaked over the wall on that cart," Bener-ib explained. "We heard lots of incriminating things from his mouth."

"Me too. They and Djed-har are working together!"

Mut-tuy made an incredulous noise. But Bener-ib, ever practical, said, "Shouldn't we get out of this neighborhood? They may double back when they can't find us ahead."

The young women joined hands and crept silently through the grove to the other side. A lane wound lazily past between scattered houses, but in the darkness, Neferet couldn't say which direction led where. She would have given anything for a glimpse of the temple of Montu or the boat canal.

What they encountered instead was a block of soldiers marching quickly along by the light of torches. Wild with relief, Neferet led her companions to the men. At their head was Menna, her father's friend, armed and armored in his leather-scale cuirass with a padded scarf over his wig.

"Lady Neferet!" he cried, his dark face lighting up with surprise. "What are you doing here in the middle of the night?"

"We've just escaped from the people you've probably come to arrest. Some of them are on the streets, looking for us, but if you hurry, you'll find the rest of them at the house of the priest Pu-im-ra." She gave them general directions to reach the residence. "It's far and away the biggest one around there."

As the troops jogged past, she called, "Isn't Papa with you?"

"He and Lord Maya were coming separately." The men disappeared into the shadowy palm grove with a muffled clang of weapons.

"I hope that means Brute made his mission understood." Neferet stared after the soldiers. "Maybe we should follow Menna. It would be pure chance if we encountered Papa otherwise."

Bener-ib looked doubtful. "I would feel safer if we were farther away."

"But we're just going to get lost," said Mut-tuy. "There's less danger with the soldiers."

Bener-ib agreed reluctantly, and the three made their way back through the dark trees. Neferet felt so secure in Menna's proximity that she said in her regular voice, "It was hugely brave of you to follow those people. Why did they come in the first place?"

"To find you, from what they said. I... I think they intended to kill you. They obviously knew who we were and where we worked."

"And we figured that if we knew where they were

holed up, we could tell your father, and he could direct his soldiers there."

"They have at least one confederate in the police," Neferet said. "And probably in the flower fields, even after Sen-em-iah's death. And I'd be surprised if there wasn't one in Sen-em-iah's household. They seem to know everything that's going on."

"And Djed-har, you say. I'm disappointed." Bener-ib shook her head.

"He provides them drugs, I think. No surprise he's involved with something louche if you think about that house of his. How could he live like that on the income of a neighborhood healer?" She twisted her mouth in puzzlement. "It surprises me that they just knocked the dogs and the guard out instead of killing them, though. Makes me think it wasn't our Hurrian and his assassins."

"No, they were just servants."

Between the fronds of the date palms, the sky was starting to grow light, the stars paling. The short summer night would soon be over. Pa-iry would go home with his wife, and the guards would change at the dispensary. Lord Ptah-mes would get the complete version of the break-in— if he weren't already en route. In a few hours, the three young women would be home safe, with their case solved and their persecutors locked up.

Neferet's stride was broken by a jerk, and before she could react, somebody had her pinned against him, a knife chill at her throat. Bener-ib screamed and thrust Mut-tuy behind her.

Neferet's heart seemed to stop. Her arms were pinioned uncomfortably behind her by a grip of uncommon strength, but she could see nothing of her captor. She could only hear his sawing breath, smell the stench of sweat and fear, and feel the heat of his body against her back—and the threat of the sharp blade under her chin.

"Shut up," he said roughly in an accented voice. "Don't make a sound, or I'll slit her throat. You two—ahead of me. Get moving."

The three of them moved as if stunned. They stumbled on before him, and he manhandled Neferet with an occasional prod behind the knees. She dared not resist—the cold bronze was too close to her flesh.

"You, girl, are my safe pass out of here," he growled.

That means he won't be quick to kill me, she thought. But there were plenty of things he could do to her that might be worse than death. If the raiders of the dispensary had been unaccountably gentle to their victims, Ullum-tishni had not. She remembered Sen-em-iah with his entrails hanging out. She remembered his wife, her throat cruelly slit by the pressure of the garrot.

"But my father's hiring you," she stammered. "You're supposed to kill Rabbit."

"Whoever pays me most gets my loyalty," the Hurrian said with a grunt that might have been laughter. "Rabbit had a chance to pay me double your father's bid, and he thought it worthwhile. Smart move for such a jackal prick."

What a piece of crap. He'd sell his own mother for gold. Somehow, contempt drove out some of her fear, and she shuffled along in a swelling desire to see the man fall.

Ahead of them, in the growing dawn, Bener-ib and Mut-tuy walked quickly, hardly daring to look back now and then. The rigidity of their backs betrayed how frightened they were.

If only they could get away safe, I might be able to try something. But she couldn't say what. The man's one-armed grip was painfully tight, and his knife never budged. She could feel it bite into the skin now and again as their steps lurched over the uneven ground.

At last, they passed from under the trees into the street from which they'd originally come. A shadowless twilight filled the lane. The two girls in advance stopped and looked back questioningly, and Ullum-tishni directed them to the right, away from Pu-im-ra's house, where some major fracas must now be taking place. He took advantage of the growing light to hustle Neferet along still faster.

All at once, something struck the Hurrian with the force of a chariot collision and a noise like a lion. The two of them heaved forward.

Neferet could feel the blade press into her throat and tried to crane her head away. She thudded painfully to the ground, barely breaking her fall with a hand, and Ullum-tishni crashed on top of her. But he had troubles enough without hanging onto his prisoner. A great muscular brown creature had him pinned beneath its paws, snarling and tearing at his head and shoulders with slavering teeth. The knife fell from the man's hand, and he tried to protect himself with his arms. Neferet writhed out from under him, gaping in amazement. Brute had returned.

Neferet scrambled to her feet and skittered away from the twisting mass of man and beast, seething with growls and shrieks of pain, only to see her father and husband and a small group of armed servants running toward her. Bener-ib and Mut-tuy got there first and dragged her to safety.

"Don't let him hurt Brute!" she cried. But there didn't seem to be much danger of that. The dog was definitely getting the best of the human being.

Papa and Lord Ptah-mes ran up, armed and grim. Hani embraced the three young women, while Ptah-mes gave a piercing whistle, and Brute pulled back from his attack like a tide that had gone out. He stood proudly panting at his master's feet, blood dripping from his grinning lips. Ullum-tishni lay still, gore soaked but alive, judging from his heavy breathing. It looked as if he had lost at least an ear.

"Tie him up and take him to the garrison. The king will decide whether he's to be executed for his crimes or not." Ptah-mes gestured with his battle-ax, and two of the servants managed to scrape the dog-savaged man from the road. There wasn't much left of his face.

"Brute, my boy. You saved our lives!" Neferet threw herself on the mastiff's neck and caressed his wrinkly head, despite the blood.

"In every sense," said Ptah-mes with a thin smile. "He led us here. We would have had no idea where you were otherwise."

"I might have headed for that abandoned house," said Hani. "But Brute took us to a large private residence, where we found Menna and his troops already at work."

"We directed him there. It was that priest Pu-im-ra's house. Rabbit. Did you see him, Papa?"

"I saw somebody who resembled a rabbit, yes," Hani said with a grin.

"What are you three doing here?" asked Ptah-mes. "Did these blackguards kidnap you?"

"Well, no. They wanted to. They wanted to kill me, apparently. But Ibet and Mut-tuy hid from them and tracked them down. When I got back, I thought they'd been carried off, so I had Brute lead me to them. But then I was captured, and Ibet and Mut-tuy set me free. Everybody's saved everybody." Neferet was effervescent with relief at the night's happy ending. It had just sunk in how terribly different things might have been. If not for her friends' courage… if not for Brute's unerring nose… if not for Papa and Lord Ptah-mes and Menna…

"I'm curious to know what shady business united these characters," said Papa as the little group began a leisurely progress toward the house of Pu-im-ra. "What was it that Sen-em-iah tried to pull out of that precipitated his death?"

"Contraband, Papa. They were moving it somehow in his bouquets. I don't yet know what it was. But they have spies all over in that florist business. Every time we talked to Sen-em-iah's son, somebody reported us."

"Even Djed-har's in on it," said Mut-tuy eagerly.

"Who's he?" Lord Ptah-mes asked.

"That lying witch doctor near the palace magazines. The one who destroyed our dispensary. Now we don't know whether it was professional rivalry or a threat to back off this case."

"And the police are involved," said Mut-tuy.

Neferet shot her an admonitory look. "So it seems. And Mahu is probably looking to get his cut of it too."

Papa gave a whistle. "*Yahyah*, this is quite a network. A lot of institutions are going to be compromised if everybody is dragged out into the open. It's disgraceful enough that two high-level priests of the Hidden One are involved—as hard as we've all worked to get them back into power."

"Will they be punished, Lord Hani, or will the other priests protect them? Maybe they judge their own," Bener-ib asked shyly.

"If this is a case of passing contraband, it falls under my jurisdiction," said Ptah-mes. "After all, anything they move illegally is not having taxes paid on it. That means the vizier and the king himself will be involved. Only the king has the power to stand up to the priests unless they cooperate willingly."

"Let's go see how our troops are faring. They should have everyone mopped up by now." Papa clapped Neferet on the back and started to move out, but she gave a yelp of pain.

"Careful, Papa Duck. I'm all sliced up by sharp stones back there."

"We are too," said Mut-tuy. "Our dresses are all shredded."

"Second one ruined since yesterday." Neferet snickered.

At Pu-im-ra's house, the soldiers had the two priests and all the servants tied up, kneeling on the floor. The master of the house, his wig askew and face crimson with outrage, was expostulating haughtily nonetheless.

"This is not to be endured. We are servants of the god. You have no right to treat us like common criminals."

"Then you shouldn't act like common criminals," said Menna with his accustomed simplicity. "You're prisoners of the king now. He can do whatever he wants with you, priests or not."

Pu-im-ra saw Hani and Ptah-mes enter then caught sight of the girls behind them. "There are your criminals!" he shouted in a dramatic voice spoiled by his speech impediment. "That man contracted to have me killed."

"Apparently, you outbid him," said Neferet. "But your bravo is out of commission now anyway."

"And he will be dealt with according to the rules of international law." Hani smiled peaceably. His own role in the affair was concluded, but he wanted to know who else was involved in what seemed to be a wide network of smuggling. "I'm sure if you fellows cooperate and tell us what you know, the king will be inclined to show mercy."

He glanced at Lord Ptah-mes, who was his senior in rank. The treasurer's arms were folded, and his handsome face was granite. He didn't look like a man from whom much mercy could be expected.

"What punishment is severe enough for cheating the Hidden One and laying violent hands on women?" Ptah-mes said coldly. "You'd better have some extremely useful testimony…"

Brute pushed his way forward. Although his expression was calm, his jaws were covered in blood.

"Or we may consider leaving you to the same fate as that of your confederate."

Pu-im-ra's air of defiance crumbled. His close-set eyes grew round with fear.

"I'll tell you anything you want to know!" babbled the fat priest behind him.

Hani gave a snort. *Human nature at its most unsavory.*

They'll be competing to rat out their fellow the more completely, especially if they see the condition of Ullum-tishni. "Who're your accomplices among the *medjay*, and how have they been aiding you?"

Both men started to talk at once, but the fat one spoke more loudly. "My name is Tetiky. I'm an honest man whom this reprobate, who was my superior, tempted and corrupted."

"Answer my question," said Ptah-mes implacably, tightening his grip on his ax.

The man gave several names, of which Hani, wishing Maya were present, made mental note. "Someone should record their testimony," he murmured.

"I will, Lord Hani," said Bener-ib.

"Get her some papyrus and writing implements," Ptah-mes directed one of the servants.

Thus supplied, the girl sat on the floor with crossed legs and applied herself to her secretarial duties. Hani enjoyed the look of surprise with which the priests' eyes followed her actions.

"What about Mahu, the chief of police?" Hani asked.

"He was aware and wanted in on it. He was deliberately going slowly with the investigation, waiting to see if we wouldn't cut him in. He said if we didn't, he'd say he had been investigating his renegade *medjay* and would turn us all in."

He's seen to it that it's going to be hard to prove anything against him, thought Hani, disappointed. But it was reassuring that his instincts about Mahu had been on track. "Who were your confederates in the florist business, other than Sen-em-iah?"

"His foreman in the flower fields and several of the workmen. A gardener at his house. His wife and steward were aware of what was going on, but they weren't wholeheartedly part of us. That's why we had to..." Tetiky trailed off, realizing he was incriminating himself.

So has the steward been eliminated as well?

"What role did Djed-har play in this business?" Neferet looked as forbidding as her husband, with her hands on her hips and her straight brows drawn down.

Now it was Pu-im-ra who contended to be heard, afraid, perhaps, that all the clemency should fall upon his confederate. "He processed our *sepen* for us. He's a crucial link in the chain. He should be punished more harshly than we."

"Did he kill anyone?" asked Ptah-mes.

"No, but only because he's been sick. And if you consider all the people who may have died along the way..."

Hani realized he wasn't following. "What were you smuggling? How did that kill people, if that's what you mean?"

The two priests exchanged looks of hopelessness, and Pu-im-ra said, hanging his head, "*Sepen*, like I said. We were sending poppy juice upriver. We concealed it in bouquets to hide the smell."

Neferet gaped at her father then turned accusingly upon the priest. "How much were you sending? That's as expensive as can be."

"Not anymore," the bucktoothed priest said. "It can be grown here. And Sen-em-iah had fields of it. Some he used for the flowers, of course, but the rest was sent to Djed-har to process into juice. The men of Ta-nehesy were willing to pay almost anything for it."

"But how much do they need? It's only used sparingly in medicine."

"We're not talking about medicine," the fat priest said with a bark of laughter. "Some of the aristocrats use it for diversion."

Neferet was having none of it. "They knock themselves out for diversion? It would be cheaper to have a servant hit you over the head."

To everyone's surprise, Bener-ib spoke up from her place on the floor. "I've heard of that, Lord Hani. In mild doses, it has an effect like water lily—a kind of euphoria, like being drunk."

Neferet stared at her, uncomprehending. "Who would do that?"

The smaller woman shrugged. "People who like to get drunk."

"There are lots of them, believe me. And not just in Ta-nehesy. We sent it that way because it was less risky. We can ship it among cult bouquets for the Great Temple of Amen-Ra up there, and the customs officials don't even look at it." Pu-im-ra seemed pleased with his own cleverness.

"Have you no shame?" Ptah-mes spat in disgust. "Defiling the good name of the god like that and cheating the king of his taxes."

"Not to mention harming people. You have to know how to dose poppy juice, or it can kill a person," Neferet said hotly. "That Djed-har is as worthless as I suspected."

Lord Ptah-mes turned to Menna. "Take these men to the garrison and keep them under guard and send someone to arrest Djed-har. The vizier will want to know what's been going on. And I'll notify the mayor that his *medjay* are riddled with corruption. He can deal with them."

He spun on his heel and left the house, Hani at his side. Bener-ib scrambled to collect her writing tools, and Neferet and Mut-tuy hung back to accompany her. He heard Neferet say, "So much for friend Djed-har."

The young women caught up with them as the two men crossed the garden to the gate.

"I suppose we should notify the First Prophet about his two wayward shepherds. He'll need to replace them in their duties," Hani said.

"We never told In-hapy to make those vessels we were going to give the temple. I guess we can forget about them now." Neferet strode along at his side, seeming well pleased with herself.

But Ptah-mes said firmly, "No, no. You promised them to the god. Go ahead and donate them. And the flowers."

"Shouldn't we tell Pen-buy what has happened? He was trusting us to find his father's killer, and we did." Mut-tuy wasn't shy about making herself heard.

"He'll be wondering why soldiers have seized some of his employees, after all," Neferet said, nodding.

Hani, relieved that the danger was past, agreed. "No reason not to." He gave his daughter a squeeze around the shoulders. "You ladies have done a marvelous job in ferreting out these scalawags. I, er, I hope it won't become a habit." He grinned at her.

But she didn't return his smile and instead gave a sniff. "I fail to follow your logic, Papa."

CHAPTER 21

M ORNING WAS WELL ILLUMINED BY the time the
little party split off from the soldiers, who marched
the two miscreants and their servants back to the garrison.
Others had been dispatched to arrest Djed-har and the
complicit employees of the florists' establishment. Neferet
realized a pattern had formed: those who had shown
themselves hostile to the girls' investigation had been
hiding their own guilt. They wouldn't have wanted to see
anyone getting involved in uncovering the truth.

"Even Djed-har," she said to Bener-ib as they walked.
"Of course he didn't want us around. His whole posture as
a healer was probably a front for his trade in *sepen*."

"I think he took it himself and too much of it," said
Bener-ib sadly. "Between that and wine, he isn't in good
shape. I don't suppose he'll last long even if he isn't
executed."

"I'm curious how they hid the juice in bouquets,
though. As liquid? Dried in those awful, smelly blocks?
Mixed with wine and saffron?"

"We can look when we get to Pen-buy's." Mut-tuy was as energetic as if she hadn't been awake the entire night, running and climbing walls.

"I'm splitting off here," said Papa. "Bed calls, if there's a little time to rest before I go to the Hall of Royal Correspondence. Try to get some sleep, girls." He hugged the three of them and headed up the lane, a broad, solid figure with a rocking gait.

Neferet watched him go, her heart swelling with affection. For all that Papa could be annoying, he was the best of fathers. One always felt safe and loved with him around.

"If we want to see Pen-buy, though, we have to see him before everybody leaves the workshop and goes to sleep," she said, not without a note of regret.

"You ladies will forgive me if I go on," said Lord Ptah-mes. "I have to be at the Double House before too much longer. I have an audience with the king this morning—he's here for the festival."

"Thank you for all your help," Neferet said, sincerely grateful. If he'd been anyone else, she would have hugged him, too, right there in the street. "And the best thing of all was the gift of Brute. He saved our lives several times over."

Lord Ptah-mes smiled, his austere expression softening. He looked like a man who had been up all night, with no rest in sight. With a courteous nod, he and his servants headed off to their busy day.

Mut-tuy smothered a yawn. "Why is everybody going to work? Isn't there a holiday coming up?"

"The Beautiful Festival of the Valley is tomorrow,"

Bener-ib said. "The florists will be busier than ever tonight. We'd better talk to them soon."

"All right, people. Now's the time. We can go to bed afterward. To the workshop!" Neferet said.

They set off with the brisk, indefatigable steps of the young. By the time they reached Sen-em-iah's establishment, the night workers had dispersed, and only Pen-buy and a few of his high-level workmen were around, seeing off the porters with the final pole bouquets.

He looked up with red-rimmed eyes at the girls' approach. "Where have you been? I tried to get in touch with you yesterday evening to tell you my steward was found strangled."

"We were captives of his murderers," Neferet said grimly. "The deaths will stop now—the case is solved. Have you had any communication with your flower fields? Because that foreman, what's-his-name—"

"Imi-seba," said Bener-ib.

"And some of your workers were part of the plot. The soldiers have arrested them."

Pen-buy's eyes widened in confusion. "Arrested? Plot?"

Neferet explained the whole sordid affair—how his father and the two priests had been in league with a neighborhood healer to produce and smuggle valuable *sepen* over the southern border, concealed in flowers.

The florist gaped at them in incomprehension, then his plump face grew scarlet, and he said angrily, "You must be mistaken. My father couldn't have been involved with this vile business. He was the most honorable man to walk beneath the rays of Ra."

"He wanted out, but the priests threatened him. That's

why they killed him," said Bener-ib in her most consoling tone.

"No. I refuse to believe it." Pen-buy turned away, staring into the shadows.

Neferet would have sworn his lashes had grown starry with tears.

"Your stepmother was in his confidence, and the steward knew about it too. The priests couldn't leave any of them alive."

"No. Anybody but him. You never knew Father. He was a good man. Ask anyone. All his workmen loved him." But his knit brow suggested Pen-buy was thinking hard. After a moment, he said with less confidence, "He was troubled about something. He didn't want me to see his books."

Neferet said nothing, just let acceptance grow reluctantly in the man. She understood how hard it must be to believe that his admired father had been in the heart of something so dishonest and even impious. She tried to picture her own beloved papa involved in some nefarious scheme and found it impossible. It was easier to imagine the Lord Ra falling from the sky.

After a long time, the florist asked in a strained voice, "Does that mean he can't have an honorable burial?"

"Oh no," Neferet assured him, although she had no idea if what she said was true. "He must have had his reasons. That's between him and the judge of souls." *Lucky for him, he died before he was disgraced, unlike the priests.* But she didn't feel sorry for them.

Pen-buy's whole body sagged with the weight of his growing comprehension and shame. "That young wife of his always wanted more. He had a whole second family to provide for."

"What we don't understand is how they hid things in the bouquets," Mut-tuy said with her usual forwardness.

Only a stack or two of the festive bouquets remained in the warehouse, awaiting their delivery to the temple. Pen-buy led the young women over and cut the colorful bindings of one with his penknife. He proceeded to pull the short-stemmed flowers out until only the bundled-reed staff was left. He opened the long, slender outer stems and exposed the sturdier skeleton of the structure. But instead of consisting exclusively of thick reeds that extended from top to bottom, several of these were hollowed out in the middle—essentially consisting of a top part and a bottom part, with a gap between them. And into the gap were tucked numerous little packets wrapped in large leaves. He drew one out and unrolled it, exposing a rock of a substance that looked like dark amber and smelled like cat piss. He looked up at the girls, his jaw dropping in astonishment.

"*Yahyah*," Neferet whispered. "So that's how."

Pen-buy cut open a second and third then a fourth and a fifth bouquet. Only two of them were solid. The others all contained a hidden surprise. The florist's face had grown set as if he was struggling with the painful but inevitable conclusion.

"Look!" Bener-ib said. "The ones with poppies at the top have *sepen* inside. The ones with other flowers don't."

"That's how they marked the ones to send south." *Pretty clever.*

"Three out of five? So few of the day's bouquets are real

and destined for the Ipet-isut? That's shocking," Pen-buy stammered. "No wonder the books were confused."

Neferet shrugged. "Maybe most of the contraband came at the very end of the night like this. Perhaps they thought you'd be less likely to examine the flowers closely after you'd seen thousands of them and time was running short."

Pen-buy pinched the bridge of his nose as if he was overwhelmed. "No matter how closely I looked, I wouldn't have seen anything. How can I thank you for bringing this all to light? Take this *sepen*, I beg you. You're doctors. You can use it for something good."

"We'll take a few blocks, but it really belongs to the king. It's contraband, after all. We'll tell the soldiers to collect it." Neferet picked a nice rock or two and pushed the rest away. "They may make you tear up your poppy fields."

"That's all right. Beautiful as the flowers are, I'd rather not remember this awful experience."

They bade the man goodbye and wished him a blessed festival on the morrow. It was, when all was said and done, the commemoration of the family dead, and he had more than his share of them all at once.

As they trudged away toward home, readier than ever for a few hours of sleep, Bener-ib said, "I really would like to see Djed-har one more time. He must have lost much of his arrogance. I think most of it was defensive anyway. We must have posed a terrible threat to his profitable side business."

"No point in tending to his health now, Ibet, my girl,"

Neferet said dryly. "They'll probably put him to death before he dies of natural causes."

"Oh, I know," she murmured, dropping her eyes. "I just…"

Neferet realized that this was something Ibet really wanted, although she would never push for it. She always formed an extremely close bond with her patients. "Well, why not? We can say hello to Pa-kiki while we're at the garrison. Papa said he's become chief scribe down there."

Mut-tuy rolled her eyes and made a dramatic expression of martyrdom, but despite her, the three continued past their own neighborhood, where their beds awaited them, down to the vast walled enclosure of the garrison, with its grim towers at every corner. It had the look of a place where malefactors might be held, to emerge only as corpses.

"I'm the sister of the chief scribe, Pa-kiki," Neferet announced at the gate. "May we speak to him?"

"I'm sorry, my lady," said the soldier on guard. "He's in consultation with General Har-em-heb's adjutant and can't be disturbed."

"Ah! Pa-ra-messu is here in Waset? That's all right. We'll see him tomorrow. Please take us to see the prisoner Djed-har, then. We were part of the party that arrested him."

The soldier looked conflicted. "I'm not sure I can."

"Ask Commander Menna. We were with him."

He dodged off to consult with Menna, and a moment later, that officer himself appeared, as cheerful and welcoming as always, despite the sleepless night of activity.

"Lady Neferet! Still up? What can I do for you?"

"We'd like to see the prisoner Djed-har, if you don't mind. Professional courtesy, you might say."

His toothy smile faded. "Oh, my lady, you weren't aware, were you? When we went to arrest the healer, we found him dead. I seized his old servant, just in case he could answer any questions. If you want to talk to him…"

Neferet and Bener-ib exchanged looks of surprise and sorrow.

"All right. Let's see him," Neferet said.

In a somber mood, they trooped after the officer into the courtyard of one of the buildings. Tied up to rings in the wall were all of those arrested in the affair. Imi-seba and several sun-blackened workmen occupied a reluctant proximity. The two priests kept to themselves, away from the lower-caste men who surrounded them. Djed-har's desiccated old servant crouched by himself, his face in his hands.

"Hello," said Bener-ib, touching his shoulder.

The old man's head jerked up. He gaped at the three women expressionlessly. "My master is dead."

"That's what they tell us. Was it his liver after all?" Bener-ib squatted at his side.

"No, mistress. He… He ended his life. He said he didn't want to be tortured and put to death by the soldiers. I'm sure the gods will forgive him."

"They may forgive him that, but I don't know about making *sepen* to smuggle to the men of Ta-nehesy. That would go against his oath to heal," said Neferet severely.

"He meant no harm," said the old man, all his hauteur drained out. "He always said the gods liked to see people happy and relaxed. It was sacred, like drunkenness."

"But he had to know that without a doctor to set a precise dose, that stuff is really dangerous. It's not like water lily. I'm afraid he was lying to himself, just like he lied to everybody else about us and about his qualifications. I suppose he wrecked our dispensary too."

"N-Not personally. He sent me to do it. He said it wouldn't hurt anybody. You could afford to replace everything."

Neferet made a noise of disgust. "As if that makes any difference. There are people who had to go untreated because we didn't have supplies. I'm afraid your master was just making excuses for himself. He was a baaad man."

Bener-ib got to her feet. "I'm sure they'll let you go," she said kindly. "None of this was your doing."

From across the court, a peremptory voice that couldn't pronounce its *R*s said loudly, "You, over there! Have you come to set us free?"

Neferet shot an impatient glance at Pu-im-ra. She'd had about enough of men who thought they could do anything they wanted. "Wait your turn," she said in an equally loud voice.

With deliberate slowness, she strolled over to the two priests. They were in the full morning sun and had to squint to look up at her. A trickle of sweat already dribbled from beneath Tetiky's wig.

"Good morning," she said cheerily. "I have just one question. How did you meet Djed-har? He seems a little below your circle of tony friends."

"Through a servant of mine. He lived in the old man's neighborhood and knew he had flexible morals." Pu-im-ra seemed pleased with his ingenuity. Perhaps he'd misinterpreted Neferet's dangerous good humor.

"He's dead, you know. He preferred to die rather than

face what you're going to suffer. Say goodbye to your nose and ears, friends."

Pu-im-ra froze for a moment. "Hasn't the First Prophet intervened? He'll get us released."

"I don't know anything about that," she said with a careless shrug. "If he has any honor, he'll surrender you to the worst sort of capital punishment. You've stolen from the god and from the king."

"But we're priests. We're *hemu-netjer*. You can't do that to us!"

"I'm not doing it. The king is. Or he could just turn you over to a large and ferocious dog, like your fellow conspirator."

The two men exchanged wide-eyed looks of horror.

"Or impalement," said Muy-tuy with gusto.

"Who's that bloodthirsty child?" demanded Pu-im-ra in an unsteady tone.

"The voice of the people, Rabbit, my friend." With a smug smile, Neferet and her companions turned and moved away.

Behind her, she could hear Pu-im-ra murmur, "'Rabbit'? What does she mean by that?"

And Tetiky, in a voice that suggested he enjoyed breaking the news to his superior now that he had nothing to fear from him, said, "That's what those common criminals called you, my lord. We all did."

✦

The next day was the festival in which the king and the Hidden One and his family mounted their golden barques and journeyed across the River to pay their respects to the late kings of the Theban dynasty. Of course, the last few rulers had been buried in the hellhole known as the Horizon of the Aten, so mostly, that meant the late, lamented Neb-ma'at-ra and his ancestors. And with the gods, the inhabitants of Waset flocked to the west bank to feast with their own dead. It was one of those holidays that was a little somber and mostly joyous—a celebration of family, living and dead.

Just as she had done when she was a child, Neferet's nieces and nephews had made little boats of papyrus to set loose on the River and leave at the family tomb. Bener-ib and Mut-tuy had tried to show the orphans how to make some for their own father, but most of the children were too small, and all of them were too unruly, so Hu-may and his elder sister had done it themselves. Soon would come the best part of the day—the uninhibited family banquet with their deceased relatives, right there in the courtyard of the tomb. Plenty of beer and picnic dishes. And meat roasted at the edge of the desert over fires that twinkled into the twilit sky until late in the endless summer evening.

Neferet and Bener-ib had herded the children to Neferet's parents' house early in the morning so they could get into position in the floating procession. Now they waited on the deck of Papa's cheery red-and-green yacht, while Sati and Maya and their brood and Pa-kiki and Mut-nodjmet and their little ones clambered on board, laughing and screeching, papyrus boats clutched in their hands. Aha would join his wife's family until later, when he'd make a visit to his own ancestors.

Neferet leaned on the gunwales with her forearms, gazing out across the sparkling waters at the magnificent divine barges gathering at the temple quay. Everything was as bright and full of color as a tomb painting—or the flower fields. She took a deep sniff of the rich, overripe River.

"Could things get any better?" she dreamily asked Bener-ib at her side. "Ma'at has been done, and all's right with the good gods' creation. Here we are with our family, and everybody's healthy, and it's a beautiful day."

Bener-ib leaned against her with her shoulder. "It's wonderful, all right. I just wish my parents weren't buried so far away."

Neferet turned to her with her mouth open. She'd never actually thought about that. "Oh, that's right. They're buried at Sau. Some year, we need to go up there for the Beautiful Festival of the Valley so you can feast with them."

"But nobody celebrates it up there."

"No?"

"There are no kings buried there. And no Ipet-isut."

Neferet gave a pondering *hmmm*. So many things she had never considered. "Well, you're part of our family now, anyway, my Sweet Heart."

From farther down the boat, Uncle Pipi's voice, excited as a child's, rose. "The User-het-amen is raising its anchors. They're getting ready to move, everybody!"

The whole family crowded to the same side of the yacht, squeezing together for the best view of the divine barque as it glided majestically into the stream in the wake of its tugboat. Neferet lifted Tiry in her arms, while Qen and Shu-roy and the older orphans glued themselves to the gunwales.

"How many boats are there, Tiry?" Neferet asked the toddler.

"*Hamtau*," Tiry answered promptly with her favorite number. As if to confirm, she held up four stubby fingers.

Mut-tuy snorted and shook her head in disgust. "Stupid. You said three, but you held up four fingers. Neither one of which is right."

Neferet was on the verge of correcting the adolescent for spoiling the day's joyous atmosphere with her bad temper, but it occurred to her that it probably wasn't very happy for Mut-tuy. On this feast of family closeness, she had to be highly conscious that she herself had no family except for her siblings—her father and grandfather were dead, and her mother had abandoned them all. Neferet would have slipped an arm around the girl, but such a gesture probably wouldn't have been well received.

The little girl in Neferet's arms began to chew on something she was holding.

"Wait, what's this, Tiry?" Neferet said, extracting a crumpled papyrus boat from the child's fist. "You were supposed to put this in the water—and I don't mean the water inside your mouth." She straightened it out and noticed that there was writing on it, which wasn't unusual—Lord Ptah-mes had given them a sheaf of used papyrus to cut up. But the content caught her eye. And the date.

"Why, this just came yesterday—and it's addressed to me!" Neferet caught Bener-ib's eye, puzzled. "Who wrote to me? I never saw any letter." She deciphered the lines that remained and burst out laughing. "A servant must have mixed it up with the old pieces. It's from some exorcist priest. He says he lifted the curse and sent it back on the one who cast the spell. I *thought* our luck had turned!"

And so, sadly for him, had Djed-har's. Curses were powerful things and cut two ways.

Another reason to be happy. "Here, Mut-tuy—one more boat to put at your father's tomb." She passed the chewed and spindled thing to the girl with a wink. "Tiry knew what she was doing."

And Mut-tuy, who had been under the curse, too, grinned with relief in spite of herself.

Neferet threw an arm around her and gave her a sisterly squeeze. "Thanks for all your help, my girl."

After that, the User-het-amen slid the smaller barques of Mother Mut and Khonsu, son of the Hidden One, and finally the king's own gilded boat. The royal lad sat under the golden sunshade, as still and solemn as a god in his cabinet.

"That's Har-em-heb beside him and the queen, isn't it?" asked Papa. He and Mama stood arm in arm like the king and queen of their own familial nation.

Only then did the other vessels slide into the current, their backwash churning the white dots of the children's paper boats that floated like flower petals on the swirling water. Among them glided Papa's little red-and-green boat with its Bes-head prow and cargo of excited children.

"Look, there's Lord Ptah-mes's yacht. His children will all be there to visit Lady Apeny's tomb." Neferet pointed against the sun at the long, sleek black-and-green craft.

"Are you going to visit his family tomb, my love?" asked Mama. "That would be a nice gesture after everything he's done for all of us." She stooped to stroke back the hair of Beket-iset, who lay on her couch at her side, smiling with joy.

"Later," Neferet said. "It's much more fun with you people."

Grandfather chuckled. "They don't seem like a particularly jolly bunch, it's true. Whereas we…" He linked arms with his two sons. "We're one of the jollier bunches. Right, boys?"

"Right!" everyone cried in unison, and their warm laughter echoed over the water.

Neferet wished she could preserve this moment forever—all these family members in good health and in love, the woman of her heart at her side, this gold-and-blue day washed in sunshine. *But we're heading west. Isn't that what all of life is—sailing to the West in the company of those you love?*

As so often happened, Ibet seemed to have read her thoughts. She said quietly, "I guess the families of all those men who were condemned for smuggling aren't so happy today."

"But they chose to side with Chaos," Neferet said, a little miffed that her joy should be tarnished.

Bener-ib nodded, looking philosophical.

On the other side of Neferet, seemingly too far away to have heard their conversation, Baket-iset said, apropos of nothing, "Only the god knows a man's heart. Not everybody who does evil is evil."

Neferet had to admit that Sen-em-iah seemed to have been a well-loved person, and people were rarely well loved without deserving it. She hoped that Pen-buy's prayers would get his father through the Weighing of Hearts. But she wasn't so sure about Pu-im-ra and the others. She had a feeling Ammit the Devourer was going to feast.

"Did we get any of the blessed flowers?" Sati asked.

"Of course." Mama smiled. "I saw to it we got some of the ones that had been closest to the god, right in the sanctuary. They're all piled in the kiosk, out of the sun."

"From flowers to wives—only the finest for our family," Papa said fondly, pressing Mama to his side.

Exchanging a look with Bener-ib and Mut-tuy, Neferet snickered. "Better check inside those bouquets, though!"

THE END

Have you enjoyed this book? Here is a sample from the next *Hani's Daughter Mystery*, **Web of Evil**:

CHAPTER 1

I T WAS LATE IN THE season of Akhet, Harvest, and the precocious heat of spring had only intensified. Neferet and Bener-ib hadn't been sorry to deliver the children to the farm to spend a few weeks in the relative cool of the open countryside. They themselves came nearly every weekend holiday, when Mama and Baket-iset, Sati and her children, and Mut-nodjmet and her brood were also likely to be around.

"This is perfect for the orphans," Neferet said, staring after the little ones, who had just gone running off amidst a pack of over-stimulated cousins. Even the baby crawled after them, crying, until the nurse scooped him up. "If this gang can't wear them out, nobody can."

"And maybe they'll learn some manners by example," grumbled Mut-tuy. She was the oldest of the orphans, although at thirteen, she no longer considered herself a "little one." Her Horus-lock of childhood had fallen to a rebellious chop of the knife a few months ago, but the hair that would become her maiden braids still only stuck out about a thumb's length from her scalp.

It wasn't a good look, Neferet had to admit, eying the girl from the corner of her eye. Mut-tuy was tall, skinny and flat-chested. Her face promised beauty later in life, but now, everything was awkward elbows and big feet. The ruthlessly cropped hair didn't help.

The women of the family sat in the grapevine-covered side yard of the farmhouse, shelling cowpeas while lunch simmered in the kitchen court, filling the house with a delicious smell of onions. At Bener-ib's feet lay Brute the mastiff, who rarely left the two young *sunet*s' side. Paws extended, tongue lolling, he resembled a lion taking his ease.

"Maya keeps talking about buying some land in the country, but I almost hope he doesn't." Sat-hut-haru shook her skirt to empty the folds of accumulated pods. "I so love to come here. It reminds me of my own childhood. And there are always the other grandchildren around for the little ones to play with." Maya, Papa's secretary, was her husband.

Mama smiled, her slim fingers expertly splitting a pod and reaming out the beans. "It makes me so happy to hear you say that. I've sometimes wondered if it weren't time to build onto the house, though. If everybody's here at once, it becomes rather like a barrack."

"No!" everyone cried in chorus.

"Don't change anything," Baket-iset pleaded from her couch. "Leave it just as it was when we were children."

Neferet suspected that was more important for Baket-iset than for anyone, since her childhood—before the terrible accident that had left her paralyzed—must have been the last truly carefree period of her life. Back when she could still dream of being a temple dancer for the Hidden One. Of having a husband and children of her own.

Neferet turned to the woman of her heart, who sat beside her. "At least they don't have to worry about you and me and Mut-tuy during the week. We can't leave the dispensary except on weekends."

"Should we not come so often, Lady Nub-nefer?" Bener-ib asked Mama apologetically. "We don't want to be a problem…"

Mama laid an affectionate hand on the young woman's shoulder. "No, no, my love. Don't even think that way. You girls are as welcome as anybody. You're all our troupe of Lovelies, like the divine girls who attend Lady Hut-haru!" She beamed about at the group of young women who surrounded her.

And Mama, Neferet thought proudly, *the center of that bevy, is as beautiful as the goddess herself.*

Despite her name, Neferet wasn't sure she counted as a Lovely. While her two sisters took after their mother, she resembled Papa—broad and sturdy, with small eyes and a square jaw. She didn't mind a bit. The youngest of the five children, she was especially close to Papa, and it was an honor to resemble him. She was smart like him, too. She and Bener-ib were *sunet*s, physicians, who had recently given up their position at the palace and opened a dispensary in the modest neighborhood where Maya's childhood home, a goldsmith's workshop, stood. One might argue how smart that was, in fact, but it gave the two young women immense satisfaction to help people who might not otherwise have had access to a good doctor.

All at once, Brute jerked to attention, his eyes fixed on the road that led from the farm to the bank of the River. The women's heads all swiveled as if they had been pulled by a string. There, against the ferny greenery of the reeds that bordered the water, a group of men had appeared. From afar came the sounds of excited shouts.

A shudder of uneasiness rolled up the back of Neferet's neck. She shaded her eyes with her hand, straining to see. "There's Maya—but where's Papa?" The two men had gone out into the marshes that morning on Papa's little reed boat. And although the River was necessary to life, it could also be a vehicle of death. In its waters lurked crocodiles, serpents, hippopotamuses. Sometimes at night, she had heard the roar of the enormous animals right there in the backwaters near the farm.

"Oh no!" Bener-ib murmured in a barely audible voice. She had lost so many loved ones that she was always quick to expect the worst.

Everyone was on their feet now. Brute took off toward the men at a run like a chariot horse heading into battle, with Neferet close behind. She wasn't ashamed to hike up her skirts in the interest of speed. After her, the other women trailed.

Where is Papa? was the question that made Neferet's heart hammer as she pounded down the earthen road. *Great One, don't let anything have happened to him.*

Maya, recognizable by his short stature, was waving his arms at them now. The other men huddled over the drop-off at the bank, some of them kneeling. They seemed to be pulling at something, lifting it up the slope. At last, a prone form slid onto the land and lay there unmoving.

An anguished cry escaped Neferet despite herself, and she forced her winded body to a burst of speed. But at last, as she and Brute approached the men, Papa climbed up from the forest of reeds. Relief flooded through her, and she slowed down, daring to catch her breath.

"What's happened, people?" she panted, mopping at her forehead.

Apart from Papa and Maya, she didn't recognize any of the men who stood before her. They were deeply sun-darkened, like those who worked outdoors every day, and they were clad only in loincloths. The unfortunate who lay stretched upon the ground, on the other hand, was dressed in a shirt and long kilt. He was a grisly sight, water-logged and bleached by the River, starting to swell under the rays of the summer sun.

By this time, the others had caught up to the girl, and Mama threw her arms around Papa. "Thanks be to the Hidden One that you're all right, my love. We saw Maya but not you, and I feared something might have happened."

"I was below in the boat trying to lift this poor fellow up for the others to pull," Papa explained with an arm around his wife's shoulders. "These reed cutters had dragged him out of the water and asked if we could help them get him to the nearest habitation."

He turned to the four workmen with a smile and clasped their hands in turn. "We'll see to it the priests of Inpu get him and try to notify his next of kin. You're sure nobody recognizes him?"

"No, my lord," said the eldest of them. "Maybe he's a city man."

"Maybe. Thanks to you all."

Bowing and murmuring, the reed cutters made their way down the bank and onto their boats. In a moment, the soft plashes of their poles could be heard propelling the reed crafts away through the papyrus.

"Whew," said Maya, brushing down his kilt. He slipped an arm around Sati's waist. "A fellow just goes out for a quiet paddle through the marshes, and here comes a corpse."

"We need to get him out of the sun," Mama said. She seemed quite unfazed by the unsavory deposit on their doorstep. "Mut-tuy, my dear, will you run back and bring one of the servants with the donkey cart and a sheet?"

For once, the adolescent obeyed without rebuttal, and the rest of the family stood around there on the road, staring in uncomfortable silence at the dead man as Brute sniffed him with interest.

"What did he die of?" Neferet asked. "Clearly no animal got him."

"We couldn't tell, my duckling. Perhaps you and Bener-ib can look him over and tell us. We need to find out who he is."

Neferet squatted at the man's side and lifted a water-shriveled hand. "He's not stiff anymore—it must have been a day or two at least since he died, but he's in pretty good shape."

Bener-ib peered over her shoulder. "His hands aren't calloused. He's probably not just be a workman."

Papa and Maya looked at each other in surprise.

"I don't see any wounds," Papa said. "And he looks too young to have dropped dead of natural causes."

Everyone was crowding around curiously now, which helped to block the blinding sun. The man appeared to be in his thirties, his close-cropped curly hair still uniformly dark. It was difficult to make out the features, which had started to grow soft and blurry. He was slim in build despite the ominous swelling of the abdomen that had begun, with plenty of hair on his chest and limbs.

Bener-ib had continued to examine his hand. "There's just this callus on his middle finger. I think he might have been a scribe."

"Not very high position, though," Nub-nefer said. "His kilt isn't especially nice linen."

"Very observant, my dove!" Papa said approvingly. "If you ever decide you don't want to sing for the Hidden One anymore, I'll bet the *medjay* could make a spot for you on the police force."

But Mama gave a bitter sniff. "I'd rather die than work for that awful Mahu. Do we have to report this to him?"

"I shouldn't think so. We're a long way from the city of Waset. We can let them know in the village. The mayor will have jurisdiction."

The clop of hoofs and the rumble of wooden wheels betrayed the approach of the donkey cart. Mut-tuy jumped out, and Papa and Maya, with the help of the driver, heaved the dead man awkwardly into the little vehicle. An acrid odor of manure still floated about it.

Neferet spread the sheet over the corpse and tucked in the edges. "Somebody'll have to go back to the City to get the embalmer priests," she said, wiping her hands on her hips.

But Mut-tuy, looking smug under her effort at casualness, said, "Oh, the steward's already sent somebody. I told him what had happened."

Papa gave her an amused glance. "Very enterprising, my girl."

"I'd be surprised if they send someone out this far," Mama said, watching the retreating wagon through visored eyes.

But Papa gave a chuckle. "Oh, I'm sure they will. The high priest is a fellow I went to school with when we were lads. I saved his honor with the schoolmaster once, and ever since, he's been more than obliging."

The others laughed.

Mama steered Sati and Mut-nodjmet toward the house. "Well, let's go back, girls. We left Baket-iset alone, wondering what had happened."

"I told her." Mut-tuy said, and she definitely looked satisfied.

Neferet rolled her eyes. *That girl's getting above herself. She'll be telling us all what to do if we let her.* But she knew the adolescent was desperate to be part of the group—even more than most thirteen-year-olds. Her own parents had either died or abandoned her. It was her brother, her junior by a year, who took care of the little ones unless Mut-tuy was forced to. She seemed not to feel much kinship with her half-wild younger brothers and sister. She had even refused to apprentice as a goldsmith, following the path of her father and brother.

But there were more immediate problems. As the

three remaining young women trudged back toward the farmhouse, Brute at their heels, Neferet said, "We need to find out who this dead man is so we can tell his family what has happened."

"Maybe they'll know in the village," Bener-ib suggested.

"That's what I'm hoping. Perhaps if we examine him more closely at the house before the priests of Inpu come, we'll discover how he died or find some clue to his identity."

The others had installed the dead man in the center of the salon, beneath the ceiling ventilator where any breezes that entered would blow over him. The thick mudbrick walls kept out the most ferocious heat, but even so, it wasn't the time of year when one wanted a corpse around for too long.

The clatter from the kitchen made it clear that lunch was almost ready. Sati and Mut-nodjmet were already carrying stools out into the yard and setting them up under the grapevine, but Neferet said resignedly, "We'd better do this now, before we have a full stomach." She whisked off the sheet while Bener-ib retrieved the basket of medical supplies they always carried in case of accidents. With Mut-tuy's help, she turned the man on his face. There wasn't a great deal of light in the salon, but some things were clear. His back was covered in dried dirt where it had lain on the ground, and the blood was sinking, giving his back half a sinister purple hue. There was no need to look further for a cause of death. A huge lump with tattered edges rose on the back of his curly-headed skull. Bener-ib poked gently with a finger.

"It's fractured badly. Somebody hit him a terrible blow

from behind," she said. "There must have been blood, but it's all washed away in the River."

"I'll bet robbers got him and threw him in afterwards to hide their crime," Mut-tuy said. As usual, in the presence of murder, her eyes came alight.

Neferet wasn't willing to let the thirteen-year-old guide the examination. "Or maybe he fell and hit his head trying to get into a boat." She rolled the dead man onto his back once more and ran a finger along under the waistband of his kilt. Nothing was tucked there—no purse, no papers, no writing implement. "After siesta, we can go into the village and ask around. There can't be that many literate people here."

"If he's from here," Bener-ib said pensively. "If he fell off a boat, he could be from anywhere."

Neferet replaced the sheet over the man's body just as Mama's voice called from out of doors, "Girls? Where are you? We're ready to eat."

"Come on, people. Let's wash up in the kitchen. We have our task for the afternoon."

The tables were set up under the vines, where gourds as well as unripe grapes hung down. The cicadas were so loud it was difficult to hear what everyone said, but there was no mistaking the savory smells that rose from the platters of flat beans and stewed onions. Papa passed a big bowl of lettuce dressed with herbed vinegar.

"What did you find out about the cause of death, my duckling?" he asked, as Neferet heaped the leaves on her dish.

"Somebody hit him on the head, or else he had an accident. His skull is fractured."

Papa and Maya exchanged a look.

Sat-hut-haru said with distaste, "We're not going to have a report here at the table, are we?"

Neferet made a face while her sister's head was down. "Some of us are going to have to go back to the city tomorrow afternoon, so if we're going to learn anything to tell his family we have to do it as soon as possible." She turned to Papa and continued as if her sister had said nothing. "Where exactly was the victim found, Papa?"

"As I understood it, the reed cutters came upon him floating face up among the papyrus down near the end of that little island—you know, where there's a kind of stream between the main bank and that separated hummock. It all gets flooded during the Inundation. I've taken you down there before."

"He could have floated there from somewhere else, then. How long would you say he'd been dead, Ibet?"

"At least a day or two. He's no longer stiff."

"*Iyah.*" Sati sprang up from her stool and stalked away toward the house. "I'm going to eat with the children in the kitchen court."

"If that doesn't take away her appetite, nothing should," Mut-tuy said under her breath.

Maya, who had obviously heard, gave her a dark look.

Mama turned to feed Baket-iset a spoonful of her food, and said dryly, "Perhaps when they've sickened us all, the girls will have some nice emetic to offer us."

Neferet let out a big guffaw. "Funny you should say that, Mama. I cut an armload of castor beans and leaves out by the goose pen. I hope you didn't have any other plans for them."

"That's fine, my love. I never poison anyone till the middle of the week."

Everyone laughed, but Bener-ib gave a glance that might have been uneasy at her plate.

"Perhaps I ought to…*ahem*," Maya edged up from his seat, his eyes flickering toward the house.

"Go on, my boy. I'm sure Sati would appreciate your company." Hani chuckled. His secretary hustled off through the wide-open doorway, barely having to duck the rolled up fly mat. Being a dwarf had its advantages.

"Well, people, we're going into the village to ask around about our dead man." Neferet rose from her stool and brushed out her skirts.

"I'll go with you in case there's anything I can add. Nub-nefer, my dove, if the priests come for our Osir, you know what to do."

"Of course, my love."

Papa and Neferet headed for the gate of the little low-walled yard, and after a moment's hesitation, Bener-ib and Mut-tuy hustled after them. Brute ambled alongside with his calm, possessive stride. The little party set out along the road that paralleled the River, surrounded by a cloud of dust. The sun hammered down on their heads and bare shoulders.

"This wasn't the best hour, probably," Neferet admitted. "Everybody may be sleeping."

"We can wake the mayor. A dead man washed up on the shore is his responsibility." Papa fanned himself with his wig. "You ladies are going to look like field workers after this noonday sun."

"We'll fit right into the neighborhood, then." Neferet snickered.

A quarter-hour's walk brought them to the small local village. They shopped there occasionally and attended local festivities, but the girls didn't know it well. It was mostly unwhite-washed brick, the color of the surrounding land, shaded with palms and figs and pomegranates. The packed-earth street was sprinkled with modest houses surrounded by their yards, walled or otherwise. Pigs and geese wandered at liberty, foraging. A trio of young children ran shrieking around a house until someone yelled from the doorway, "Quiet, you brats! People are trying to sleep!"

Papa chuckled. "I doubt if we'll have to wake the mayor after all." He looked around, then pointed to a solid-looking house a little back in a grove of date palms. "Last time I came here, the mayor lived right there. He's a man named Pa-shedu."

There were no garden walls. The trampled earth and bushes might or might not have belonged to the mayor, and the guinea hens that gobbled and pecked seemed to be the same ones that roamed up and down the village. A donkey was hobbled in the shade of a fig tree. It looked up in curiosity as the little troop passed, but Brute didn't dignify the animal with a glance.

The door stood open in the heat, the fly-mat hanging. Papa called out softly, "Is anyone home?"

Almost immediately, a wiry little woman on the far side of middle age pushed aside the mat and said in a deep voice, "What can I do for you?"

"We're looking for the mayor, Pa-shedu, mistress. I hope we're not waking the household."

"Well, you won't wake *him*. He flew into the West more than a year ago. I'm his widow. It's me who's mayor now."

She turned and led the visitors into her modest salon. Brute, a gentleman if ever there was, took his seat modestly outside the door. Neferet, surprised and delighted to find a woman mayor, expected that the widow might take her seat in a chair of office, with a scepter of authority. But apparently village life was less formal than life in Waset. Instead, their hostess settled herself cross-legged on the floor and offered her guests the cushions strewn around. Her expression was intense and businesslike.

"Now, how can I help you? My name is Kem-sit."

ACKNOWLEDGMENTS

The author gratefully acknowledges all those who have helped her in the production of this book. To the wonderful women of my writers' group, for their critique and encouragement, my thanks. To Lynn McNamee and her editorial team at Red Adept—Rashida, Sarah, and Virge—profound gratitude (and Lynn, for so many other forms of help). To the flexible and talented gang at Streetlight Graphics for the cover and map. To my cousin and her husband, my technology guru: thanks, guys. And most of all, to my husband, Ippokratis, who put up with the months of fixation it takes to write a novel, many, many thanks.

ABOUT THE AUTHOR

 N.L. Holmes is the pen name of a professional archaeologist who received her doctorate from Bryn Mawr College. She has excavated in Greece and in Israel and taught ancient history and humanities at the university level for many years. She has always had a passion for books, and in childhood, she and her cousin (also a writer today) used to write stories for fun.

Today, since their son is grown, she lives with her husband and two cats in northern France, where she gardens, weaves, plays the violin, and dances. And reads, of course.

OTHER TITLES BY N.L. HOLMES

THE LORD HANI MYSTERIES
Political intrigue and mystery in Akh-en-aten's Egypt

Finalist, Best Series of 2021, Next Generation
Independent Book Award

Finalist, Best Series of 2022, Chanticleer
Independent Book Awards

Bird in a Snare (2020) Grand Prize, Chaucer Award
2021 for best historical fiction before 1750

The Crocodile Makes No Sound (2020) Gold Medal,
Adult Fiction, The Wishing Shelf Book Awards 2022

Scepter of Flint (2020)

The North Wind Descends (2020)

Lake of Flowers (2021)

Pilot Who Knows the Waters (2022)

THE EMPIRE AT TWILIGHT SERIES
Free-standing personal dramas with a touch
of intrigue, set in the Hittite Empire

*The Lightning Horse (*2020)

The Singer and Her Song (2020)

The Queen's Dog (2020)

The Sun at Twilight (2021)

The Moon That Fell from Heaven (Red Adept
Publishing, September 2023)

The Mountains of Freedom (Red Adept
Publishing, *Vella*, coming soon)

THE HANI'S DAUGHTER MYSTERIES
Neferet carries on the family curiosity in the reign
of Tut-ankh-amen with cozy mysteries

Flowers of Evil (2023)

Web of Evil (January 2024)

Made in the USA
Columbia, SC
31 August 2023

22321077R00195